REBEL

The Galactic Syndicate Book 2

N.C. Madigan

MORE BOOKS BY

N.C. Madigan

The Galactic Syndicate Cycle
Psychogen
Rebel
Dyad (Forthcoming)

Between the Realms
Book 1: *Demon*
Book 2: *Witch*

1

Gael Daniels admired the glittering blue gem nested on his right index finger. The antique silver ring held a mysterious blue gem called Astarte, and Gael had the largest piece ever found. As he tilted it in the light, the astarte sparkled. Lowering his hand, he turned his attention to the mining operation taking place below him. As the current CEO of the family-owned Walnad Interplanetary Corporation, Gael Daniels was responsible for checking on his various mining operations. He drew in a long puff on his cigar held between the fingers of his left hand.

He knew the temperatures outside the building were nearing 43 degrees C, but the room he stood in was comfortable at 22 degrees C. Gael leaned over and plucked a glass of Sun Whiskey from the nearby table. He lifted the glass to his lips and let the taste of Sun Whiskey mingle with the flavor and smoke of his cigar. Gael could see a ghostly reflection of himself in the window. His dark skin was marred by two scars on his face, one above his left eye and one on his left cheek. The cause of the scars was innocuous, but he never told the truth about how he'd gotten them. Gael found it much more interesting to embellish the stories.

Based on the last report he'd read, the production line below progressed smoothly. Aside from the occasional mishap, of course. Those were to be expected: a severed limb here, a dead body there. Hazards of the workplace. Dehydration was the biggest culprit, but there wasn't much to be done about that. Liquid water was difficult to transport outside of the environmentally controlled buildings, and too many frequent breaks would push the schedule back too far. There were deadlines to meet and shipments to send. Far below the tower in which Gael stood, on the surface of Planet 1531B, workers stood in lines along a constantly moving conveyor belt, picking through the useless rubble to find the tiniest bits of Astarte. The bits of astarte were tossed into buckets while the debris fell from the conveyors into a large crevasse. The gemstones glowed so brightly that the reflected sparkles shone like high-powered lights even from a considerable height.

The door to the room closed with a snap, and footsteps crossed the smooth tiled floor. In the reflection of the window, Gael saw the Overseer of 1531B, Bill Reade. For whatever reason, Reade insisted on wearing his red Solar System Authority uniform, even though he was no longer employed by that organization. Walnad was paying him now. It didn't help that Reade's cousin was an officer of the SSA Supersensory Division. Without Lieutenant Howard's insistence, Gael would not have hired Bill Reade. He was too much of a live-wire.

"Mr. Daniels?"

"What is it?"

"The foremen in the mines believe this planet has been stripped of all astarte," Reade said.

"This is hardly a planet," Daniels remarked, his gaze still lingering on the workers below. He saw Reade's reflection roll its eyes.

"Dwarf planet, then. Regardless, it might be time to move on to a new location."

"My last report stated that only fifty percent of the astarte had been extracted," Daniels grunted in reply.

"Fifty? Impossible, sir."

"Is it?"

"Yes. You've heard about the quakes. We've practically mined this planet hollow," Reade argued. Daniels said nothing and stared through the window at the workers. Numbers and charts ran through his mind as he tried to remember exactly what he'd last read about this mining operation. Perhaps he was wrong, though Gael would never admit that to a man like Reade.

"Put a proposal together for abandoning operations here, then," Daniels said. "Get it to me soon. I will check with my scouts to see where the nearest opportunity is for you." Grim-faced, Reade nodded and turned, leaving Daniels alone once again in the tower.

Gael Daniels made a point of never sticking around his mining locations very long. He found that his appearance at the mining operations was necessary for keeping the workers *motivated*. Not to mention, many of his foremen and overseers were former SSA, and Gael questioned their loyalty.

The small, two-person ship, *Pioneer*, waited for Gael in the docking bay. Painted black and white, it was a purchase Daniels made right after their operations expanded to mining. With a powerful FTL jump drive, he could quickly visit several locations in a short amount of time, then return to his corporate headquarters on Sun Station Alpha without missing any meetings.

Bill Reade entered the docking bay, his hands laced behind his back. Gael hung back, waiting. "I will get that proposal to you soon," Reade said, coming to a halt beside *Pioneer*. "Your ship is refueled and ready to go, as well."

"Thank you." The forced interaction with the stoic-faced overseer made him uncomfortable.

"Safe travels." Reade bowed slightly, then tapped the center of his chest with his fist, thumb against his breastbone. Gael returned the gesture, turned back to the ship, and passed through the narrow gangway tunnel. Inside his ship, he secured his belongings in the storage bin and slipped into the pilot seat.

Pioneer undocked from the bay, and the engines flared, pushing the ship past the minimal atmosphere surrounding 1531B and into space. Gael set his ship's coordinates to the nearest transportation wormhole and settled back in his seat. Closing his eyes, he tried to let his mind calm enough to get some sleep, but an unfamiliar feeling of unease settled in the pit of his stomach.

2

Liza Strange was absorbed in reading articles on the Sol Network when an alarm blared over the intercom system of the *Gypsy Star*. She tossed aside her tablet, whipped her blankets off her body, and simultaneously rolled from the bed, gracelessly falling to the floor. Her roommate, Gwen Adan, slipped from the upper bunk and landed lightly on her feet beside Liza.

"Come on, then," Gwen said, lowering a hand to Liza and hoisting her up.

"All hands." The command was shouted over the intercom from the bridge. The crew already knew what the alarm meant: they had reached their next target. Gwen pulled clothes from their shared wardrobe and tossed Liza's to her.

"Thanks," Liza said, stumbling over awkward limbs. She managed to get into her pants and shirt and pulled her jacket up over her shoulders. Using an elastic tie, she pulled her dreads back into a knot behind her head. Gwen did the same, and together they left the room.

In the ship's hallways, Liza and Gwen parted ways. Gwen walked toward the lift that would take her to the bridge while Liza descended a metal stairwell down one level of the ship, where the gunner stations were located. She found the twins, Weed, and Speed, already pulling on their gunner suits, thin spacesuits designed to give temporary life support, should the gunner station become separated from the ship. Their identical faces lit up in grins when Liza arrived.

"Master Gunner," they said together, saluting her. Liza shook her head.

"Hardly," she replied, pulling her own suit from a locker.

"Captain's orders," the twins countered. Though the twins and Captain Dominik Rhyne thought she was a capable Master Gunner, Liza couldn't accept their praise. She hardly knew anything about the systems. The twins were much more knowledgeable, and they continued to teach her everything they knew. Gwen joked that Liza was part of "upper management" now, which made Liza wrinkle her nose.

"Sixty seconds to intercept." It was Becce's voice, which meant that Dom was piloting the ship. Weed and Speed pulled their helmets on and scrambled into their respective gunner stations. Liza jogged to the ship's bow to the control room, where she could watch the action outside of the ship, monitor the guns, and fire the ion cannon, if necessary.

She dropped into her chair and paired her helmet communication lync to the rest of the ship. The monitors flickered on, showing interior and exterior camera shots. Gwen was on the bridge beside Becce, both looking over the holographic layout of the target ship. Aside from Dom, the rest of the crew waited in the decompression chamber, including Vely Strange, Liza's younger sister. In the last two months, Vely's hair had grown out, her roots white-blonde, leaving the lower half of her hair still dyed brown. It was an odd look for her. Her hair disappeared under her helmet. The others in the chamber followed suit.

Vely had been convinced to join the recon team since her psychogenic ability wouldn't accidentally blow a ship apart. Her job was to knock out anyone who tried to get in their way. Vely preferred this option; she really didn't want to kill people.

The sisters were in disagreement on that point.

"Ten seconds to intercept."

One of the largest people in the decompression chamber, Corbin, *Gypsy Star* cook and recon team member, held a long, thin device that would fire a grappling hook into the other ship's hull. Beside him, Vely waited with a heavy bag slung over her shoulders. At the ten-second announcement, Corbin readied his posture and aimed the device at the door. Tsuto, the shape-shifting alien, who was in his favorite shape of a giant praying mantis, stood ready at the door, his strange appendage on the door lock.

"Interception complete."

Tsuto hit the door lock, and it opened with one smooth motion. Corbin fired the grappling hook towards the merchant ship, and it latched onto the hull. Vely adjusted her bag and grabbed hold of the cable. Liza watched as each recon team member leaped from the chamber, holding onto the line attached to the merchant ship.

Liza changed her monitors to the cameras mounted on the exterior of the ship. She rotated a camera around so she could see various weapons of this merchant ship. The ship didn't seem too heavily armed, but then, she wasn't getting a complete view. Liza tapped a button on the panel to lync her with Weed and Speed.

"Be on your guard. Their guns aren't moving yet, but I'm sure we'll see some fire," Liza said. The twins chirped a response. The lync line beeped softly when another connection joined.

"Liza?" It was Dom.

"Aye, Captain," she said, smiling to herself.

"You and the twins are ready for action?" he asked.

"Aye, sir." She heard him huff. He never should have told the crew that he disliked formalities.

"Gwen is sending you the ship layout with the recon team's tracking signals. If something happens, we'll need an alternative exit strategy," Dom said. As he spoke, a file arrived at Liza's control panel. She opened it and set it to one of the monitors. She could see the blinking green lights that indicated each of the crew members. "Stand by."

3

Vely Strange leaped from the *Gypsy Star* and allowed the cable to skim through her gloved hand. She bumped hard against the hull of the merchant ship. Holding tight to the line with one hand, she opened the canvas bag slung over her shoulder and drew out a compact laser saw. It was a contraption that the twins created. She flipped the switch, and a beam of red light issued out from the end. The usual high-pitched whine of the device disappeared in the vacuum of space. She aimed the laser at the hull, and the metal began to heat and weaken. Corbin appeared beside her, still holding onto the cable.

After another moment, the hull was weak enough for Corbin to press the metal inward. Vely shut off the laser and stowed it in her bag while Corbin used his shoulder to press against the soft metal. The panel collapsed inward, creating a hole. Corbin and Vely scrambled through the hole while Tsuto, Doctor D, and Cedrick traversed the gap between the two ships.

The team assembled inside the merchant ship away from the hole. "You all remember your routes?" Doctor D asked over the spacesuit lync. The crew nodded. "Let's go."

Tsuto, Doctor D, and Vely went in one direction and Corbin and Cedrick in the other. Corbin and Cedrick were tasked with ransacking the ship's galley, while Vely and her group needed to find a specific, valuable bit of cargo. She had memorized the route required to reach the cargo hold on the ship, a course she followed with Doctor D and Tsuto on her heels.

If her guess was correct, they had entered the ship three levels above the cargo hold. As Vely trotted along the corridor.

She pictured the ship's map in her mind, trying to remember the lift and the stairwell location.

As expected, the corridor ended at a stairwell and lift. Vely led Doctor D and Tsuto down two flights of steps. This corridor was mostly deserted, except for a few armed guards standing near a door. Vely and Doctor D crouched down out of sight.

"That room would be my guess," Doctor D said.

"I'll take them out," Vely said. She pulled the canvas bag from her shoulder and handed it over to Doctor D, who slung it over his back. Vely removed her spacesuit gloves and tucked them away, leaving her hands bare. She stepped out of her cover with a deep breath and walked down the corridor towards the guards.

They were alerted to her presence as soon as her footsteps echoed off the metal floor. Both turned towards her, their weapons lowered. Vely had never seen those types of guns before. Thankfully, Doctor D was able to supply her with information.

"Those are microwave guns, Vely. Be careful. The guns are silent, so you will not get any warning," he said through their lync.

"Got it," Vely said. From within, she pulled on her Tranquility. The cool sensation flowing over her body, calming her as it began to emit from her exposed hands. She could see the delicate blue mist surrounding her, filling the corridor as she walked. "Emitting Tranquility. Keep yourself covered, Doc," she added to him. Despite numerous experiments, Vely and the crew were unable to determine if a person could avoid the effects of Tranquility when entirely covered by a space suit and breathing tanked oxygen. Sometimes it worked, and sometimes it did not.

"Who are you?" one of the guards yelled as Vely approached. Up close, she could see they were not SSA. Their uniforms bared some insignia that she'd never seen before. Walnad maybe? Vely smiled, her face partially hidden by the visor of her space helmet.

"No one important," she said. She increased the flow of her Tranquility until the area was thick with blue mist. She watched their expressions slacken and halted the release of Tranq. The guards leaned against each other and slid to the ground, their eyes gazing at something that was very far away. Their weapons rolled from their hands.

Vely turned to the door. It appeared to be a simple electronic lock. It would pose no problem for a small explosive.

"How's it going down here," Doctor D asked.

"The guards are down. You can try to come down here," she said. The Tranquility was dissipating, but not very quickly. "Door appears to just have an electronic lock. I'm going to blow it."

"Aye, aye," Doctor D replied.

Vely pulled a small explosive device from a pocket and stuck it to the door, right along the edge of the keypad. Before she pushed the button, she picked up sound coming from the guards' communication lyncs.

"We're breached! Shoot any intruders!"

Vely shook her head and muttered, "Took you long enough."

She punched the button for the explosive and jogged away from the door. With a muted blast, the explosive detonated, releasing the electronic lock on the door. By the time the smoke cleared, Doctor D and Tsuto had joined her.

"Any problems?" she asked, and Doctor D shook his helmeted head. He turned towards the metal door, stuck his fingers in the gap caused by the explosive, and pushed the door open. Metal screeched against metal until there was a large enough gap for Doctor D to squeeze through. He passed into the room first, followed by Vely and Tsuto.

The lights in the room did not come on automatically, as one might have expected. Vely searched around on the wall beside the door for some kind of control panel, her fingers finally grazing over something. She tapped, hoping she'd hit the right button. Nothing worked. Instead, she registered a hissing noise.

"What is that?" she asked. She couldn't see Doctor D or Tsuto. They had moved forward into the darkness, away from the small amount of light coming through the door.

"What is what?" Doctor D asked.

"Don't you hear that?"

The hissing grew louder, and Vely's hands began to burn. She yelped in pain and stumbled out of the room, pulling her gloves back onto her hands, not bothering to check. "There's something in there! Some kind of gas," she shouted into her lync. "Get out!"

"Hold on." A light illuminating a bit of the darkness, but Vely could barely see anything inside. "Shit, you're right," Doctor D said, his voice panicked. He and Tsuto stumbled from the room. Tsuto appeared to be unaffected by the gas, but the exterior layer of Doctor D's suit was peeling away. He glanced at his arms and then at Vely. "This room is a set up. There's nothing in there except..."

"Except what?"

"Bodies."

4

"We've got incoming fire," Liza said to the twins. "Switch to neutralizers and stop those blasts."

"Switching," the twins said. Liza's eyes flicked from monitor to monitor, watching the blasts fired from the merchant ship. A flurry of *pings* sounded in her ear as the entire crew was dropped onto the same lync line.

"We got a problem, Cap," Doctor D said.

"What is it?"

"The room we thought was for material storage? It's not there. There was something else in the room."

"What was it?"

"Piles of dead bodies." Silence buzzed on the lync. Liza froze. "There was some sort of corrosive gas in the room, too. Possibly to destroy the bodies."

"Was the room guarded?" Dom asked.

"Yeah. Vely took them out."

"Get back to the ship," Dom said. "We'll incapacitate the ship and leave it at that."

"No, wait!" Vely interjected. "I think I found something."

"Vely..." Liza growled in response, a warning to not disobey. Liza's agitation ignited her power, and she felt it crawl around her skin. She took several deep breaths to try and calm herself.

"Doctor D, come down here! This is the room. It was locked with a tether, but I got it open," Vely said. A long silence followed. Doctor D and Vely must have muted their microphones.

"What are they doing over there?" Dom asked though Liza didn't think he was expecting an answer.

12

Doctor D came back on the line. "Vely found some of their cargo. We're packing it up now."

"Cedrick and I cleaned out the galley. We're heading back to the ship," Corbin said.

"Liza," Dom said. "Plan on blowing out the cargo hold area of the ship. After everyone is back on and we release the grappling hook, I'll turn the ship around so you can use the ion cannon." Liza glanced at the layout of the merchant ship. She tapped the screen to zoom in on the cargo hold location.

"Aye," she replied. On the control panel, she engaged the ion cannon. It would need a few moments to charge.

"Shit! We have a problem!" Becce interrupted, her voice high pitched.

"What?" Several people asked at once.

"The ship is pulling away from us too quickly. The grappling cable is going to snap," Becce said. Liza flipped one of her screens back to the exterior shot of the *Gypsy Star* and honed in on the decompression chamber. The cable tightened as the merchant ship tried to pull away.

"I'm on it," Gwen announced. "I'll disconnect it; otherwise, it's going to rip our ship apart."

"Wait! Cedrick and I are almost there," Corbin said. Liza watched the activity on her monitors, annoyed that she couldn't do anything to help.

"Changing targets, boss," one of the twins said. "Taking out thrusters." The gunner station rotated, the barrel aimed at the merchant ship's thrusters. One by one, blasts from the gun took out the thrusters, making escape more difficult.

"Cedrick and Corbin are boarding now," Gwen said. "Becce, can you lock down this section of the ship. They've got several crates."

"Locking down."

Liza's diagram of the *Gypsy Star* blinked where doors closed, protecting the rest of the ship from the pressure differential. They wouldn't be able to use the decompression chamber with such large cargo.

13

"If we're going to be doing raids of this size, Dom," Becce said, "we need to use the cargo hold doors and lock down that level of the ship."

"I know." Liza had been part of those conversations. Dom was against using such a large door, leaving them more vulnerable to counterattack.

"Cedrick and Dom have boarded. Vely. Doctor D. Where are you at?" Gwen asked. Liza could see on the monitor that she was ready to release the grappling hook from the *Gypsy Star* side.

"Almost there. If you can hold off a little longer…"

"I'll try," Becce said. A pause. "Shit!"

"Now what?" Liza asked, not meaning to shout at loud as she did.

"They've given up escape and are deploying their guns. I don't think our gunners will be able to reach them," Becce said. Liza switched cameras again and saw what Becce was seeing. Panels on the merchant ship slid open, revealing extra weapons. Usually, merchant ships didn't have that much firepower.

"You've gotta try," Liza said to the twins, who acknowledged her.

"Just another minute," Gwen said. Doctor D, Vely, and Tsuto were climbing through the open door on the ship's side, several bags weighing them down. Liza watched as Gwen pulled Tsuto through the doorway, and at the same time, threw her Katho power at the grappling hook, removing it from the merchant ship and pulling it back into the *Gypsy Star*. Once it crossed the open doorway, Gwen closed the exterior door of the ship.

"We're detached," Gwen said.

"Pressure restoration process initiating. It'll be about ten minutes," Becce said.

"Liza, is the ion cannon ready?" Dom asked.

"It's ready."

"You should be able to get a good shot in," Dom said. Liza

felt the ship maneuver into a tight turn. The ion cannon was positioned on the bow of the ship. Dom needed to move them around and get behind the merchant ship for her to get a good shot.

"Incoming," the twins said rather calmly. Liza saw their attempt to neutralize a blast from the merchant ship, but it missed. She braced herself, and the *Gypsy Star* shuddered with the impact. Liza sighed. Repairs would need to be made.

Liza tapped a button on her control panel, and a thin screen slid up from the panel and flickered to life. A red crosshatch surrounded by a circle was in the middle of the screen. Liza stretched her hands to the sides and placed her fingers on the controls for the ion cannon. She hadn't practiced much, and the controls were delicate. Luckily, she had a large target.

Dom shifted the ship around to the back of the merchant ship while the twins continued to neutralize blasts. They missed another, and the ship shuddered once more, shaking Liza's crosshatch on the screen. The *Gypsy Star* continued to move until the stern of the merchant ship was in sight. Liza adjusted the barrel of the ion cannon, gently nudging the controls with her fingers. She locked onto the lower corner of the ship.

"Locked," she said, tapping a button with her thumb.

"Fire."

She pressed the button with her fingers. She felt the rumble of the ion cannon, and from the screen, she saw the blast impact the ship. The explosion began a chain reaction that included the stern engines, which started to break apart.

"We have SSA ships on our tail," Dom said. "We're going to FTL. Everyone hang on."

Liza pulled the harness on her chair around her chest. She barely had it buckled when the *Gypsy Star* lurched into the jump.

5

Vely sat on a bed in the medical bay, her hands resting on a cool, metal table. Doctor D stood on the other side of the table, applying a cooling salve to her hands, which were red and blistered from whatever gas was used in the room of bodies. There had been no time to discuss that particular issue after the pressurization process was complete. Vely rushed to the medical bay to have her hands treated while the rest of the crew cared for the loot.

Liza leaned against the wall, a scowl plastered on her face. Vely couldn't tell if it was her usual expression or was actually annoyed about something.

"What's wrong, Liza?" Vely finally asked. Doctor D set aside the salve and picked up some white bandages, and carefully wrapped her hands.

"Nothing," Liza said, her arms tightening across her chest. She was lying. Vely met Doctor D's gaze, and he smiled at her.

"The operation went fine, didn't it?" Vely asked. "What's bothering you?"

"Nothing," Liza repeated.

"I know you're lying," Vely said. Liza pushed herself from the wall and began to pace the room.

"You shouldn't have gotten hurt," Liza said, her eyes darting between the floor and Vely.

"You don't have to be overprotective," Vely said. "I'm fine." Liza wrinkled her nose in disagreement.

"Vely performed very well," Doctor D said after he stepped away from the bedside. "You have been excelling in all the training you have received from the rest of the crew. Both of you have been progressing well with your psychogenic abilities as well. You hardly need your Dyad anymore. Liza stopped pacing, but her limbs twitched with agitation. "Relax, Liza," Doctor D added with a calming smile. She said nothing but nodded to Vely and disappeared from the room.

Vely glanced at Doctor D. "I don't know what's wrong with her," she said. Doctor D shrugged his giant shoulders.

"I don't try to understand women," he said. "All the science in the world cannot explain their wiles." Vely snorted, and Doctor D grinned. "You're all set. Come back tomorrow, so I can change the bandages."

"I will. Thanks, Doc." Vely hopped off the bed and left the medical bay. Cedrick waited for her in the galley. He rose from the chair he'd been lounging in and rested a hand on her shoulder. Vely couldn't help but notice that the pallor of his skin and the dark circles around his eyes hadn't improved since joining the crew. She thought that his escape from the SSA would have been kinder to him. She couldn't understand it.

"How are your hands?" he asked.

"Gross looking," Vely said. "They're all blistered." Cedrick took her hands in his and touched them to his chin.

"Doctor D will make sure they heal properly," he said.

Vely nodded, allowing him to fold her into his arms. She could hear his heart beating in his chest. "Why did you wait out here?" she asked him. He didn't answer right away. Vely glanced up at him. "Because Liza was in there?" Cedrick's cheeks turned pink.

"She still doesn't trust me," he said.

"She doesn't trust anyone."

"I thought she would understand after I explained everything," Cedrick said. Vely could only shrug her shoulders. "You understand, don't you?"

"I understand that we all have things in our past that we've had to do to survive," Vely said. "What matters now is that you remain honest, at least to me." She paused, smiling to herself. "We are *pirates,* after all."

A sad look passed over Cedrick's face for a moment. "Denny hated pirates so much," he mumbled. "Can you imagine what he'd say if he could see us now?"

"I'm sure he'd be properly appalled," Vely replied, leaning her cheek into his chest. His arms tightened around her, and they stood in silence for a moment, remembering their fallen friend.

6

The Walnad Interplanetary Corporation headquarters was a sprawling complex that made up several city blocks inside Sun Station Alpha. Each smaller six-story complex was connected by pedestrian tubes that crisscrossed the Sun Station. Gael remembered seeing old pictures from when humans lived on Earth, pictures showing tall buildings jutting into the sky, hundreds of stories tall. He wondered what it would be like to have a structure that rose up into the unknown reaches. Alas, he would never see such a building in his lifetime.

Gael stood at the large windows of his office, looking over the colony. Gael's office afforded him a view of the popular gastro-neighborhood. The restaurants in the area had attempts at creative and unique food. Gael found most of them to be too similar. There was only so much to be done with the genetically modified food grown in the Sun Stations' greenhouses.

The intercom on his desk beeped. Gael turned and tapped the screen, connecting him with his assistant, Charles Mann. "What is it?" he asked, dropping back into his chair.

"Ms. Foste and Mr. Gammon have arrived," Charles said. Gael sighed.

"Send them in."

It was a moment before the doors to his office slid open, revealing the two people that annoyed him the most in the galaxy: Director Alis Foste and Assistant Director Lynwood Gammon of the Solar System Authority. Alis Foste was a tall woman with a floating mass of black, curly hair.

Her expression was a permanent scowl, and the arch of her eyebrows gave the impression that she was judging everyone. She probably was. Lynwood Gammon was marginally friendlier than Alis. He usually dealt with personnel issues within the organization. Lynwood was slightly taller than Alis, with light brown hair and light eyes. His face was more open, but he kept his mouth closed more often than not.

They were a formidable team, and when Gael agreed to the joint venture between Walnad and the SSA, he had no idea he'd be dealing with those two. An underling maybe, from their accounting department. Not the director of the entire organization.

Alis swept into the room, her floor-length jacket trailing behind her. She dropped into one of the armchairs on the opposite side of Gael's desk. Lynwood sat beside her with less flourish.

"To what do I owe the pleasure?" Gael asked, folding his fingers together over his desk. Alis arched an eyebrow.

"You lost another merchant ship," Alis said.

"I know." He'd already heard the ship had been ransacked and incapacitated by the pirate ship *Gypsy Star*. He still hadn't admitted to himself how much of a loss that ship was, and he certainly wasn't going to tell Alis.

"We had some of our officers investigate the remains of the ship," Alis said.

"Could anything be salvaged?" Gael asked.

"That's not the problem," Lynwood interjected. Gael glanced between the two.

"What is it?"

"There was a room full of dead bodies and a high concentration of hydrochloric acid," Alis said. She leaned forward in her chair. "I don't care what you do, as you know. But you have to tell me about these things so I can mitigate any repercussions." Gael stared at her. He turned slightly in his chair to face his computer. He brought up the report of the destroyed merchant ship and read it over. Alis and Lynwood

20

stared at him, waiting for some kind of response.

1531B. That's where the ship had left from. Gael pressed his lips together and shifted his gaze back to Alis. "I will make sure to inform you of all activities next time. I think this time was just a communication gap."

"You're saying you were not aware of this particular incident?" Lynwood asked.

"I'm afraid not," Gael said, lacing his fingers together. "I will look into it, of course, and remind my ship captains to inform me of any activities they may have on their ship."

Gael watched Lynwood and Alis exchange a glance. He was pretty sure that they didn't believe him, but he wasn't sure what else they expected. Sure, Walnad had some bad press about their mining and manufacturing practices, but dead bodies? That could be a crippling blow to the company. The SSA would suffer, too, at least from those who still trusted them. It was a good thing the Sun Station colonists rarely paid attention to anything outside of their pitiful lives.

"Was there anything else you wanted to discuss?" Gael asked. "Surely you did not come here from your headquarters just to talk about a few dead bodies."

"Piles, actually," Lynwood correct.

"Either way."

"There was something else. You will have to increase our budget if you want your new wormholes protected," Alis said. "I have already sent you the proposed increase." Gael glanced back at his computer. He hadn't checked his messages all day. He probably should have; he could have been better prepared for this surprise meeting.

"I'll look at it and let you know," he said, dismissing the topic. He saw Alis's gaze darken considerably. It was a gaze that Gael preferred not to experience. "Was there... anything else?"

"No." Alis rose from her chair, and the back of her legs pushed the chair across the ground, screeching against the tile floor. She stepped around the chair and strode to the door, leaving a wake of anger. Lynwood stood up, trying to maintain a degree of calm, and followed his boss out of the office. The door slid closed again. From his desk, Gael locked the door. Using his intercom, he messaged his assistant.

"If anyone else stops by today, tell them I am busy," he said to him. Charles confirmed the message, and Gael turned off his intercom.

He released a long breath. Mining operation 1531B had been shut down, as Bill Reade had suggested. Their transport ship returning to the Walnad Warehouse was intercepted by pirates, and dead bodies were found on board. The SSA wasn't around to protect that ship, so he supposed he could push some responsibility back on them. Gael knew that Bill Reade regularly had problem employees from the mining operations, but getting rid of them was easy. Why the sadistic acid treatment? Gael leaned back in his chair and laced his fingers in front of his face. He would have to get to the bottom of this little problem.

7

A portion of the *Gypsy Star* crew gathered in the bridge. Dom and Becce stood side by side at the table in the center, a holographic projection hovering in the center. Doctor D lounged in a chair, listening to the conversation between Becce and Dom. Liza leaned against the wall near the lift, one boot propped up against the wall, her arms crossed over her chest. Liza remained plugged into her communication lync. The twins were outside the ship, repairing the damage caused by the merchant ship's blasts. She was on standby should they need more help.

In the meeting, the subject of the dead bodies had come up. "How many were there?" Becce asked, staring at Doctor D through the holographic projection.

"Over a dozen? I didn't get a good look. After I realized what was going on, and the gas started filling the room, I hustled out of there," he said. "They were in... varying states of decay." Liza wrinkled her nose. She wasn't sure she had the stomach for dead body talk.

"And those guards you found?"

"Their uniforms were unfamiliar to me, and I didn't recognize the symbol." Doctor D rose and stepped up to the table. He tapped a button on the console, and the projection of the solar system disappeared, replaced by a faint green cloud. Using a finger, he drew two curved triangles, one pointing up and the other pointing down with a line through the middle of each triangle. Dom and Becce both stared at it, eyes narrowed.

"I've never seen it either," Dom said. "I think those Corsair bastards are flying under the SSA, aren't they?"

23

"Yeah," Becce confirmed. "It's just so disturbing." Liza lifted her head.

"It's like what they did to the Moon colonists," she commented. The others glanced in her direction.

"You're right," Dom said. "Did you ever find out who was running the operations on the Moon?"

"Walnad owned the fields. SSA had Enforcers stationed there. I can only assume it was a joint operation of the two," Liza said, shrugging her shoulders beneath her dark jacket.

"I imagine that's the case for most locations," Doctor D said. "It was a similar situation on the shit colony where Corbin and I were born." Liza raised an eyebrow.

"Shit colony?" she asked.

"SC-203. It doesn't exist anymore. All of the life support systems failed. Much like your Moon, Liza, anyone who couldn't get off the colony ended up dead," he said. It was unusual for such a dark expression to take hold of Doctor D's features. Liza had forgotten that Doctor D and Corbin were cousins. She should have remembered since their features were so similar. "We went to Mars and learned our trades there."

"Whatever is going on under Walnad and the SSA's noses, we don't care about," Becce said. "Just throw a blanket over all of them and call them enemies."

"Until we hear otherwise, that's exactly what we'll do," Dom confirmed. He shifted his weight, leaned down to the console, and brought up the map again on the holoprojector. "We have a meeting with Captain Thane Lezal," Dom continued. "He wants to meet us at the L2X Rad Station. Liza, you'll recognize it as the first Rad station you visited with us. It's closer to our current location than the Cove."

"I don't think the crew has recovered from the last time we were on the Cove," Doctor D said.

"That was two months ago," Liza commented. Doctor D chuckled. Vely had told her about the Cove being moved and how spectacular it was, and about playing in zero gravity. She'd never admit it, but Liza was a tiny bit jealous.

"We'll be meeting him in a room at the Rigel Tavern. I have a feeling that Lezal is pulling together a fleet of ships," Dom explained.

"Why?" Becce asked. "That would just make us a bigger target."

"But we can take down bigger targets. I don't know yet, though, Bec. We'll have to wait to find out. He isn't transmitting any additional information over communication lyncs right now," Dom said. "The twins had to decrypt the location," he added with an annoyed expression.

"Something must have happened to make him more paranoid," Doctor D suggested.

"I think this is standard for him, especially after Warwick and Zimir betrayed his trust," Dom said. "Becce is going to set up our route, probably have one FTL jump. I'll let the crew know at dinner."

"Aye," Doctor D said, pulling himself up from the chair. He stretched his arms over his head. "I'm going back to my lab if you need me." He stepped into the lift, patting Liza on her shoulder as he passed and disappeared. Becce moved to a different spot at the table and took over the control console. She began typing, immediately pulling herself into her own world.

Liza was about to head down to her room when Dom appeared beside her. He took her gloved hand. "Come on," he said and led her into the lift. She allowed him to led her down to his rooms.

Inside, Dom turned to her. He was smiling, but in a concerned sort of way. "You have been quiet today," he said. Liza shrugged and sat down in one of the plush chairs. "You know that I value your opinions."

"I just don't know much about all this," Liza said. "I haven't been here that long." Dom sat down in the chair opposite her.

"You're learning," he said. "What's wrong? You have

25

been distant." Liza looked away.

"Nothing," she answered. Dom raised his eyebrows.

"You and I both know that's a lie," he said. "You can talk to me." Liza released a sigh. He was right that she was lying. There were many things in her head, things she didn't feel like discussing with anyone. Especially Dom. Liza threw herself up onto her feet and paced the room.

"Are you sure it's okay for Cedrick, Gwen, Vely, and I to be here?" she asked, her hands planted on her hips as she strode around the room. Dom watched her with amused eyes.

"Of course, I'm sure," Dom answered. "Why?"

"None of us are exactly experienced at... being pirates."

"You were confident about it a few months ago. Why the hesitation now?" Dom paused, watching her. "Do you want to quit?"

"No, of course not," Liza said, stopping abruptly. "I just wanted to know."

"What else is bothering you?" Dom asked, standing to cross the room to her. He stopped her fidgeting by resting his hands on her shoulders. Liza tried not to shy away from his touch. "You are still having problems trusting Cedrick." It wasn't a question.

"Yeah," Liza admitted. "But Vely trusts him."

"If he is an enemy, I'd rather have him here, where we can keep an eye on him," Dom said. Liza couldn't help the appreciative smile that crossed her face.

"I'm worried about Vely getting hurt. Not just on raids, but by him, too," Liza added. To her surprise, Dom shrugged his shoulders. Where was all this word vomit coming from?

"I know you want to protect her, Liza, but we have to let people get hurt sometimes. I remember when Becce and I first joined a crew. She fell for one of the gunners, and he turned out to be a pretty terrible guy. It was hard to see her so upset, but she became stronger because of it," Dom said. "We learn from all our mistakes." Liza tried to fidget again, but the weight of Dom's hands on her shoulders kept her in place. In response, she felt the tingles along her skin, her kathokinesis waking up to cause trouble.

"How do I know..." Liza began but stopped herself. Dom stepped closer, and the distance between them shrank.

"What?"

Liza bit her lip and felt arcs crawled down her arms and spine. Except there was nothing on her arms when she glanced at her skin. There were only little bumps, causing her arm hair to stand on end. She had chills.

"How do I know I'm not making a mistake right now?" she asked, her heart pounding in her chest, jolting her entire body. A devious sort of smile formed on Dom's lips.

"That's part of the fun, don't you think?" Liza scoffed and punched him lightly in the ribs. He chuckled and released his hold on her. "I'm only joking. You'll just have to trust me, I guess."

"I'm bad at that," she said.

"You'll learn." Dom touched her chin with his first and middle finger, tilting her face up towards his. She froze in an automatic response, her mind racing, her eyes furiously searching his, looking for intent. He stopped his face inches from hers. "Why do you look so scared?" he asked. Liza opened her mouth to reply, but nothing came out. Dom pulled back, his fingers sliding from her chin to her neck.

"This is all new for me," she managed to stumble out, trying her hardest to stop her heart from racing.

"This?"

"You," she said. Dom raised an eyebrow; he was toying with her. "Everything." A slight tilt of his head, a silent encouragement for her to keep talking. Liza sighed, feeling herself deflate slightly. Only Vely knew the things that were about to pour out. "Back on the Moon, *if* there was someone I was interested in, they usually ended up dead, one way or another. Killed in the fields, killed in the streets by the Enforcers; even my parents died that way. I allowed myself to feel attached once. The devastation afterward was horrific.

Vely said I wasn't going to die, but it felt like I would. I vowed to never feel that way again." Liza paused, looking down at her boots. "Then you came along." Her face heated with a blush. She could feel it creeping down her cheeks and up into her hairline.

"You are allowed to be happy," he said. "You need to give yourself permission to feel those emotions. Let go of your fears." Liza flicked her gaze up to his. He caught her cheek in his hand, his other arm sliding around her waist, palm resting on the small of her back. That sensation crawled up and down her spine once more. A smile lit up Dom's face. She saw it just before his lips closed over hers.

8

Inside the office of the Director of the Solar System Authority, dark-colored tiles struggled to reflect back the white lights shining from the ceiling. Most of the light in the room was absorbed into the darkness. The furniture and decorations, such as they were all straight lines and sharp angles, with minimal extra color beyond white, gray, and black. The room oppressed those who walked in, purposely draining them of whatever resilience they might have had before arriving. Alis Foste preferred it that way.

She sat at her desk, looking through several reports that glowed on transparent screens mounted to her desk. Supersensor recruitment was up, though actual completion of the rigorous training courses was down. Many were failing out. Lack of dedication, lack of willingness to serve. Lack of determination to live.

Using a finger, Alis pushed the reports away and opened another file, one that had been grating on her nerves for the past two months. Three pictures appeared on her screen: a young woman with unkempt dreads and a woman with neatly braided dreads. Both Kathokinetic. The third picture showed a young man with dark blonde hair. Augur. All three escaped on a ship called *Wasp*, most likely using their Kathokinetic ability to bend the pilot's will. The docking port of the Supersensory training facility sustained severe damage due to an errant gamma blast. Apparently, the two escaped kathos had deflected it. The ship managed to get away without a tail, and so far, no one had been able to track them down.

Alis tapped the picture of the dark-skinned girl, the only

thing about the entire situation that made her feel like it wasn't a complete failure. Alis would bring in Colonel Jeffry Morre, whom she'd managed to not murder after the escape, to discuss her plan with him in due time.

The door to her office slid open, and Lynwood stepped inside. His boots made loud clicking noises on the tiled floor as he walked that echoed around the room. Alis watched him through the screen. When he reached her desk, he set his tablet down and crossed his arms over his chest.

"Mulling over the Strange case again?" he asked, grinning. Alis closed the file and pushed the screens, sliding them off to the side.

"You know my detestation for weakness," she said, seating herself in her black faux leather chair. "But it has become something of an obsession." Lynwood smiled.

"Your secret is safe with me," he said. Alis gave him a dark look.

"What do you want?"

"I received some information from the officer who investigated that merchant ship," he said, lowering himself into one of the chairs on the other side of the desk. "He looked into the insignia on those guards' uniforms."

"And?"

"Well, nothing came up from that. But," he added quickly when her face became angry. "But we found out who was the commanding officer of the ship." Alis raised an eyebrow. "Bill Reade, former SSA officer, as you may recall, was previously stationed on a colony called SC-203. He was the commanding officer there as well, and after the life support systems failed, he was dismissed. We think that these guards, whatever their insignia stands for, have some link to Reade."

"Interesting."

"As far as we can tell, he lied extensively when he applied at Walnad. He didn't take responsibility for the life support systems and claimed that the death of the colonists was a heavy burden. Fake sympathy. Walnad hired him and made him an overseer for their mining operations."

"Why is all of this important?" Alis asked.

"It's a hunch, but I have this feeling he's hiding something. Something big. Perhaps he could be of use to us."

"He sounds completely unstable," Alis said. She pulled her screens back towards her, their mounts sliding across the track in her desk. She quickly accessed the SSA personnel records and found Bill Reade. Lynwood waited for her to skim through his discharge report. "Yes. Unstable." She glanced back to Lynwood. "There's suspicion he killed the life support systems on purpose."

"We never found evidence of that," Lynwood said. Alis sighed and leaned forward, bracing her elbows on the desk. She rested her chin on her interlaced fingers, her dark hair falling over her shoulders.

"I hate those poor, pitiful humans just as much as the next person, but if every colony is destroyed, we will lose the money that comes in from taxes and Walnad subsidies," she said. "What happened with the investigation of the Moon?" Lynwood colored.

"The officer in command of the Moon colonies fled. We still haven't found him," he replied. Alis growled low in her throat.

"Put a tail on Bill Reade. I want to know what he's doing," Alis said, leaning back in her chair. "Rogue SSA officers are dangerous, even former ones." Lynwood rose from the chair and picked up his tablet, tucking it under his arm.

"Of course, ma'am," he said. Alis waved a hand towards the door, a silent dismissal. Lynwood spun on his heel and clicked his way out the door.

Alis watched him leave before turning back to her screens. She stared hard at the photo of Bill Reade from the SSA personnel files. There was something about his expression that almost chilled Alis to the bone. That is if she was capable of feeling such a thing as *fear*.

9

Over dinner, Vely only half-listened while Captain Dom explained the scheduled meeting with Captain Thane Lezal from the Galactic Syndicate. She knew she should be paying attention to his words, but her sister was a distraction. Liza was a bundle of nerves, her willpower fighting to escape her skin, sitting beside her at the table. Though Vely couldn't see Liza's power the way her sister had described it, as little arcs that crawled and jumped around her skin. And Liza could not see the delicate, blue mist of Vely's Tranquility. Since their reuniting, however, they had become tuned into each other's abilities. They could feel each other's power and could feel the emotions behind the power. Since they had restored their dyad, the sisters had fewer psychogenic accidents.

Right now, something was agitating Liza, and her control over her own ability slipped.

Vely reached out and touched Liza's arm, where there was a bit of exposed skin. Liza glanced at her, eyebrow raised. Vely shook her head and allowed her Tranquility to seep into Liza, calming the agitation. Liza visibly relaxed, and Vely could feel Liza's power calm down.

"Thanks," Liza whispered. Vely nodded and shifted her hearing back to Dom, who was still talking about the meeting with Lezal. She had missed most of the information, and now it sounded like Dom was speculating or guessing about the meeting's agenda.

"Calm down, Cap, and eat your dinner," Corbin said, not looking up from his own plate. The crew chuckled. Dom grinned and seated himself. Conversation swelled around the table. The twins chattered to each other, speaking too quickly for anyone to follow, Becce engaged Gwen and Liza in conversation, and Corbin and Doctor D talked about the food. Cedrick, who was beside Vely, touched her arm.

"I'm heading back to my room," he said. Vely turned to look at him. She was about to ask why when she noticed how pale his skin was, the dark purple bags, and the bloodshot veins running through the whites of his eyes.

"Are you alright?" she asked.

"Just not feeling well. I'm going to try and get some sleep," he said. Vely nodded and watched him rise from the table, pick up his plate, and wander to the galley to deposit his food. No one around the table paid him any attention except Liza, who watched him with a stern expression. Vely sighed.

"You're never going to like him, are you?" Vely asked her sister. Liza shrugged her shoulders, and Vely felt Liza's agitation rise again.

"We can discuss this later," Liza mumbled, returning to her plate.

Vely leaned back in her seat, staring up at the ceiling. Something was wrong with Cedrick. Since he escaped from the SSA training facility with Liza, he'd been acting strange, and whatever was ailing him was causing severe physical symptoms. She wondered if Cedrick had talked to Doctor D at all. She'd have to ask him later.

Liza was another matter. Try as he might, Cedrick couldn't break through Liza's outer shell. Liza had listened patiently, albeit skeptically, to his explanation for what he'd done before he ended up on the Moon. The murder of his father and Augur mother by the SSA, trying to make money to survive on the Sun Stations by using his ability to rig illegal gambling rings. If he had been unable to pay the bills, he would have been sent to another colony anyway. He only prolonged that inevitable. Liza had brought up the accusations against him that he murdered his parents. Vely didn't give Cedrick the chance to answer that question, for she scolded her sister for being heartless. An insult Vely later apologized for.

But the tension between the two was thick, and Vely felt caught in the middle. She loved her sister, and she felt strong feelings for Cedrick, whatever they were. And he still maintained the same care for her that he'd shown before his arrest by the SSA. He always referred to them as "us" and "we," as if they were a couple. It hurt Vely that she couldn't discuss this with her sister. Wasn't that part of the reason for even having a sister?

Vely glanced down the table, where Becce and Gwen were still chatting with Dom. Perhaps one of them could be her confidant. At least they might be slightly less judgmental than her sister.

After the meal, the *Gypsy Star* made a short FTL jump towards their destination. When the FTL jump was over, Becce gave the crew the all-clear to leave their harnessed seats. The crew gathered in the bridge, strapping themselves to seats lined along the edge of the walls. Cedrick hadn't appeared from his room. Vely hoped he used one of the harnesses that could be accessed in case of emergency instead of sustaining the force of an FTL jump without restraints.

Slipping out from her harness, Vely followed Liza and Gwen back to their shared room. Apparently, they had been roommates at the training facility and were used to it sharing a room. Vely never thought Liza would willingly allow a roommate other than Vely herself.

"What's wrong with you today?" Vely asked Liza, who sat down on the bed to remove her heavy boots. Vely closed the door to the room and hopped up on the desk mounted to the floor, reinforced with welding should Liza blow it up again.

"Nothing."

"Liar," Gwen said. Liza glared at her. "Your defenses are down."

"I thought we agreed not to prod into each other's minds," Liza said. Gwen shrugged and smiled.

"You need more practice, anyway," Gwen countered. Vely smiled at their banter.

"So now you have to tell because otherwise, I'll just bribe Gwen to tell me," Vely said. Liza's face turned pink, and she glared between Gwen and Vely. She removed her other boot and dropped it on the floor with a clunk. She pushed herself up onto her bed, leaning against the wall. The bunk over top of hers, Gwen's bed, obscured part of her face.

"Dom kissed me earlier," Liza said after a prolonged silence.

Vely shrieked, and Gwen said, "Is that all?" Liza glared at them. Vely hopped off the desk and sat down on the bed with Liza.

"I thought you cared about him," Vely said. "Why does him liking you back throw you off balance?" Liza couldn't lie about that. Vely could feel it.

"I don't know."

"No one can compete with Liza's heart of ice," Gwen said, absently pacing the room, floating objects around with her kathokinesis. "I realized that right after I met her." Vely touched Liza's arm, not to give her more Tranquility, but to show solidarity and support.

"I know our childhood was tough," Vely said. "People who live in other places don't experience the same things we did."

"No kidding," Liza said bitterly. Vely tilted her head to the side. Liza was going to handle the situation in her way, no matter what anyone said. Vely thought of Cedrick and the first time he'd kissed her. The ensuing emotions and feelings were overwhelming and exciting. For Liza, who worked so hard to keep people away, maybe the feelings were stronger than usual. No wonder she was so off-balance. Vely also knew that soft words and encouragement weren't going to work. Instead, Vely released her hold on her sister, pushed herself off the bed, and planted her hands on her hips.

"Well, Liza Strange, someone finally likes you, so don't

screw it up," she said. Liza met Vely's eyes, a confused expression on her face. Vely returned a glare of determination. Scoffing, Liza crossed her arms over her chest.

"Thanks, little sister," she said sarcastically. Vely turned to leave the room, but she caught the grin that spread over Liza's lips. Marching through the door, Vely smiled and winked at Gwen, who was holding back a laugh.

Vely made her next stop at Cedrick's room. She tried the door and found it to be unlocked. Cedrick lay on his bunk, arm thrown over his eyes. Vely was relieved to see that the emergency harness had been deployed from the wall. Vely crossed the room to Cedrick and sat down on the edge of his bed. He stirred.

"Vely?" he asked without moving his arm.

"How are you feeling?" she asked. His response was a groan. "Have you talked to Doctor D yet?"

"No."

"Why not?"

"I doubt he can help me," Cedrick said.

"He's a doctor," Vely protested, but Cedrick shrugged his shoulders. "I'm only saying this because I care, but you have to talk to him to figure out what's wrong. Otherwise, the rest of the crew will think you're useless, and they might leave you somewhere else." Cedrick shifted his arm to reveal one eye, which was looking at Vely. "Dom is fair, but he won't tolerate someone who can't pull their own weight."

"I suppose you're right about that," he mumbled. Vely nodded, eyebrows raised. Of course, she was right.

"You're still part of the SSA wanted list, and you moved up a few spots since your escape from them," Vely said, unabashedly admitting that she'd been monitoring the "Most Wanted" list on the Sol Network. "So you'd be arrested right away if anyone found you."

"Alright, I'll talk to him," Cedrick mumbled. He threw his arm to the side and pushed himself into a sitting position. He still looked terrible.

"Are you not sleeping very well?" she asked.

"Not at all," Cedrick replied. "It started at the training facility," Vely pressed her lips together in a frown.

"Did they do anything to you?"

"Not that I remember."

"Come on. Let's go see Doctor D."

10

Liza sat on the floor of Weed and Speed's workroom, the soles of her boots pressed together, her knees splayed to the sides. With a metal screwdriver in hand, she attempted to pry apart a small component she'd removed from the bridge wall. Dom said he thought it was part of a security system, but no one had ever used it. Interested, Liza pulled the box down from the wall and tried to open it to see what parts were inside. Weed and Speed tinkered with a broken taser they'd picked up on the Cove.

The screwdriver wasn't working very well. Liza dropped it to her side and reached out for a nearby pile of tools. She concentrated her willpower on the tool she needed and sent arcs out to the pile. It wiggled free from the pile, and Liza snatched it from the air with a hand. With the narrow, pointed tip, Liza wedged the casing open and pulled the device apart.

Liza had noticed the difference in her control over her willpower. She could use her Kathokinesis to pull tools, electronics, or other random items to herself without issues if she was concentrating. It was when her mind was wandering and unfocused that she had less control. Gwen had observed this and confirmed. They wondered if it had to do with practice or if having Vely around helped balance Liza's power. Liza suspected it was a little of both.

The door slid open, and Tsuto stepped into the room in praying mantis form. He carried a metal box in his appendages. Liza watched him from her peripheral vision but continued to prod around inside the security device. Tsuto dropped the box on the work table in the center of the room, and the twin looked inside.

"Something from Doctor D?" they asked together, and Tsuto bobbed his head. "Broken?" Another bob of his head. Liza glanced up from what she was doing. Weed lifted the device from the box. It was one of Doctor D's enhanced microscopes. They both began to poke and prod at it and removed the outer case to expose the insides. Tsuto approached Liza, and as he walked, he shifted shape, taking on the form of Vely. Liza looked up.

"My sister wants me?" Liza asked. Vely's head nodded to her. Liza set aside her project and pushed herself to her feet. Tsuto shifted back to his mantis form. "Where is she?" Tsuto just tilted his head to the side. "I'll find her." Tsuto was only as helpful as he felt like. Liza nodded to the twins and left the room. She tromped up the metal steps to the next level of the ship, heading towards Vely's room. Cedrick's door opened, and Gwen stepped out. The expression on Gwen's face put Liza on edge.

"There you are," she said. Liza nodded in greeting.

"What's going on?"

"There's something wrong with Cedrick," Gwen said. She grabbed Liza's gloved hand and pulled her along to Cedrick's room. They entered to see Vely kneeling beside Cedrick's bed while he lay, thrashing violently in his sleep.

"Did you send for Doctor D?" Liza asked.

"He's on his way," Gwen said. They watched while Vely tried to restrain Cedrick's thrashing arms. He whispered something, but Liza couldn't hear what he was saying. Doctor D burst into the room, already wearing his white lab coat. Gwen and Liza moved out of his way as he knelt down beside Cedrick.

"When did this start?" Doctor D asked.

"I was going to bring him to see you because he hasn't been sleeping. Before I could get him out of bed, he fell asleep. I figured I'd let him sleep, which had been for about an hour. It was a few minutes ago that he got violent," Vely said. "He said

39

he hasn't been sleeping since he was at that facility with Liza."

Liza frowned and crossed her arms. She remembered how badly he looked while they were with the SSA. He had said something to her about not sleeping. Liza supposed, looking at him now, that she hadn't been paying him much attention. He certainly looked worse than before.

Doctor D checked Cedrick's vitals while dodging his erratic movements. "Gwen. Liza. Please come hold him down." They stepped to the bed, and Liza gently pushed Vely away. Between the two, Gwen and Liza were able to restrain his arms and legs. It was a surprise that he wasn't waking up, despite essentially manhandling him. "His heart rate is way too high," Doctor D said. He leaned forward and pushed up Cedrick's eyelids, beneath which his eyes were rapidly moving from side to side. "It's normal for REM during dreams," he said, but more to himself than the gathered crowd. Doctor D rose to his feet. "This will be unpleasant, but we need to wake him up."

"How?" Liza asked. "He hasn't woken up yet." Doctor D pressed his lips into a thin line. With a heave, Doctor D grabbed Cedrick under the arms and hoisted him from the bed. Liza and Gwen stumbled out of the way. Though he was upright and almost on his feet, Cedrick was still in the throes of some nightmare. Doctor D sighed and gave Cedrick a hard slap to the face. Vely shrieked.

Cedrick's eyes wrenched open. He looked around the room, his eyes moving frantically while his chest heaved. Doctor D rested Cedrick on his feet and kept one stabilizing hand on his shoulder.

"What's going on?" Cedrick asked, his voice panicked. Vely slid up to him and wrapped her arms around his midsection. "Did I hurt anyone?"

"Of course not," Liza said automatically, not controlling the scorn in her voice. Gwen elbowed her in the side.

"You were having some kind of violent nightmare," Doctor D said. "We couldn't wake you." Cedrick shook his head.

"No, it wasn't a nightmare," he said. "It was a vision."

Cedrick's knees gave way, and he sank to the bed, slipping from Vely's arms and dropping his head between his knees.

"What was the vision?" Vely asked.

"I don't know for sure…" Cedrick said. "But I know there was a lot of destruction and pain." He closed his eyes and shook his head as if trying to remove the images from his mind. Liza couldn't help the narrowing of her eyes. She hadn't spent much time learning about Augurs, but their ability seemed too subjective to take seriously.

"I need to do some research," Doctor D said. "But I might have an idea of what's wrong with you."

"Thank you, Doc," Vely said, looking up at him, worry in her eyes. Doctor D nodded and left the room. Gwen touched Liza's shoulder. Liza had trouble reconciling her sister's feelings for this guy when she couldn't feel anything for him.

"I want to talk to him. I think I have the same idea he does," Gwen whispered. Liza nodded, and Gwen followed Doctor D from the room. Vely touched Cedrick's arm, and Liza sensed the cooling sensation characteristic of Vely's Tranquility. She turned and left the room.

11

Gael Daniels had a headache. With fingers pressed to his temples, he tried to massage the pain away that continued to throb. He tried to think of what could have caused the sudden headache, but the only cause he could come up with was stress.

He had forgotten about the incident report from Bill Reade's ship for a few days. When he had a few minutes to himself, he scanned the report from the SSA investigator. As always, it was meticulously detailed. The investigator reported every dead, partially decomposed body found on the ship, along with information about the type of gas used to accelerate the decomposition process. It all made Gael's stomach churn.

Naturally, he put up a front when Alis Foste questioned him about the incident. In reality, he had only known that a pirate ship had attacked and looted the ship, destroyed the engines, and stole several crates that held a large quantity of astarte. That was a normal occurrence, and because of it, Alis' proposal for increased SSA coverage was going to be approved by the Walnad Executive Board. Gael hoped the increased coverage would cut back on the number of successful raids by the pirates.

But the bodies were disturbing. He didn't know who those people were or why they had been killed. And if they had committed a crime, why weren't they dropped off at an SSA prison or left in the brig? And if Bill Reade was behind it, what was his motive?

Gael sent a message back to Alis, giving her a cold response that he'd read the report and had no additional information. She'd probably call bullshit on him, but what else was there to do?

"Mr. Daniels?" Charles Mann called to him over the intercom.

"Yes?"

"Don't forget about your dinner meeting with Mr. Breton," he said. Gael groaned and felt the headache dig deeper into his skull. Dorian Breton was the democratically elected Sun Station representative and, unfortunately, had non-business-related ties to Gael. An insufferable man with no tact, horrible manners, and an empty brain. He was supposed to act as the liaison between Walnad, the Sun Station, and the SSA to ensure the Stations were getting their end of the bargain for putting up money to fund the SSA. Gael Daniels thought he was an idiot, and Alis Foste felt as much disdain for Dorian as any human could feel for another. This was a source of amusement for Gael. Sometimes he called meetings with Dorian just to watch Alis squirm.

"Thank you. I'll leave now," Gael said into the intercom. He shut down his computer terminal and lifted his suit coat from the rack in the corner of his office. He slipped it on over his shoulders and left his office, locking the door with his state-of-the-art biometric authentication security system - BASS.

Outside the Walnad headquarters building, Sun Station Alpha was temperature controlled at 22º C. At night, the temperature dropped to 16º C, which was supposed to be the optimal temperature for sleeping. Colonists could adjust the temperatures inside their own homes if they preferred warmer or cooler temperatures, becoming expensive. Most of the solar power collected from the sun went to manufacturing, farming, and colony maintenance activities. Most Colonists were content, however. They knew nothing different than what had always been.

Gael strolled down the sidewalk towards the restaurant where he was to meet Dorian Breton. The restaurant was called

Scorpio's Tail and boasted spicy and ultra-hot fare. Gael had been to Scorpio's Tail once before and found the food to be adequate. Dorian had picked the place, his penchant for spicy food being the only exciting thing about his personality.

Dorian was waiting for Gael outside the door to Scorpio's Tail, apparently using his communication lync to talk to someone. His hands flew through the air as he spoke, though the person he spoke to couldn't see him. Dorian was a large man with ashen skin, light-colored features, and consistently committed fashion faux pas. Gael shook his head and approached. Dorian saw him, quickly said goodbye, and turned off his lync. Gael tapped his breast bone with a closed fist, his thumb against his breast bone.

"Gael Daniels! A pleasure to see you again, my friend!" Dorian said and skipped the greeting, opting instead for a friendly hug. Gael froze under the gesture, resisting the urge to push the other man off of him.

"And you, Dorian," Gael said, plastering a fake smile on his face. "Shall we?" Dorian led the way into the restaurant and informed the young hostess of his reservation. They were led to a table near the back of the restaurant, the one with the most privacy.

"Have you been here before, Gael?" Dorian asked. He pushed the button for the menu screen to slide up from the middle of the table.

"Once."

"Ah, then you know how fantastic the food is!" Gael grunted in response. His eyes were scanning the cheesy names and descriptions of dishes. Dorian was already tapping his order into his side of the screen. "I highly recommend the Spitfire Tofu. Excellent flavor."

Gael picked something at random, and the menu retracted into the table. Gael laced his fingers together on the table and leaned forward. "The reason I wanted to meet you-"

"So, how have you been?" Dorian interrupted. "It's been a while." Gael bristled.

"Just fine. I wanted to discuss something with you," he said. "Business." Dorian flapped a hand at him.

"There's always time for business talk later," Dorian said. "Did you hear that my daughter had a child?"

"Ah, yes. Congratulations. The first?" Gael asked. Dorian nodded, already pulling his tablet from a pocket to bring up images of the child. Dorian showed him picture after picture of a tiny baby wrapped in a white blanket, cheeks still red and eyes mostly closed. Gael nodded at each image, making cursory noises of approval. Finally, after what felt like a few hundred pictures, Dorian replaced his tablet and leaned his elbows onto the table. A middle-aged waiter dropped off drinks and food to their table without a word.

"So, what did you want to discuss?" Dorian asked, already picking up his fork to eat. Gael swallowed a sigh.

"Another merchant ship coming back from a mining operation was raided by pirates," Gael said.

"That's terrible," Dorian said, without irony.

"Yes. Alis Foste has created a proposal for increased coverage by SSA officers and ships. The Executive Board of Walnad will most likely approve the proposal tomorrow. Do you think the Sun Stations will contribute?" Dorian took his time to answer. He took several bites and chewed slowly, either thinking or savoring the flavor. Or none of the above.

"They might be willing, but you know, we've already increased taxes," Dorian said. "I'm not sure how much higher we'll go before Colonists start to complain."

"Understandable," Gael said, glancing at the dish in front of him. None of it looked appetizing, but Dorian was staring at him expectantly. Gael picked up his fork and stuffed a bite in his mouth, and pretended to enjoy the food. It was bland.

"Perhaps we can work something out?" Dorian asked, already halfway through his plate.

"Like what?"

"The Sun Stations need more farming space. Perhaps Walnad builds that new addition we need, at cost, of course."

Gael tried not to let his mouth fall open.

"At cost? But that's..." Dorian was staring at him again with his innocently blank expression. Was Dorian actually intelligent? Was this an act? "Let me take it back to the board," Gael conceded. Dorian smiled and thumped the table with one fist.

"Excellent! I'm sure your execs will agree since it benefits everyone," Dorian said, spreading his hands wide. Gael nodded, feigning agreement, but he was still trying to figure out if these suggestions were Dorian's or perhaps planted in his mind by the Sun Station's governors.

Dorian excused himself to use the restroom, and while he was gone, Gael wondered what Alis would think of this development. Knowing her, she'd still think Dorian a complete idiot. Perhaps the man had picked up a mentor somewhere. Clearly, he was improving his negotiation skills somewhere. Gael would have to stay on his toes if he was going to keep controlling Dorian's every move. When Dorian returned from the restroom, Gael watched him with a stoic eye, wondering what was in his head. But Dorian proceeded to talk about his daughter and new grandchild for another hour, keeping Gael at the table long past the time he would have preferred to go home. Finally, there was no food left on their plates, and Gael's head was swimming with Sun Whiskey, and Dorian proclaimed that he *must* be going. They rose together, Gael fronting the bill, of course, and left the restaurant. They parted ways outside with a closed-fist tap to their chest.

12

The *Gypsy Star* docked on the L2X Rad station. Vely felt a slight jolt as the docking mechanisms locked into place and the gangway tunnel attached to the passenger door. Liza and Becce wanted to show Vely and Gwen around the Rad station, but Vely was in no mood. Doctor D ran tests on Cedrick, attempting to solidify his diagnoses, which he had yet to reveal to either of them.

Liza stopped by the med bay one more time before leaving the ship. "Are you sure?" Liza asked, glancing at the three in the room.

"I'm sure," Vely said. Liza lifted an eyebrow, shrugged, and turned to leave the room. Vely looked back to Cedrick, who was sitting up in one of the patient beds.

"I bet she wishes I was dead," Cedrick said, his eyes heavy-lidded. The dark circles under his had gotten worse. He looked as if he might pass out at any moment.

"That's not true," Vely said. Cedrick shook his head in disagreement. "We'll just have to keep trying." He shrugged his narrow shoulders. He had lost a lot of weight since his kidnapping from the Cove, and despite Corbin's best attempts, he hadn't gained back any. Doctor D pushed himself back from one of his lab benches and rose to his feet. With a tablet in hand, he moved to stand at Cedrick's bedside.

"I'm still not one-hundred percent on this, but all the symptoms are consistent," Doctor D said. "Gwen was able to provide some interesting insight as well."

"What is it?" Cedrick asked. Doctor D sighed. Vely knew it wasn't going to be good.

"I believe you are suffering from a condition called Augur sickness or vision sickness. Gwen's information about what kind of training Augurs undergo at that facility really gave me the final clue I needed." Vely's chest tightened unpleasantly.

"I've never heard of that," Cedrick protested. Doctor D nodded, his lips pressed together.

"It is not very common," Doctor D admitted. "Though many Augurs may have gone undiagnosed, just appearing to have gone insane." Cedrick frowned. "The condition is caused by the excessive use of the Augur ability to force visions onto oneself. Gwen said the SSA trained you by forcing you to have visions."

"Yes."

"And it causes the types of symptoms you're having: the sleeplessness, the vivid dreams or visions, the violent reactions to the visions you are having..."

"So, what does this mean?" Vely asked.

"There are a few suggestions for treatment, but none of them have proved to be effective. The tough thing about Augur sickness is that no cure has been found," Doctor D said. "We could try sedatives to help you sleep; you can try resisting your visions and generally avoiding using your ability too much. Of course, all forced visions must stop immediately." Vely saw Cedrick swallow with difficulty. "You are not currently forcing visions, are you?"

"Of course not," Cedrick snapped. Vely felt a twinge in her mind. *Lie.* She shook her head and pushed the thought away. Why would he be lying, and why would he be forcing himself to have visions? That didn't make any sense.

"I am going to suggest that we try the sedatives, and I'll monitor you here for a few nights," Doctor D said. Cedrick shrugged once more, looking down at his hands. Vely wanted to reach out to Cedrick, but something about his posture and demeanor told her to leave him alone.

"Do you need anything from me, Cedrick?" Vely asked

after Doctor D had stepped away and was rifling through a cabinet.

"No, Vely," he said. "I want to be alone." She reached out and tentatively touched Cedrick's shoulder, then quickly withdrew her hand and whirled out of the room.

Vely, however, did not want to be alone. As far as she knew, everyone else had left the ship. With nothing better to do, Vely left the ship and entered the bustling Rad station.

A large holographic map of the Rad station hovered in the center of open space outside the docking bay. Vely glanced it over, searching for the Rigel Tavern. Finally, the small building on the map caught her eye. It wasn't too far away. Vely memorized the directions and set off.

The L2X Rad station was a bustling metropolis of stores, restaurants, bars, and other establishments to entertain visitors. Vely knew she should be interested in all the different people she was seeing, be fascinated by all the things they never had on the Moon, but everything had a dull film over it. Her mind continually returned to Cedrick and the diagnoses that Doctor D had given him. She didn't know anything about Augur sickness, and she knew that she'd be spending the rest of the day worrying about it and researching it. Perhaps if Doctor D had been more upbeat about the whole thing, Vely wouldn't feel so nervous. But he made sure to say that there wasn't anyone known cure if one even existed. What happened to the other Augurs with this sickness? Doctor D said they would go insane. Would that happen to Cedrick? A part of her mind that she tried to ignore, the one that sounded suspiciously like Liza, said, *They die.*

"Shut up, Liza," Vely mumbled to herself.

The Rigel Tavern came into view. The building reminded her of the faux wood buildings on Mars, but it was only painted. She stepped up to the red door, and it slid open to admit her.

Inside was a rowdy crowd of whom Vely could only assume were pirates. Their behavior resembled the behavior on the Cove, and to her surprise, Vely recognized a few faces. She looked around for her sister among the crowd but with no luck. Finally, she saw twin heads of spiky green hair sitting off in one corner. Vely maneuvered her way through the tavern until she reached the far corner table where the crew sat with drinks in front of them. Gwen scooted over on the bench to make room for Vely.

"Where's everyone else?" Vely asked after she sat down. Corbin pointed to the ceiling.

"In a room upstairs with Lezal and some other Captains," he said.

"And Liza?"

"She's up there, too," Corbin said, unable to stop a grin from forming on his face.

"What's so funny?" Vely asked.

"Just amused by the Captain's actions, that's all," he said. Vely frowned and glanced around the table, and everyone else was grinning, too. Clearly, she was missing something, but at the moment, she didn't care. Tsuto sensed her distress and dropped an appendage on her shoulder in an attempt at a comforting gesture.

"Thanks, Tsuto," Vely said. A waitress from the Tavern appeared at the table and dropped off a round of drinks. She asked if Vely wanted anything. Deviating from her previous promises to herself, Vely said, "A Sun Whiskey, please."

13

Dom sat at the large table in the upper room of the Rigel Tavern, Liza and Becce flanking his shoulders like bodyguards. Becce's hands were planted on her hips while Liza had her arms crossed over her chest and her usual brooding expression on her face. Several other pirate Captains and their Quartermasters sat around the table, and Captain Thane Lezal sat at the head, his own cronies flanking him. He had removed his large hat and set it on the table. After taking a swig from his drink, he gestured to his cronies, who passed small devices to the Quartermasters. Becce took the device from the other cronies and pocketed it. Liza was curious about what the device was for.

"I have just given you all critical information about our mission here," Lezal said as he folded his fingers together over the table. "First, you now have a list of all the pirates who have deserted the Syndicate for the Corsair Collaboration. Names, ship names, communication identifiers, and so on. Second, that storage chip contains the most up-to-date information about Walnad routes, wormholes, current Walnad operations, and SSA locations. And last, we have uncovered extensive information about tracking SSA ships. Please don't jump into that too heavily. Many of their ships are much more powerful than yours."

Lezal glanced around the table, meeting the gaze of each person in the room. Liza glared hard at him when he met her gaze. He gave her a brief smile before moving on.

"As some of you are aware, we recently discovered that Shad Warwick and Zimir Tchesova were receiving large sums of money for capturing and sending Psychogens to the SSA, which only helps to bolster their Supersensory Division. We have one present here today who managed to escape that facility." The pirates leaned together, whispering, but Lezal did not reveal her identity. "As far as we can tell, they plan to use the Kathokenetics in long-range attacks on our ships, which we will be unable to fight against. We will only be able to try and escape. This presents a problem. Second, the SSA has asked for more money and resources from Walnad and the Sun Stations, and there's no reason why they'll be denied. Their fleet will grow. Not to mention, our escapee has informed us that the SSA has been created fake psychogens, but we don't know how they're managing that just yet. Additionally, Warwick and Tchesova have been released from the SSA prison where they had been confined," Lezal went on. Liza hadn't heard this, and neither had Dom or Becce.

"What?" Dom cried. Lezal shook his head and held a hand out to Dom, indicating for him to sit back down.

"We believe they have agreed to join the Corsair Collaboration and will be hunting us, with the SSA's blessing," Lezal said. "Their information is included on the storage ship. My point in bringing this up is that we must always be wary of traitors. Yes, we exist to steal and pilfer, but we do not exist to help the enemies of this solar system." To Liza's surprise, no one countered Lezal's words. They seemed to be more willing to condemn Warwick and Zimir for their actions, despite the amount of money they made from selling Psychogens. Pirates were strange creatures. Or perhaps they hated the SSA that much. Liza couldn't blame them.

"The reason I called this particular group together was to create a fleet. Some of you have probably guessed as much. We have five ships here, and together we're going to start taking out Walnad warehouse colonies, SSA hubs, and of course, their ships. We need a stronger foothold to rebel against their attempt to take over this solar system. After all, why exist if we don't cause as much trouble as possible." A round of cheers rose from the gathered pirates. Lezal grinned behind his bushy beard.

"One more matter…" Lezal said, gesturing for the pirates to quiet. "Warwick *was* my Underboss, but he is no longer. I'm passing that responsibility onto Dominik Rhyne, Warwick's former second." The eyes in the room turned to Dom, who froze under their stare. "Captain Rhyne, who is your second?" Lezal asked.

"I am," Becce said. "Becce Kerry." Lezal nodded.

"Excellent. We will be here for a few days. Fuel your ships, stock up on supplies. I will contact everyone when we are to leave."

Chairs scraped across the floor as the pirates stood, some turning to greet each other. Lezal made his way around the room and slapped Dom on the back. "You'll do fine, son," he said. Dom forced a smile, but Liza could see how nervous he was. It was a strange look for him.

"Thank you, sir," Dom said, pushing himself to his feet. Lezal moved on, and Becce rounded on Dom.

"You are a good Captain, you know," she said, somewhere between a scold and a compliment. "Lezal wants to groom someone young to take over for him when the time comes. We need to work on your confidence in public."

"He has no problem with it behind closed doors," Liza murmured, and Becce burst out laughing. Dom blushed, and Liza gave him a sardonic smile. He shook his head and dropped his hands on the two women's shoulders.

"Thanks," he said. Together, they left their room and made their way to the rest of the crew.

Just as Liza hit the first floor, she heard someone yell through the crowd.

"Hey, Strange!" Liza bristled and was ready to beat someone when a familiar face appeared in the crowd.

"Wayne River?" Liza asked in surprise. The tall, handsome pilot she had forced to help her escape was striding through the crowd towards her. He gripped her hand and pulled her into a rough hug. "What are you doing here?"

"Taking you up on your original offer," he said. Liza raised an eyebrow. "I'm joining the Syndicate."

"You are?"

"Not that it's *your fault*," he began, "but ever since I assisted you with your escape, the SSA has been after me. I don't think they want to throw me in prison, but once they find out that I willingly helped you, they might."

"Oops," Liza deadpanned. Wayne shook his head.

"It's fine. I have a small crew now, and I have a meeting with Captain Lezal. I believe I'll be joining this little fleet of yours," he said. Liza couldn't help the crooked smile on her face.

"I think you'll fit in just fine," she commented. Wayne slapped her shoulder and pressed past her towards the stairs.

"I'll find you later, Liza Strange," he said and disappeared up the shadowed stairwell.

14

Bill Reade sat at one end of a conference table, his hands bound in front of him, accompanied by two SSA Enforcers. He did not look happy.

Gael, Alis, Lynwood, and Dorian Breton sat around the conference table, having gathered for the sole purpose of finding out just what Bill Reade was doing with a room full of dead bodies. Reade hadn't made himself easy to catch once the merchant ship was destroyed. That only made him appear guilty in Gael's eyes. Not to mention, Reade would have to answer to a higher power if things went sideways during this meeting.

"So what exactly happened?" Dorian asked, his eyes shifting from Reade to Gael.

"He had a room full of dead bodies that were slowly disintegrating from an acid mist," Alis answered in her usual monotone. She held up a small remote and pressed a button. An image of the room appeared on the wall behind Reade. Dorian shrieked. Reade glanced back over his shoulder and smiled at his handiwork. Even Gael shuddered.

Lynwood rose, a tablet in hand and Alis removed the image from the wall. "Bill Reade. You're here to explain your actions. Do you understand?"

"I still don't understand why you're so uptight about this," Reade said, his eyes dark and menacing. "How are my actions any different than those of the SSA?" Gael had to resist shaking his head in disgust.

"Do you understand why you are here?" Lynwood repeated, his voice firmer this time.

"Yes," Reade finally answered.

"Who were those people?" Lynwood asked. A glint appeared in Reade's eyes. Malice? Amusement?

"They were your best workers, Gael Daniels," Reade said. Everyone in the room flinched, except for Reade.

"What?" Gael asked, rising halfway from his chair. Alis shot him a dark look, and he sat back down.

"That's right. Your best foremen as well." A heavy silence fell in the room while Gael, Lynwood, Dorian, and Alis processed that information. Gael had assumed that they were workers but not that they were his best workers.

"Why?" Gael asked.

"They challenged my authority."

"That hardly seems like a good reason to kill a bunch of people," Dorian commented. He was about to speak again when Reade gave him a slithering smile. Dorian closed his mouth and curled into himself.

"You told me 1531B was completed mined out. If it wasn't, why did you leave?" Gael asked, feeling sweat bead on his forehead from the effort of remaining calm.

"Oh, I lied about that," Reade said. Gael felt his anger rise and take over his disgust.

"Why would you lie about that?"

"I had to," Reade seemed to pause for effect. "They were traitors. They were plotting against Walnad and the SSA." Alis slammed her hand on the table and stood up, a gamma pistol in her other hand, aimed at Reade.

"Cut the cryptic comments and tell us what's going on here," she growled at him. Though her anger wasn't directed at Gael, he still flinched at her aggression.

"You should understand me, Gael," Howards said, throwing a meaningful look at him. Gael frowned deeply. Alis turned to him, her eyes blazing. "The traitors wanted us to be caught by the pirates. With all the astarte on board, the pirates would have gotten their hands on the entire shipment! You should be more grateful we hid most of it so they couldn't find it."

"He's insane," she hissed. Gael shook his head, his own fingers itching to draw his gamma pistol from its holster.

"We've been controlling the solar system for ages!" Reade cried, his hands spread wide. Dorian's face hardened, and he glanced up at Gael. They shared a brief moment of understanding. Gael could not allow this to continue. "Those people…" Reade went on. "They were a threat to us! And there's more out there, scheming under your noses!" Reade's eyes were wide and glossy, and sweat poured from his temples, wetting his hair.

"Who are you talking about?" Gael asked, fighting to keep his voice calm. Howards laughed, an unsettling sound that pierced the walls of the room.

"The *Cosmic Resistance!*" Howards shouted. His hysterics mounted, and Gael wrapped his fingers around the gamma pistol, hidden by his suit coat. "We must show them our power and might! We must show them what happens when you disobey!"

"Who is he talking about?" Alis asked, her voice low. Howards turned to Gael, his hands wide, his eyes pleading.

"We must stop them. They're a threat to us all! The Temple must— "

He barely had the last word out when Gael fired his gamma pistol, obliterating Bill Reade. Dorian cried out in horror while Alis merely winced. The SSA officers who had been guarding him both turned a sickly shade of green.

"We could have gotten more information out of him," Alis mumbled. Gael holstered his gamma pistol.

"He gave us enough information," Gael said. "Whatever this Cosmic Resistance is… it needs to be eliminated."

"How do you expect us to do that without his information? And what is this 'temple' he was talking about?" Alis asked.

"I have no idea. You're the one with the military power," Gael retorted. He rose from the table and patted Dorian on the shoulder. "Come on, Dorian. I just received some excellent Martian cigars. And a full bottle of Sun Whiskey." Dorian rose on shaky knees, his eyes wide and face pale.

"I'll inform Lieutenant Howards about his cousin, then..." Lynwood said, rising slowly from his chair, his face pale. Gael escorted Dorian from the room, and they left Alis behind, fuming.

15

The Rigel Tavern remained crowded, every table full of people. The Gypsy Star crew had spread out among the other tables to chat with pirates they knew and discuss Captain Lezal's plans. The noise in the room rose and fell with laughter, and loud discussions as each group tried to talk over the noise of the others. Vely, Gwen and Liza remained behind to save their table. With some reservation, Vely told Gwen and Liza about Doctor D's diagnosis for Cedrick.

"That's what I thought it might be," Gwen said. "I've seen it happen before."

"What is it?" Liza asked.

"In some of the bad cases I saw back at the SSA, the Augur would just go insane, trying to distinguish reality from their visions. Some of them stopped sleeping altogether. The human body can't really survive without sleep," Gwen explained. Vely pressed her lips together in worry. Cedrick wasn't that bad yet, but would he end up that way?

"What would eventually happen to them?" Vely asked, not really wanting the answer.

"Some would die from sleep deprivation, some might attempt suicide, and some would just... disappear."

"Disappear?"

"We always assumed the SSA took them away and did something with them, but we never knew what," Gwen said. "But it's not pretty."

"I don't want any of those things to happen to Cedrick," Vely said. "There has to be a way to cure it." Gwen smiled, but it was a sad smile.

"The SSA has been researching a cure, but so far, they haven't figured anything out," Gwen said. Vely hung her head and considered ordering another shot of Sun Whiskey. She felt a gentle pressure on her shoulder. She glanced to the side and saw Liza had a gloved hand resting there.

"We'll figure out something," Liza said. Vely smiled, and though she knew it would upset her sister, she threw her arms around Liza and gave her a hug. Liza patted her back in return.

"Thanks," Vely said after she released Liza. Gwen reached across the table and covered Vely's hand with her own. They fell into silence for a moment until a voice cut across the tavern, drawing their attention.

"Liza Strange!" Liza looked up from her drink, craning her neck with a moderately annoyed expression on her face. The crowd parted slightly, and a slim young man appeared. He dropped down at the table beside Gwen. "Gwen! I didn't know you were here, too!" he said, throwing an arm around Gwen's shoulders. She raised her eyebrows.

"Wayne River," Gwen said, a smile on her face. "What are you doing here?"

"Didn't Liza tell you? I'm joining the Galactic Syndicate."

"Are you drunk already?" Liza asked. He simply nodded, and his eyes landed on Vely.

"Who's this?"

"This is my sister, Vely Strange," Liza said. Vely reached across the table to shake Wayne's hand. "This is Wayne River. He helped us escape."

"Completely willingly," Wayne added with a wink to the girls.

"What made you change your mind?" Gwen asked. Wayne motioned for a server to bring him a drink.

"After I dropped you off, the SSA tried to get in contact with me. They assumed I was controlled by you, so I let them believe that. As a few weeks passed, their messages got more violent and aggressive. Then my weekly stipend of Simlars from the SSA stopped appearing in my account. Got a little spooked after that, so I figured I'd join the Syndicate to give myself some protection," Wayne explained. Gwen looked despondent.

"I didn't think about how it would affect you," Gwen said, dropping her chin. Wayne waved a hand to dismiss her concern.

"The SSA doesn't tend to keep people like me around very long. Once we start learning secrets, we're usually... dispatched," Wayne said. "This is a better option for now."

"Will you be traveling with Lezal's fleet?" Liza asked, and Wayne answered by nodding his head, drinking deeply from his cup. He set his cup down.

"He was surprised at my small crew," Wayne said, "but he was happy to hear about my E-class speeder that I keep on board. You know, just in case."

"We could have stolen your speeder instead of taking your entire ship?" Liza asked. Wayne rolled his eyes.

"Like you'd be able to pilot it." Liza just shrugged her shoulders with a mysterious grin on her face.

Vely noticed the way Gwen and Wayne kept throwing sidelong glances at each other. Vely smiled sweetly at the exchange and tried not to laugh.

Vely, Liza, Gwen, and Wayne eventually left the tavern to wander back to the spaceport. The others were tipsy or drunk while Vely led the way, being the only sober one. It seemed as if most of the people still wandering the Rad station were very drunk, all trying to make their way back to the spaceport or to the various hotels scattered around the station.

Halfway back to the spaceport, a loud shout cut through the crowd. Everyone froze, looking around for the source of the cry. A few people moved, and Vely was able to see three SSA Enforcers standing over two men on the ground. Beside her, she felt Liza tense, and her willpower swelled; Vely could feel the power pressing against her body. She reached out to grab her sister's arm, to stop her from pushing forward into the crowd.

"What's going on up there?" Gwen asked.

"Those Enforcers are hurting people," Liza growled. Vely tightened her hold.

"Don't go rushing in there, Liza," Vely said. "You'll get hurt, or someone else will get hurt."

"I can't let them do this," Liza said. The crowd dispersed, and Vely could see the Enforcers pulling their weapons from their holsters. The crowd began to run away, fearful of the gamma pistols.

"Your sister is right, Liza," Wayne said, pushing past Liza to block her way. "Don't get mixed up in this. You'll draw attention to yourself and the others." Liza growled in the back of her throat. Gwen dropped a hand on Liza's shoulder. Vely saw a look pass between the two, and Liza grinned. They were up to something.

Both turned to look at the crowd, and both their faces set in concentration. Vely watched, feeling her own fear and anxiety welling up inside, worried that something terrible was going to happen. A tingle on her skin alerted her to Liza using her powers. The Enforcers turned towards Gwen and Liza and broke into a run towards them. Vely saw Liza rip her glove from her hand, and when the first Enforcer reached them, Liza planted her hand on his face. Vely felt the force of Liza's willpower slam into the Enforcer's body.

"Liza!" Gwen cried. Vely blinked. The Enforcer that Liza touched was frozen in place, his eyes glazed and distant. "You Snapped him." Liza dropped her hand from his face and stepped back.

The other two Enforcers stopped moving, and with Gwen's command, holstered their gamma pistols back inside the holsters. The men who had been attacked were bleeding profusely and trying to get back to their feet. A few people from the crowd rushed to the men on the ground, ready to give aid. The two remaining Enforcers walked away, their gazes blank and uninterested. The Snapped Enforcer remained standing where he was.

"Oops." Liza didn't sound very sorry.

"She what?" Vely asked, interrupting Wayne, who was asking the same question.

"Snapped. It's when a Katho bends someone's will too far, and it breaks," Gwen said. Liza didn't look affected by this at all.

"What will happen to him?" Vely asked, remembering how she'd accidentally flooded a man's mind with Tranquility, turning him into a drooling vegetable.

"He'll probably commit suicide," Gwen answered. Vely tried not to wince.

"That's harsh, girl," Wayne said. He strolled through the crowd towards the Enforcer that was still standing perfectly still among the quickly vanishing crowd. Wayne stopped in front of the Enforcer and examined him, peering into his face. He touched the man's chest but received no reaction. "He's like one of those things... what were they called..." Wayne asked, tapping his foot on the ground in thought. He snapped his fingers. "Zombies! From old Earth literature!" Vely raised an eyebrow. She had never heard of anyone else who had read anything from Earth.

"Should we do something about him?" Vely asked. Gwen and Liza both shrugged. "

"Just leave him here," Liza said, grumpier than she'd been a few minutes prior. "Let's go back to the ship."

"But-"

Liza, Gwen, and Wayne were already walking. Vely glanced back at the Enforcer once more, the one who'd been Snapped. A guilty feeling gripped her head. She didn't like the Enforcers any more than the next pirate, but this fate seemed strange and harsh. Against her better judgment, Vely tore her eyes away from the Enforcer and jogged to catch up with the others.

16

It was unusual for Alis to oversee the new Corsair recruits as they received their equipment and ships, but a new annoyance had taken hold of her mind, and she was determined to make sure everything was done correctly. Finding out that somewhere in the galaxy, there was a resistance group calling themselves the Cosmic Resistance. It was just another thing she didn't want to deal with.

As it was, she came down from her proverbial tower to greet several new arrivals. She may have gone to see the recruits anyway. Shad Warwick and Zimir Tchesova had arrived after being picked up from an SSA prison and brought to the headquarters. When Alis heard about how their crew had mutinied and turned them in, she became interested in the two. Alis was aware of their past dealings with the SSA, such as bringing in new Supersensory recruits, and was willing to assist them now that they were shipless. Their knowledge of the inner workings of the Galactic Syndicate could be helpful.

She watched the two former pirates disembark from an SSA ship. They were wearing obvious hand-me-downs from the prison, old worn trousers, and oversized prison-issued shirts. Their haggard appearance put quite a damper on Alis's enthusiasm. It also appeared that the prison did not allow haircuts or shaves.

Alis approached the two men with Lynwood trailing at her side. She smiled and held out a hand in greeting. "Welcome to the SSA headquarters, gentlemen," Alis said. "My name is Alis Foste, and this is Lynwood Gammon." Warwick was the first to shake her hand, followed by Zimir. Alis had heard rumors that Zimir was a Bloodhound. If that were true, it would certainly make things interesting.

"Pleasure to finally meet you in person," Warwick said with a sick sneer. Alis tried not to show how disgusted she was by his expression. A chill crawled up her spine. Her previous dealings with him had not prepared her for the real thing.

"I heard about how you ended up in that prison. I thought you might have information for me in regards to the pirates that I will find useful," she said. Warwick and Zimir exchanged glances.

"That's a possibility," Warwick said, stroking his beard with one hand.

"We have a different sort of revenge planned," Zimir said. Beside her, Lynwood shuddered at the sound of his voice. She shot him a glance.

"Oh?"

"Zimir means to say that we would like to have a chat with our former crew," Warwick said. Alis fought a grin from appearing on her face. "I should have left that meddling Katho and her sister her in the middle of space to die when I had the chance," Warwick mumbled. Two months in prison must have given the two men a lot of time to think and sulk.

"I'm sure we can arrange for you to confront your old crew," Alis said. "In the meantime, please make use of our facilities to enhance your wardrobe and receive any grooming you might prefer. Your ship and a small crew will be assigned to you soon."

"Thank you," Warwick said, bowing his head slightly. Zimir simply stared at her with his hard, unfeeling eyes. Alis stared back. She could tell that he was like her, but his tastes for vengeance were very different.

Lynwood accompanied Alis back to her office. She sat down at her large desk and tapped her fingernails on the smooth surface. Lynwood watched her for a moment before speaking.

"Do you think it wise to send them after the *Gypsy Star*?" Lynwood asked. Alis pressed her lips together.

"I'm not sure I'm ready to decide that just yet," Alis said. "I'd like to get more of a feel for how insane those two went while in prison."

"They weren't there very long," Lynwood commented.

"True, but there's something in their eyes…" She trailed off, staring off into the distance. "Anyway, make sure the turnaround on these new Corsairs happens quickly. I have received a report stating that there are many pirates at Rad Station LX2 right now, and I'm sure they're up to something."

"Shall I send a fleet?"

"Not yet," Alis said. She felt him stare at her a little longer, but she had no other words for him. Finally, he made a quarter-turn towards the door.

"I'll see to the recruits. Contact me if you require anything," Lynwood said. He crossed the office and left through the sliding door.

Alis leaned back in her chair, her fingertips pressed together. She knew that Lynwood wouldn't understand the mild feeling of excitement in her gut from the thought of a three-way showdown. There was no way the Cosmic Resistance could gain a foothold in the galaxy, and the pirates, though numerous, could be quickly snuffed out. Their egos allowed them to do as they pleased as if no one would ever catch them when their guard was down. But Alis had a plan, and it was sure to cause quite a stir among the pirates when she activated that plan. Her manufactured Supersensors were going to bring the solar system to its knees.

Alis turned on her communication lync and alerted Lynwood. His voice came through a moment later.

"Yes?" he asked.

"Bring me Jeffry Morre."

17

"Lezal's plan is to travel as a group to TRAN67, a wormhole that will take us to the Hestia II solar system," Dom said, addressing the gathered crew in the bridge. "Walnad found that wormhole several years ago and most likely has been mining whatever planets and moons are on the other side. Lezal sent a group of pirates to follow the Walnad ships and find this wormhole, and they finally succeeded."

Becce tapped a few buttons on the holoprojector console, and a map of the galaxy appeared. She zoomed in towards a location where a glowing light pulsated. "That's where the wormhole is located," Dom said, pointing to the pulsating light. "While on our way to this location, we'll likely run into some other merchant ships. We'll have a chance to destroy and loot those ships. The biggest issue with this plan..." Dom zoomed out away from the wormhole on the map, and Becce tapped another button. "There are no nearby Rad stations. I'll be purchasing a backup J-Jar for extra fuel. We'll make our final Rad station stop here-- " Dom pointed to a spot on the map, "and continue on our way. We will not be able to make an FTL jump until we're near the wormhole. That's the only safe way through the wormhole, so we have to save our fuel."

"This seems dangerous," Vely whispered to Liza, who raised an eyebrow.

"Of course, it's dangerous," Liza whispered back.

"We'll be leaving in two days," Dom said, closing down the holoprojector. "Wrap up whatever business you have here. Dismissed."

The crew stood from the chairs in the bridge and began to head towards the lift. Vely stopped Liza before she could disappear.

"Are you sure we should do this?" Vely asked, trying to keep her voice low. Liza shifted her weight on her feet and dropped a hand on her hip.

"Why are you concerned?" Liza asked.

"Aren't you? We're following a bunch of pirates into a *wormhole*," Vely said. Liza almost wished she had Vely's power to calm her down.

"I don't think Lezal is going to send us all into a wormhole if it was going to kill all of us," Liza said. "He would die, too. I don't think that's his plan."

"But it's dangerous."

Liza shrugged. In fact, Liza was itching to fight, to use her power. Her frustrations towards the SSA grew more and more each day, and the tattooed identification code on her arm was a constant reminder of what they'd tried to force her to become. Liza had not told anyone about the growing anger inside of her, but she had a suspicion that Gwen knew. But even Liza's desire for vengeance had limits, and if her sister wanted to avoid a perilous mission, Liza wouldn't get in the way.

"If you're scared, have them drop you off somewhere," Liza said. "We'll circle back and pick you up after." Vely tilted her head.

"That's crazy," she argued. Liza shrugged.

"I'm not afraid of this mission," she said.

"I'm not afraid..." Vely mumbled. Becce approached the sisters, her hand on her hip.

"What's going on?" Becce asked, showing concern. Liza shrugged, but Vely spoke.

"I'm concerned that this mission is dangerous," Vely said. Becce shrugged her shoulders.

"Well, we can always come to find you afterward," Becce said, "if you'd rather wait here. I don't know how long we'll be gone. Maybe a month or two in Earth time." Vely shifted her weight, still uneasy about the situation. "Well, you have a few days to decide before we leave this Rad station." Becce stepped away, dropped her hands to her sides, and disappeared down the lift. Dom was still in the bridge but didn't appear to be paying them any attention.

"Sorry, Vely," Liza said, spreading her arms to the sides. "This feels right to me, and I want to go on this... adventure." It was hardly the right word, but Liza could think of nothing else. 'Murder quest' was hardly an appropriate way to describe something causing her sister distress.

"Adventure..." Vely repeated. Liza gripped Vely's shoulder, silently demanding that her sister meet her gaze.

"If you want to make a future for yourself, do it. We can do anything now. And even if we do part ways, it's not as if we will never see each other again. Besides, we have both learned to control our abilities. I'm not afraid of our Dyad breaking again," Liza said.

"I suppose you're right about that," Vely said. "But we finally found each other again, only to go in opposite directions?" Liza smiled.

"This time will be by choice. That's different," she said. Vely tried to smile. Liza hesitated a moment but released her insecurities and pulled her younger sister in for a hug. Vely returned the hug with force but only prolonged it a moment. They released each other and stepped back.

Vely stepped around her sister without another glance and disappeared down the lift, leaving Liza behind in the bridge. Liza sank into one of the chairs and crossed her arms over her chest. In all honesty, she wasn't thrilled about the idea of Vely leaving the ship, but she certainly wasn't going to stop her. Liza surprised herself with the words of comfort she managed to speak and had no idea where they came from. It almost felt like she was channeling her mother.

Dom looked up from the command console on the holoprojector.

"That must have been difficult for you," he said. Liza

gave him a curt nod in affirmation. "But I think you're right. There's nothing wrong with the two of you following your own aspirations." Liza pushed herself back onto her feet.

"It's strange to have that freedom," she said, her hands dropping to her hips. "Am I selfish for wanting to do something for myself?" Liza didn't expect an answer, but Dom gave her one anyway.

"Of course not," he said. He stepped away from the command console. He stretched an arm around her shoulders. "I think you handled that well. If Vely decides to do something else while we're gone, then, of course, we can find her again later. This time, you'll have ways to keep in contact with each other." Liza grunted in response, and Dom chuckled. "Don't worry. Everything will work out."

"I hope you're right."

18

Vely still felt uneasy after leaving the bridge. Liza had made her feel a little better about their differing opinions, but there were still things of which she was afraid. Liza could die on that mission, and they'd never see each other again. Or something could happen to Vely while Liza was gone; she could end up hurt or dead. An uncomfortable realization came over Vely as she made her way to her room on the ship.

I always rely on others to help me.

Vely entered her room and allowed the door to close and lock behind her. Sinking into the thin but comfortable mattress on the bunk bed, she closed her eyes. Memories of her childhood flashed before her eyes. All through their childhood, Liza had been her protector, her defense against anyone who would want to harm her. Or her parents. Vely managed on her own only a few days after her mother's death, and Vely had to run away to survive. Even then, Cedrick had come to her rescue after she'd inadvertently started a riot.

She should learn to protect herself and learn to use her power. She should stop being afraid of what could happen and focus instead on what she can accomplish and live for the moment.

"Like Liza does," Vely said to herself. She rose from the bed and paced her room. Vely could go on her own adventure and choose her own way, just as Liza wanted to do.

Someone knocked on Vely's door. She pressed the button beside the door to unlock it, and the door slid open, revealing Gwen in the doorway.

"Vely, do you want to go out to the station? Wayne and

I are going back to the tavern," Gwen said. Vely shrugged her shoulders.

"Sure." Vely grabbed a long jacket from her closet and pulled it on over her shoulders, and followed Gwen from the room. As they stepped back into the hall, the door to Cedrick's room opened. He stepped out, looking haggard but awake. He brushed his hair back from his forehead.

"What are you girls doing?" he asked.

"Going to the tavern for a drink. You look like you could use one," Gwen said with a smile. Cedrick nodded his head and joined them in the hall. "I think a few of the others are already there."

"Let's go, then," Vely said, and allowed Gwen to take the lead, so she could fall in step with Cedrick. "How are you feeling?"

"Doctor D's sedatives have been helping," Cedrick replied. "They make me a bit groggy, though."

"But you can sleep without visions?"

"For a few hours."

"I had a thought," Vely said. "if you want."

"What is it?" he asked, his hand circling Vely's back to rest on her waist.

"You didn't hear Dom's explanation of Lezal's plan, but I can fill you in later. I'm afraid," she said.

"Of what?" Cedrick asked.

"Of the mission."

"So, what do you want to do?" he asked. Cedrick and Vely followed Gwen from the ship, traversing the gangway.

"I don't know yet, but... well, Liza said I could make my own adventure." Cedrick laughed with a smile on his face.

"She's not wrong," he said.

"If I chose not to go on this mission, would you come with me, wherever that ends up being?" Vely asked.

"I would go with you," Cedrick said. "Unless your plan is to turn yourself into the SSA. I can't agree to that."

"Not a chance," Vely said with a grin. "I checked recently.

I'm still on their 'Most Wanted' list. Along with you, Liza and Gwen. I even saw Wayne River on there, too." Cedrick chuckled.

"Impressive." Cedrick stopped Vely, allowing Gwen to keep walking ahead. He held her with his hands on her biceps. "I had originally planned to try and make us all a team, a team of Psychogens. But I think right now, that plan is not feasible. Besides, at this point, there's not much just the three of us could do." Vely raised her eyebrows.

"What were your plans?" Cedrick shook his head.

"They're not important right now. But I will come with you, wherever you want to go," he said. Vely blushed and smiled.

"Thank you." Cedrick leaned forward and brushed a kiss to her lips. When he released her, he kept his hand entwined with hers, and together they continued the short walk to the tavern.

Inside, Gwen had already joined a table with members of the *Gypsy Star* and Wayne River. Liza and Dom were absent. Vely and Cedrick sat at the table with the others, who scooted down on the benches to make room. Doctor D leaned forward.

"Sleeping alright?" he asked Cedrick.

"Better than before. Thanks, Doc," Cedrick answered, shouting over the noise of the tavern to be heard. Doctor D smiled and raised his glass to Cedrick. A server appeared at the table, took the order for another round of drinks, and disappeared into the chaos.

Vely watched the crew laugh, talk, and drink with a slight sadness in her chest. If she did decide to leave the crew, would she ever see them again? She cared for them all. The crew had been kind to her, yet Vely felt she had not repaid their kindness.

On the Moon, Vely and Liza didn't even know there were pirates in the solar system, terrorizing ships, stealing, and making trouble for the SSA. Vely had learned enough from history that pirates were regarded as being ruthless and evil, and yet she had met many pirates now, in the last few months, who were not nearly as scary and horrible as she would have expected. There were a few exceptions, of course, but overall, they were decent to their own. Vely couldn't deny that she'd learned a lot from them as well, and they helped her grow into a stronger person. But now, she knew, despite her misgivings, that she needed to do something on her own. To break away from her reliance on others.

The tavern door opened once more, and Liza and Dom entered, followed by Captain Lezal. Vely wondered what they had been doing; many pirates from Lezal's crew were already in the tavern, already drunk. Lezal followed Liza and Dom to their table and joined them when enough room was made for them on the benches.

"Where were you?" Corbin asked who was closest to the three.

"Negotiating the sale of an extra J Jar for your ship," Lezal answered. "I have some excellent contacts on this station."

"It will be delivered tomorrow, and we'll set it up in the cargo bay," Dom said. "We're going to need the help of our resident Kathos to move it when the time comes," he added, pointing to Gwen and Liza as he spoke.

"Not a problem," Gwen said. More drinks were ordered, and soon their corner of the tavern was loud and rowdy with laughter.

As much as Vely tried, she couldn't feel a part of the group. She had already mentally removed herself from the crew. When she did leave, she thought she might leave silently, only saying goodbye to her sister to avoid answering any awkward questions. She'd leave a note with Liza and would be gone before the rest of the crew could try and stop her.

The night wore on, and Vely's eyes drooped. With each blink, it was harder and harder to open her eyes. Cedrick looked tired as well; his chin dropped down to his chest, only to jerk up after a loud burst of laughter. Vely stretched her arms up over her head, feeling her muscles stretch and her spine crack. She lowered her hands and pushed them into her coat pockets. Inside one of her pockets, her fingers brushed against a thin, metal square. She drew the square out and looked at it.

Ren Para of Mars.

The fog of indecision parted in Vely's mind.

It was very late when the tavern emptied of pirates and other patrons, most of whom could barely walk under their own volition. Vely held up Cedrick, who wasn't so much drunk as exhausted and followed behind the rest of the crew. Liza carried Dom, the twins attempted to carry each other, and Tsuto had changed into an oversized version of Corbin and carried Becce on his back. At the same time, he held up Corbin and Doctor D. Gwen and Wayne walked side by side, apparently not too intoxicated, their heads close discussing something. Something was going on between them, and Vely thought it was cute. Vely smiled.

The mass of people heading towards the docking port moved slowly, their desire for their beds hindered by the amount of alcohol consumed. That was why, when gamma pistols began to fire, the crowd was slow to react.

Blasts of gamma fired off in different directions, taking down a few people. Vely pulled Cedrick down to the ground to avoid the blows. Others dropped to the ground too, but Vely could not tell if they had been hit by a blast.

"What's going on?" Cedrick asked her.

"I don't know," Vely said, trying to peer through the bodies to find her sister. Liza was nearby on her hands and knees, a ferocious look on her face. "Liza!"

Liza turned her head and saw Vely.

"Stay down!" she shouted back. Liza pushed herself to her feet and searched the bodies for Gwen. Dom tried to rise. He grabbed Liza's hand and implored her not to get involved. She shook him off. "Gwen!"

The other Katho rose up out of the bodies. More gamma blasts were fired wildly into the air. Already, several structures had been hit and were boasting large, smoking holes. If any of the blasts hit the exterior shell of the Rad Station, everyone would be doomed.

"I have to help," Vely said, barely realizing what she meant as she spoke.

"No, stay here," Cedrick protested, but Vely ignored him and rose up. She stepped around people on the ground, who were still trying to hide from the blasts. Now that she was standing, she could see the group of people firing their gamma pistols. It was a group of men and women, all wearing a dark blue armband around their biceps. The SSA logo shone from the band. They had the attitude of Enforcers but were hardly dressed like usual SSA crones; they were rag-tag and scruffy, scarred. Even so, these new SSA monsters were flanked by several orange-uniformed SSA Enforcers. Vely caught up to Gwen and Liza, who were already drawing willpower from those around them.

"Who are they?" Vely asked.

"I heard someone say they're from the SSA's Corsair Collab," Liza said. Vely could feel Liza drawing more and more power, and she worried about just how much her sister could handle.

The group of Corsairs moved forward, followed by the Enforcers. They stepped on and over people who were still trying to hide by lying on the ground. Vely wasn't sure, but she thought their gamma pistols were spent and needed time to recharge before they could be fired again. At least that could buy them some time to retaliate.

"Any pirates here who wish to remain alive can willingly turn themselves in now," one of the Corsairs shouted over the crowd. "You'll be brought to the SSA headquarters to be *recalibrated*." Vely heard Liza mumble a very long string of swear words.

"We need to destroy their weapons first," Gwen said. "We don't need to Snap them all."

"Why not?" Liza asked. Gwen gave her a dark look.

"Fine."

Vely didn't know how she could help. Lately, she had only used her Tranquility to dampen Liza's errant power. That wouldn't be helpful now. She looked around to the people lying around her feet. Some were crying and screaming, holding to each other for dear life. Vely released a long breath and allowed her Tranquility to seep from her skin, to calm those who were afraid. In her mind, she imagined a barrier around Gwen and Liza to avoid affecting them. She didn't know if it would work, but it was worth a try.

Liza and Gwen reached out with their willpower. The gamma pistols in the hands and holsters of the Corsairs, one by one, exploded. The Corsairs cried out when their pistols were reduced to scraps of metal.

"What the--?"

Liza and Gwen pushed against the Corsairs and Enforcers, forcing them back, away from the other pirates. They stumbled over each other, knocked each other down, and pushed each other out of the way. They cried out in anger, unable to explain how their bodies moved contrary to their desires.

"What should we do with them?" Liza asked. "Since you don't want to Snap them." Gwen chewed her lower lip for a moment, then glanced at Vely.

"You can blank their minds, can't you?" she asked.

"I have to be touching them," Vely answered. She was glad she had an excuse; she did not especially want to harm anyone.

"Bend them just enough to send them on their way," Gwen said, her attention back on Liza. "We'll send them to Jupiter."

"Won't they come out of it eventually? We can't maintain it forever," Liza said.

"It will last long enough to get them out of here and to keep these people safe," Gwen replied. Liza nodded. Vely felt the nature of Liza's willpower shift to a more direct effort against the Corsairs' minds. It was a good plan to send them away from the Rad Station if they could have gotten that far.

A group of ten pirates, those who were furthest away from Vely's Tranquility, rose up from the ground once they realized that the Corsairs and Enforcers were now weaponless. With shouts of anger, the pirates descended on the Corsairs. Vely shut her eyes and turned her head away when the first attack came. She felt Liza and Gwen's power die away.

"So much for that plan," Liza commented, watching the violence.

"That will be on their conscience, not ours," Gwen said, turning to face Liza. "We have to be careful, Liza. We don't want to become what the SSA tried to turn us into." Liza's face fell as she contemplated this angle. It had been evident to Vely that her time at the SSA training facility had changed her sister, had given her some new purpose. But it was a dangerous purpose that Liza had chosen. Gwen knew it, too, and Vely watched as Liza began to struggle internally with what she wanted and what was morally right.

19

Pirates helped each other from the ground, brushing themselves off, shaking off the effects of Vely's Tranquility from their minds. Liza barely acknowledged the activity around her. She could hear the voices of her crew, asking each other if they were okay, confirming that they were not injured, but her mind barely processed their words. Gwen was still staring at her, an eyebrow raised.

"Come back, Liza," Gwen said, shaking her with a hand on the shoulder. "It's okay. I understand how you feel."

Did she? Liza turned further inward, trying to decipher the tangled web of thoughts and emotions that made up her brain. Liza could hear Dom trying to talk to her outside and Gwen calmly asking him to give Liza her space. Then Gwen was inside her mind.

I know you are desperate to try and make up for the horrors you experienced on the Moon. I know you wanted to destroy them. But there are other ways to accomplish that. Taking down a few people at a time won't do anything. Bloodying your hands will change nothing.

Liza blinked, her vision clearing slightly, and she could see Gwen again, her hand still on Liza's shoulder.

"There you are." Liza shook her head and stepped away from Gwen's touch. The crowd around her was still reeling from the attacks. Crews looked for each other, hoping none of their friends were the ones caught by gamma pistol blasts. Liza tried to calm her racing heart and silence the voice telling her to find the Corsairs and Enforcers on the Rad station and eradicate them. She rubbed at her arm, where the SSA identification tattoo still shone black against her pale skin. Gwen touched her own tattoo, a gesture of solidarity.

"Come on. You drew a lot of willpower. When your body catches up, you're going to be exhausted," Gwen said, taking Liza's bicep in her hand and guiding her towards the spaceport. Gwen glanced over her shoulder at Dom. "I'll take care of her." Liza heard Dom's voice respond, but she didn't listen to what he said.

Anyone walking to the spaceport had to pass by the Corsairs that her been attacked by the pirates. All valuables from the now-dead Corsairs had been stripped by the attackers. Looking at their bloodied faces, Liza thought the vacant expressions of someone Snapped was better than the results of physically pummeling someone to death.

Liza woke up to Dom entering her room; Gwen seemed to be absent. Her body still felt drained and exhausted. She collapsed in bed before the worst of the exhaustion could overtake her, but she knew she'd need more time to recover. Dom sat down on the edge of her bed. Liza pushed herself up onto her elbows.

"Something wrong?" she asked. Dom shook his head.

"I just came to see how you were doing," he said. Liza shrugged and dropped back down, her head sinking back into her pillow.

"The usual: overdo everything and deal with the consequences later," she said. He chuckled. "Is everyone else fine?"

"Yeah, they're okay. Corbin is almost done making food if you're hungry," Dom said.

"Probably should," Liza replied.

"Cedrick and Vely spoke to me this morning," Dom said. "They plan to find a ship that will take them to Mars."

"Why Mars?"

"She didn't say, other than knowing someone she met when she was there before," Dom said. "You're okay with this?"

"Yes and no," Liza replied. She pushed her blankets from her and stretched her body out along the length of the bed. Her muscles protested. "She shouldn't stay if she doesn't want to participate in this mission. And maybe she'd be safer somewhere else."

"I understand," Dom said. "And Cedrick?"

"I guess I hope that if he's sick, he won't be as much of a danger," Liza said.

"Not the best way to look at it," Dom said, shaking his head.

"I know."

Dom rose from the bed and held out his hands. Liza allowed him to take her hands and hoist her from the bed. For a moment, their bare hands touching, Liza's willpower raced to Dom, wanting to control him. She fought back and quickly removed her hands from his.

Stop it, she scolded, but she really had no idea *who* she was scolding. Her own Katho power? Liza yanked her gloves on before Dom could touch her hands again.

"Vely hasn't left yet, has she?" Liza asked to cover the awkward silence.

"No. I'm not sure she has the details planned yet," he said. Still wearing the clothes she'd fallen asleep in, Liza followed Dom from the room.

"The new J Jar is scheduled to be delivered when we're done eating," Dom said. "Do you think you're recovered enough to help us move it?"

"Yeah, of course," Liza said. She wasn't sure if that was true, but she didn't want to give anyone a reason to worry.

In the galley, the crew had already gathered, and some were just sitting down with plates of food. Liza had a sudden, overwhelming wish to not be surrounded by people just now. Her crew, true to form, began to ask her how she felt if her exhaustion was due to the Sun Whiskey or something else. Liza waved off their comments, citing a need for food. Liza sat beside Vely, in the spot furthest away from the rest of the crew.

"Mars, huh?" Liza asked, digging into her plate.

"I met someone named Ren Para there," Vely said. "I think Cedrick and I are going to see him."

"What does he do?" Liza saw the smile on Vely's face like it was something amusing.

"The black market. He sells things on a literal black market," Vely answered. Liza snorted a laugh.

"I would like to see that at some point," Liza said.

"You will." Vely shifted her food around and took a few more bites. "Cedrick and I found a speeder that we can rent to get to Mars. Cedrick apparently knows how to pilot them. I kind of had a thought that-- that maybe Ren might know someone who can help Cedrick. He knew I was a Psychogen without being a Bloodhound. "

"Interesting." Liza resisted her immediate urge to question Vely about Cedrick. She could tell by her sister's face that Vely was expecting something of the kind.

"You'll keep in regular communication, right? You have the lync information for my room?" Liza asked. Vely was momentarily surprised, but she nodded her head.

"Of course."

"And if I go crazy and blow everyone up, I can blame you for not keeping me in check?" Vely rolled her eyes.

"Sure. I'll be your scapegoat," she said. The sisters laughed together. When Liza glanced up from her plate, she saw Dom smiling at her from down the table. She smiled back with what she felt was a sincere smile, though it was an effort not without struggle.

20

Gael watched the initial progress of the new greenhouse on Sun Station Alpha from his speeder, Pioneer. With the proper funds supplied, construction was well underway. Dorian Betron was in the passenger seat beside him.

"What's the timeline for this project?" Dorian asked.

"Not very long. Less than a cycle around the sun," Gael said. Watching the construction workers gave Gael a specific type of pain in his wallet. Naturally, the new addition would be helpful for all the colonists of the Sun Stations, the SSA, and Gael's company, but he had been resisting this construction for some time. Gael had a tendency to resist exterior construction requiring life support. It cost too much.

Alis had received some intel that the pirates were planning to converge on the TRAN67 wormhole to disrupt Walnad operations and transportation from that area. Gael knew that Alis would try to squeeze every dollar from him to protect his ships from that situation. But as he sat in his speeder with Dorian, SSA officers and those damned Corsairs were being trained and outfitted with the equipment and ships they needed to go chase after the pirates.

"Satisfied?" Gael asked Dorian. "Have you seen enough?"

"Yes, let's go back," he replied. Gael gripped the controls of *Pioneer* and navigated the small ship back to Walnad's private docking bay. It was a short trip, only requiring a few more minutes of Dorian's company. After docking, Dorian bade him goodbye with his fist to his chest and set off for whatever it was that Dorian spent his ample time doing.

Gael called on his assistant, who appeared in a small,

battery-operated automobile. Charles Mann unlocked the doors, and Gael climbed in.

"How was the viewing?" Charles asked, navigating the vehicle from the docking bay.

"Dorian is satisfied," Gael said. "All appears to be progressing smoothly." Charles hesitated in his response. "What is it?"

"Is it right to deceive the people this way?" he asked. "There is truly a need for that farm space." Gael bristled, but he kept his anger inside. Charles was the only one he allowed to speak to him in such a blunt manner.

"It is not a true deception," Gael countered. "The board knows that this kind of expenditure was not prudent right now, but we also know that our merchant ships need more protection. More merchant ships that can make it back here without incident means more money for the company. We're not deceiving people. They will get their new farm. However, until we have the funds available for the entire project, we're giving them the illusion of more progress than we're actually making."

"How will you handle it if someone finds out about this deception?" Charles asked.

"I haven't thought that far ahead," Gael admitted, something he loathed to do. "I'll need your help when that time comes."

"Of course, sir," Charles said.

The rest of the trip back to the Walnad headquarters passed in silence. Charles dropped Gael at the main entrance, a strategic move to allow his employees to see him, a visible leader rather than some CEO pulling strings from behind a curtain. Of course, that was precisely how Gael operated, but he wanted to give the employees that *illusion* of a visible leader.

The young woman at the front desk bade him, hello, and he returned the greeting with a smile and a nod.

Back in his office, Gael had a message from Alis waiting for him on his communicator. He pressed play as he prepared one of his favorite cigars.

The ships you requested have been dispatched. I have learned some information that will make tracking these pirates laughably easy. We should have this problem wrapped up shortly.

Short and to the point. Gael leaned back in his chair, his cigar hanging between his fingers. He thought it was more convenient if Alis didn't try to remain such a mystery with her information. Much of her paycheck came from Walnad anyway. She should be more than happy to supply him with all the information he could ever want.

Perhaps he should plant a spy in her organization. Or maybe try and bring Lynwood to his side. Gael wouldn't be surprised if Lynwood knew everything that Alis knew. He followed her around everywhere she went, like some kind of lost animal.

Could he *trust* Alis to perform her side of this deal? Gael had been burned too many times in the past. He'd rather do it on his own. An idea crossed Gael's mind. Was he willing to give up something to gain so much more? Perhaps.

Gael tapped a button, alerting Charles Mann to come into his office. The young man appeared a few moments later, a tablet in hand. He crossed the room and sat down across the desk from Gael.

Before speaking, Gael appraised the young assistant. Gael had known Charles for a very long time, well before he was of working age. Charles' father sat on the board of directors for Walnad. And perhaps with a bit of a haircut and some minor changes, Charles could pass himself off as someone else.

"Charles, do you have aspirations beyond this company?" Gael asked. Charles looked momentarily concerned.

"Not really, sir," Charles answered. Gael smiled at the "appropriate" response.

"What if I presented you with an opportunity to broaden your horizons?"

"Am I being fired?" Charles asked. The sincerity and fear in his face were strong. Gael shook his head and waved a hand.

"No, no, of course not," he said, leaning forward in his chair. "I need someone to spy on the SSA for me, and I don't trust anyone else for the job." Charles' eyebrows rose in surprise.

"Spy on the SSA?"

"Yes. Alis barely recognizes her own people. It would be easy to get you into that organization and feed me back information. I need to know what she's up to."

"But she already has Lynwood. Why would she need someone else?"

"I'm sure you can make yourself useful to Alis, or at the very least, Lynwood," Gael said. Charles seemed to consider this for a moment, then shrugged his shoulders.

"Sure. I'll do it." Gael grinned.

"Wonderful."

21

Vely and Cedrick had their bags of clothes and other personal items slung over their backs, waiting for their time to depart. She had promised to wait to leave until after Liza was done moving the new J Jar into the cargo hold of the ship.

Liza and Gwen had managed to draw a crowd, and Vely watched the entire scene with amusement. They stood on either side of the Jar, using their hands to direct their power. By directing their willpower, they could lift the Jar up about a meter from the ground and glide it up the ramp into the ship's cargo hold. It was a feat, so Vely couldn't blame the spectators who came to watch the two young women move the giant cylindrical container on their own. Vely wondered if Liza should try not to make her Psychogenic power so obvious, but she figured it was a way for Liza to let everyone know not to mess with her, which was something Vely knew her sister would prefer.

Before the cargo bay door closed, Liza hopped back out onto the domed catwalk. She bypassed the crowd and joined Vely and Cedrick.

"Ready?" she asked. Vely and Cedrick nodded, and the three set off along the catwalk. The rented speeder was docked a short distance away.

Vely felt a little anxious to be leaving Liza behind, and it was a feeling she'd fought, ignored, and attempted to reconcile for the last several hours. Even now that it was time, she still felt the flutter of uncertainty in her stomach.

"I know you'll be fine without me, but I'm still worried," Vely confessed. Liza shrugged her shoulders but with a smile.

"You know I can handle things on my own," Liza replied. "You're probably just a little nervous for yourself." Vely didn't want to admit how right Liza was.

"This is the speeder," Cedrick said. He stopped walking and gestured to the small, two-person speeder docked between two others. A company name was painted on the side, but most of it was worn out. Otherwise, it appeared to be in good condition.

"Are you sure this thing will make it to Mars?" Liza asked.

"I'm told it will," Cedrick said, and Vely could tell that he was feeling a bit dubious about it as well. Vely was determined to make the best of it.

"I'm sure it's fine. Let's head out soon," Vely said but didn't add 'before I change my mind.' Liza turned to her and pulled Vely into a tight hug.

"At the risk of sounding like mom, call me all the time," Liza said. Vely smiled against Liza's shoulder and tried to hold back the few tears that were threatening to fall.

"I will," she said. Liza released her and turned to Cedrick. A silent stare passed between the two for a moment until Liza held out a hand. Cedrick gripped her hand, and Vely hoped at least a silent truce between the two.

"Let's go," Cedrick said and turned away to walk up the short inclined ramp that was attached to the speeder. He pressed a release button on the side, and the small door opened. There was barely enough room for the two of them to squeeze inside and drop their bags into a small cargo hold bin behind the seats. Vely climbed into the passenger seat and pulled her harness around her shoulders, and latched it, pulling it tight. Looking out the window back at the catwalk, she waved to her sister, who had an oddly peaceful look on her face. Or maybe it was just her usual, expressionless look that Vely had grown too used and was afraid to leave again.

Cedrick fired up the engines of the speeder, and Vely was surprised at how loud they were. He pressed a series of buttons and switches that were labeled "life support." The speeder detached from the docking port, and Cedrick carefully maneuvered it away from the other ships. After putting some distance between themselves and the rest of the docked ships, Cedrick increased the speed, and they zipped around a large, incoming merchant ship.

Riding in the speeder was unlike anything Vely had experienced before. Riding in the Gypsy Star had felt different since the ship was so big. But the small, nimble speeder could dart around other ships coming into the Rad station, swing wide around other space clutter, and speed up faster than she could have imagined. She couldn't help the wild laughter of excitement that escaped her when Cedrick looped the ship around upside down and shot off away from the Rad station.

"Is your harness tight?" Cedrick asked. Vely nodded, still wide-eyed at their considerable speed. "We're going to enter an FTL jump. This won't be like on the Gypsy Star."

Cedrick pushed a lever forward, and another component of the engine revved, filling Vely's ears. The FTL system counted down - 3 - 2 - 1.

Vely pushed back into her seat with a heavy force, so heavy she felt that she couldn't breathe. The speeder rumbled and rattled around her, and Vely tried to convince herself that the sounds were completely normal. For just a moment, she couldn't tell they were moving until the space around them blurred. Vely shut her eyes.

"Almost," Cedrick said, but his voice sounded forced and far away.

Finally, the ship lurched forward and slowed considerably. Vely felt herself strain against her harness, the straps cutting into her shoulders and chest. Mars, the rusty brown planet, looming nearer as the speeder approached, popped out of seemingly nowhere. At their distance, Vely couldn't yet see the domed enclosures that made up the livable spaces of the planet.

"I didn't know little ships like this could make FTL

jumps," Vely said, her head still reeling. Cedrick smiled at her.

"I'm sure you're feeling the effects of it, though. It's a much rougher process than with large ships," Cedrick explained. Vely pressed a hand to her head and nodded. "Some people think humans shouldn't be traveling in space like this."

"Probably not," Vely said, her eyes fixated on Mars. "We evolved to survive on Earth with those conditions. I'm surprised we've lasted this long in space."

"Good point," Cedrick said. "I've got the coordinates to the docking port programmed. I'm going to try and sleep. You should, too."

"Go ahead," Vely replied. "I'll wake you if needed."

Vely dozed off without realizing it but was woken up by a rapid beeping. When she opened her eyes, Cedrick was already awake, taking over the controls of the speeder. Mars was even closer now, and now Vely could see the domes that stretched over a large expanse of the planet, connected together by tubes. The docking port was a large dome, larger than any of the others. There were smaller catwalks encased in tubes that stretched out, where the larger ships could dock and the smaller dome where ships like their speeder could go inside. Cedrick navigated the speeder in that direction and joined the queue to pass through the airlock compartment. Before long, they joined a few other speeders in the airlock and were granted access. Cedrick docked the speeder at the nearest port and shut down the engines.

"Barely made it," he commented, his eyes surveying the control panel.

"What do you mean?" Vely asked.

"We almost ran out of fuel," Cedrick said, his voice far too calm. Vely stared at him, her mouth hanging open. He grinned.

"That's not funny," she remarked. Cedrick patted her shoulder and released the door. It popped open with a hiss.

"Come on. We made it to Mars."

22

Chaos reigned many levels below Alis Foste's office as ships and crews were outfitted with clothing, provisions, and weapons. J Jars were fueled. Not too far away, the top trainees from the SSA Psychosensory Division were moved from trainee status to full agent status, and the uniforms were made as quickly as possible. Alis fought against the notion that her plans were moving too fast. She still didn't know everything she needed to know about the pirates and about the alleged Cosmic Resistance. But while Gael Daniels was distracted with the construction at Sun Station Alpha and the pirates grouping to attack the ships traveling through the wormhole, she had to move faster than planned. There was already a chance that her Corsairs and SSA Enforcers would not reach the wormhole before the pirates went through. This was an inconvenient annoyance but not an insurmountable one.

Her greatest opportunity was the current divide in attention among the people of the solar system. Lynwood reported the increased mass of speculation articles cropping up on the Sol Network, ranging from topics of the continued expansion of Mars, what would happen to the Moon colonies, the activities of the SSA and Walnad, and of course, the activities of the Galactic Syndicate. With such a range of concerns, the solar system population would hardly notice a discreet coup, during which their government would be silently eliminated and replaced by her own people.

Lynwood's report, however, included little information about the Cosmic Resistance. He had discovered that some were grouping together to push back against Walnad and the

SSA. However, none of the speculations included confirmation that the Cosmic Resistance even existed.

The final push Alis needed to jump-start her plans was the sentiment surrounding the Galactic Syndicate. Nearly everyone in the solar system knew that the Syndicate existed, as the Syndicate themselves didn't try to hide. Alis learned that some of the solar system colonists favored the pirates with some surprise and a little horror. They were seen as archetypal 'Robin Hoods.' *Steal from the rich to give to the poor.* However, the problem with that thought process was that the pirates stole from the rich to keep for themselves. There was no sharing with the poor. Lynwood suggested the colonists merely sided with the pirates' efforts to stop the total control of Walnad and the SSA.

Whatever the reasons, Alis knew it was time to take control of the colonies. She could only do so much against the pirates at the moment; the current location of the Cove was still unknown, though Shad Warwick was able to provide details about the current leader of the Syndicate, Captain Thane Lezal, who had a talent for keeping himself off the radar.

At least, he had in the past.

Her secret weapon. A setup so perfect, she could hardly believe it happened by accident. The information had given her such joy that she'd bestowed her happiness onto Jeffry Morre and promoted him to Commander.

He sat across from her now, reading the same report that Alis had received from Lynwood. Morre's injuries from his encounter with the Katho Liza Strange had healed, but Alis had heard from his peers that his pride had been injured. She didn't care for people who allowed their pride to be broken.

Morre sat opposite Alis in her office, holding a tablet in his hands. He was reading through Alis' plan of attack.

"You are sending Carte and Howards out with the Agents?" Morre asked. He set the tablet on the edge of her desk.

"Yes."

"And you trust those two pirates to lead your fleet to the

wormhole?"

"Not really."

"Then why are you keeping me here?" he asked.

"I'm sure you'll view this as being a substandard assignment," Alis said, leaning forward over her desk. "But I need you to be the welcoming committee." He raised an eyebrow. "For when she returns."

"I'm not sure I entirely understand."

"As you are aware, I am not a supersensor. Just a regular human. I do not have any supersensors among my staff because they have all been sent to your division. I need someone here who can exhibit some control, the kind the rest of us lack."

Morre stared at her silently for a moment, then nodded.

"I understand."

"Once this little situation has come to a close, you will join Carte and Howards with the rest of the division."

"As you wish." He bowed his head slightly. "Unless there's anything else, I'd like to talk to the others before they leave with their agents."

"Of course," Alis said, holding a hand out to dismiss him. Morre rose from the chair, saluted, and disappeared from her office. Alis laced her fingers together and smiled.

When he wanted to, Lynwood could perform rousing speeches. Alis watched him from the side while he informed the fleet of Corsairs and SSA Enforcers about the plan to intercept the pirates. He managed to ignite the people's emotions to give them some fire to use in their mission. Though Alis rarely admitted her faults out loud, she had to admit that she was not proficient at public speaking. She had a habit of insulting people rather than exciting them. That was why, the first time she saw Lynwood give a motivational speech to a group of Enforcers bound for a distant drifter colony, Alis had snatched him away from the training division and brought him to work for her.

Lynwood dismissed the crews, and they dispersed, heading for their ships. Blue and orange uniforms mingled together for a moment before breaking apart into their respective ships. There were few Corsairs and Enforcers that could peacefully work together in crews. Some had the habit of maintaining former prejudices. Captain Warwick, however, had been given a rank among the SSA to ensure his authority over both sides of the fleet. She saw him with Zimir, boarding his new ship, *Belenus.*

"Are the Supersensors ready to depart as well?" Lynwood asked, appearing at Alis' side.

"I believe so. Commander Morre is having some final words with Carte and Howards."

"Was he upset?"

"Perhaps. He didn't say he was," Alis replied. Lynwood gazed at the crews, slowly disappearing onto their ships.

"It is important that he be here."

"I agree," Alis said. "Things will be much smoother that way." Lynwood turned away from the crews.

"Shall we reconvene later?" he asked. Alis nodded, and Lynwood strode away. Alis smiled to herself. Her plans were moving forward, and her ultimate goal, the one she'd been striving for since childhood, was finally within reach.

23

The *Gypsy Star* moved away from the Rad station to join the rest of Thane Lezal's fleet. The ships undocked from the Rad station and made their way out into open space one or two at a time. Lezal had set up a communication line between all the ships, so each crew could hear him when he began to speak.

"We are almost grouped together. Each ship's navigator or pilot knows the coordinates of where to come out of the FTL jump. Remember that we will be taking the FTL jump as far as possible without using all our fuel. This is gonna be a long one, so buckle in and get ready."

Liza was already seated in the bridge, her harness pulled tight over her shoulders. The twins were beside her, talking to each other so quickly that Liza didn't bother to keep up. Gwen was seated on the other side of the bridge from her, her gaze distant. Liza gently pushed towards Gwen's mind.

Stop being nosy, Gwen said to her. Liza pulled an innocent face, and Gwen rolled her eyes.

What are you thinking about?

Nothing that you need to concern yourself with, Gwen replied. Liza prodded, but Gwen's mental defenses were rock solid. Gwen gave Liza a smug look and retreated inwardly once more, leaving Liza to glance around the rest of the crew. Dom and Becce were in the cockpit, preparing for the jump. Corbin and Doctor D were comparing notes about something on a tablet, and Tsuto was shaped like a small boy, swinging his legs back and forth from the seat.

Liza sighed to herself and leaned back in the seat. It was still difficult for her to believe that she was living on the Moon just a few months ago, having lost her father and trying to figure out how to make ends meet. Liza was part of a renegade pirate fleet, about to travel through a wormhole to chase after Walnad ships. And she had what she'd consider friends, maybe family even, and wouldn't have to worry that if she were injured, that they'd steal everything from her and disappear. It was a strange feeling, but a nice feeling.

"Preparing for FTL jump," Becce said over the ship's intercom. The automated countdown began at ten. Liza closed her eyes and tried to relax her body. The others settled into their seats.

The countdown reached one, and the now-familiar pressure leaned into Liza's chest, pressing her hard against the seat. There was nothing to do now except try to sleep.

Someone shook her shoulder. Liza opened her eyes and saw Dom standing in front of her. The others in the bridge were also opening their eyes, shaking off the FTL jump effects. Liza blinked several times and took a deep breath, her chest straining against the harness. She unbuckled herself and slipped from the seat.

"We've just come out of the jump. We'll be waiting here for the rest of the ships to join us," Dom said to the crew. Harnesses unbuckled, and the crew stumbled to their feet. Liza felt a little sick. She stood and swayed on her feet a moment before regaining her balance. Dom steadied her with a hand on his shoulder. "Gwen, Liza, I want to show you something."

Dom motioned towards the lift. Exchanging a brief glance, they followed him.

What would he have to show both of us? Gwen asked. Liza shrugged her shoulders. The three descended down to the Captain's quarters, and Dom let them inside.

"Thane wanted me to show you this," he said, picking up a small metal box from the table in the center of the room. He popped the lid off and handed it over. Liza and Gwen peered inside. It was a small gemstone, blue in color. It was tiny, little more than a fleck.

"What is this?" Gwen asked.

"Astarte. It's a gemstone found in the solar system we're traveling to. We found a large quantity among the crates we stole from that merchant ship, and it sold for a lot of money at the Rad station. The profits have been shared in your accounts," he said. "Thane wants to make sure we get all the astarte from whatever ships we encounter. He doesn't care if it ends up back in Walnad's hands at some point, but he wants money for it first."

"What does Walnad use it for?" Liza asked.

"We don't know."

Liza reached into the box and picked up the tiny fleck of gemstone. Despite the gloves she wore, she felt the prickling energy of her willpower come alive. But it wasn't normal. The power swelling in her was too much, and she quickly knew she would lose control of it. Liza thrust the gemstone back into the box, and her power calmed.

"What was that?" Gwen asked. Liza stared at the small gem.

"I don't know. I felt like I was losing control of my willpower," Liza said. Gwen frowned and picked up the small astarte. As Gwen must have felt, Liza could feel her power swell, pushing against Liza's body. Gwen dropped the stone back into the box.

"What's happening?" Dom asked, who couldn't feel the willpower.

"It's affecting our willpower," Gwen confirmed. Her face screwed up in concentration. "Do you mind if I take this to Doctor D to inspect?" Dom shook his head and popped the lid back on.

"By all means," he said and handed the box over to her. Gwen thanked him.

"I'll let you know if I come up with any conclusions," she said to Liza, then disappeared out the door. Dom stared at Liza with concern.

"That was strange," Dom commented, and Liza nodded her head. Her skin still crawled with the feeling of her willpower, desperately trying to get away. It disturbed her that her power felt malicious. Like her willpower had become angry.

"I don't like that at all," she commented, rubbing her arms with her hands and shaking herself to try and release the strange feeling crawling over her. Dom stepped closer and laid his hands on her biceps, but he wouldn't feel the chill on Liza's skin. It was coming from within.

"Are you working on anything right now?" he asked, circling her with his arms. Liza snorted.

"Not really," she replied. "I could be re-calibrating the ion cannon." Dom leaned back to look at her face.

"You do that every day," he said.

"Not *every* day." Dom laughed and shook his head. He squeezed her against his chest again, and Liza fought the urge to pull away. She wished that her instinctual reactions to physical contact weren't so negative. She thought she'd gotten better about pulling away from people, but it was difficult to fight the urging in her mind. And Dom-- Dom was infinitely patient with her idiosyncrasies. Liza felt that if their situations were reversed, she would have given up a long time ago. Or not tried at all.

She supposed that was part of what made her so different from Dom and most others.

"What was your family like?" Liza asked, her cheek pressed against his chest.

"My family?" She nodded. Dom released his hold on her and looked down. "Well, around the time I was eleven or so, there was a bad flu that spread around my sector of Mars. My parents were wiped out, along with Becce's and many other kids in the area. We all become orphans at the same time. Becce and I, and a few others, we made a clubhouse out of my parents' home, and it sort of became our base. We avoided letting the SSA and the governor of Mars find out that we were orphans, or we would have ended up in a pretty terrible orphanage. Instead, we pooled our money inherited by our parents, and one of the smarter kids rationed it out for us. We managed fairly well without adult supervision. We'd pick up odd jobs here and there to make money, but we caused a lot of trouble, too." Dom chuckled to himself. "We used to play pranks on people in the middle of the night. Really freaked some people out."

"You only had parents until you were eleven?" she asked. Dom shrugged.

"Yeah." Liza frowned. "What's wrong?"

"I'm just trying to figure out why I am the way I am," she said, glancing away. "You only had your parents for a short time. I had them up until a few months ago." Dom brushed her cheek with his hand.

"Don't think about it so much," he said. "I may not have had parents, but I had a group of people who were like siblings, and we had to be close to survive," Liza growled a sigh. "There's nothing wrong with you, you know."

"Do you know how much I am resisting running away from you right now?" Liza asked, a deep frown still on her face. Dom smiled and cupped her face with his hands.

"And yet, here you are." Liza blinked at him. That was true. She was still here.

"Sorry."

"Don't be. Your past makes you who you are today. And though you might disagree, I wouldn't change that," he said. Liza felt some of her anxiety melt away, and she allowed herself to smile.

"Thanks, Dom."

"My pleasure," he said, just before he kissed her. This time, when Liza's power awakened, it was calm. Little arcs crawled around her skin, tingling the fine hairs on her arms and on the back of her neck. Dom squeezed her against his chest, and Liza felt a warm sensation grow in her heart. Maybe, just maybe, she could have a normal relationship with a man without fear.

24

Mars was no different than the last time Vely had been there. However, the sight of the green light district near the spaceport gave her unpleasant feelings of remorse. She wondered if there was someone there who didn't know that Denny had been killed and that he would never return. Someone who might never know what happened to him. Cedrick rested his arm across her shoulders and pulled her against his side.

"I know what you're thinking," he said. Vely nodded and rested her head against him for a moment. But the crowd made her nervous, and she didn't want to linger for too long.

"Let's go. We should find a hotel to stay at until we find Ren," Vely said. Cedrick nodded, and he dropped his arm from her shoulders and laced his fingers through hers. They pushed into the moving crowd. It wasn't hard to find hotels near the spaceport, but it was difficult to find a hotel that didn't rent by the hour. After an hour of searching, Cedrick pulled Vely down an alley, crossing from the main thoroughfare onto a side street. There were smaller pubs and bars, quieter streets, and hotels that rented rooms by the day.

"I wish I could remember the hotel we stayed at last time," he commented, reading the signs on the buildings as they walked.

"I don't remember either," Vely replied. "This area looks promising." Cedrick nodded and led her off the street into a hotel with an open lobby. Under the balconies' support beams, a long counter ran along the wall, and the rest of the lobby was filled with chairs and couches. Cedrick motioned for Vely to wait on a couch, and he walked to the counter to rent a room. Vely looked around the lobby. It was fairly plain. She expected other hotels to be just as colorful and outlandish from the wild colors that filled the main thoroughfare. Seemed this hotel had different ideas. She heard Cedrick thank the employee behind the counter, and he turned away, holding a card

"Let's go," he said. Vely stood up from the couch and joined Cedrick. They took the lift up several floors and stepped onto the landing. At their room, he swiped the card, and they stepped into the room. It was small and just as plain as the lobby below. But there were two narrow beds, and more importantly, a communication lync. Vely brushed inside past Cedrick and dropped her bag on the ground.

"Wait," he called after her, allowing the door to close behind him. He dropped his bag on the ground. Vely sat down in front of the communication lync and pulled Ren Para's card from her jacket pocket. "Hold on, Vely," Cedrick said, closing his hand over hers. "Don't you think we should decide what we're going to do here before we start calling random strangers?" Vely raised an eyebrow.

"He's not a stranger," she said. "He sold us that coded drive!"

"Yeah, for a lot more than it was worth," Cedrick replied.

"It got us on the Cove, didn't it?" Vely shot back. Cedrick stared at her a moment, then sighed.

"This is what you want to do?" he asked. Vely nodded. "Alright."

She turned back to the communication lync, and Cedrick let go of her hand. She set the card down and dialed the lync number. The words 'Securing Connection' blinked on the screen. It was replaced by a question: 'Leave message?' with the option to select 'yes' or 'no.' Vely tapped 'yes' and waited. Text appeared at the bottom of the screen that read 'Recording Now.'

"Ren! I'm Vely Strange! I don't know if you remember me, but you gave me your card a few months ago. I'm back on

Mars, and I'm looking for some help. Could you please call back on this line? Thank you!"

She ended the recording and shut down the lync. When she turned around in the chair, she saw that Cedrick had already stretched out on one of the narrow beds and was asleep. Doctor D had given Cedrick a bottle of sleep aid. That bottle was on the table between the beds. According to the clock in the room, it was late, and Vely's schedule had been so disjointed from all the traveling around. Space travel made following a regular sleep cycle difficult. Since leaving the Moon, Vely had simply slept when she was tired and really had no idea where she stood in terms of the agreed-upon twenty-four-hour clock.

But she was tired now. She stretched out on the other bed and rolled her face into the pillow, determined to sleep until she heard the communication lync alert her to a call.

Vely slept much longer than she intended. When she did wake up, the hotel room was dark, and it was pretty quiet outside. Cedrick was still fast asleep and appeared to be vision-free. Vely pushed herself off the bed and crossed the room. She pushed aside the curtain over the window and looked outside. There were not many people out walking, and most of them looked intoxicated. Vely withdrew from the window and glanced at the communication lync. A light was blinking, indicating a message.

She rushed to the lync and pressed play on the message. Though she couldn't have conjured Ren Para's face in her mind, when his face filled the screen, Vely recognized him.

"Vely Strange! A pleasure to hear from you," he said. "Whatever is going on, I can try to help. I have a project that I'm working on if you're interested, and we're always looking for more members. And based on the little I know of your background, I think you'd be interested. Come to our headquarters tomorrow around 1800 hours, and we can talk more." Ren rattled off an address, which Vely had to replay several times before she had it memorized. The message ended, and Vely felt a ripple of thrill run through her body.

Vely paced the room for a while, her mind too active to sleep more. Cedrick appeared to be out for the night. After a while, she turned on a light and sat on the bed. Inside her bag, she'd shoved the books that Liza had saved from the Moon. Settling in, Vely began to reread a book about the history of philosophy and the words of men who had been alive more than three thousand years ago.

Day broke with the sounds of people on the streets of Mars, talking, laughing, and hawking wares. Vely jerked awake, blinking the sleep from her eyes. She'd dozed off about a hundred pages into her book, and her dreams had been filled with ancient men with long beards, trying to teach people how to think. Vely scrambled out of bed, feeling like she was late for something, but there were still many hours before she and Cedrick needed to meet up with Ren Para. Vely turned towards Cedrick and shook him awake.

"Come on, Cedrick. I'm hungry," she said and gave his shoulder another shake. He groaned and opened his eyes.

"How long did I sleep?" he asked, his voice still husky from sleep.

"A long time," Vely said. "All the way through the night."

"Have you been awake the whole time?" Cedrick asked after he'd pushed himself to the edge of the bed, his feet touching the floor.

"No. I slept some," Vely said. She was trying to control her excitement, but she wasn't doing a great job of it. He stared at her.

"Why are you bouncing around so much?" he asked.

"Ren left a message last night. He wants us to meet him, to learn about some project he has. And we can ask him about your Augur sickness," Vely said. Cedrick frowned and glanced away from her.

"I don't know, Vely..." Cedrick said. She planted her hands on her hips.

"You said you wanted to come along with me. What did you think we'd do once we got here?" she asked. Cedrick just shrugged. "Maybe you just don't understand enough about struggling to survive," she said, her eyes narrowing to a glare. "Liza and I-- we were born into a constant need to survive. And that need hasn't gone away. Not yet, anyway."

"I know," Cedrick said, finally rising up from the bed to stand in front of Vely. She remained steadfast. He lowered his hands onto her shoulders. "I'm sorry. I'm just... not used to someone else taking the lead." Vely laughed.

"Get used to it, then," Vely said. "You lead us through the first part of our journey. Now it's my turn." Cedrick smiled and kissed Vely's forehead.

"You're right," he conceded. "Lead on, Vely Strange."

25

The hotel receptionist was able to give directions to Ren Para's location. The building was located in a smaller sector of Mars, and there was no choice but to walk. They left early, giving themselves plenty of time to arrive before the scheduled meeting time.

During the walk, Vely was wide-eyed and curious, her head swiveling in every direction to take in everything. Their previous visit to Mars had not lent itself to much exploration or appreciation of the colonies and their unique culture. They had been in such a hurry to find a coded drive and go find Liza and the pirates. Now, Vely could appreciate the buildings on the planet, made of bricks that were Martian in origin. Most buildings were only a few stories tall, some having limited upward space to grow due to the curvature of the domes. The building in the sectors they passed through were squished together, with barely any room between them. Some buildings appeared to be leaning against each other for support. It was a strange sight, compared to the Moon, where most buildings were built of metal.

Cedrick trailed along beside Vely, his demeanor quiet and sullen. Vely prodded him in the shoulder. "What's wrong?" she asked. He glanced at her.

"I'm tired," he said. Based on the pallor of his skin and the dark circles under his eyes, Vely couldn't disagree.

"Even though you slept?"

"Not enough, I guess. Trying to make up for a deficit is tough," he replied. Vely hummed in reply.

They walked on in silence, Vely once against absorbed

in the sights, smells, and sound of Mars. The people were just as different as the structures, such a contrast to the Moon. Vely remembered the Moon colonists as downtrodden and depressed, their lives based on how much they could afford to eat that day and whether or not their more sickly family members made it through the night. On Mars, those cares seemed less prevalent. More stores and shops sold various trinkets that Vely would deem useless, but the Martians seemed to love. Vely racked her brain for a moment, trying to remember a phrase she'd heard her father say.

Disposable income.

Vely wasn't sure yet how far her Simlars would take her on Mars. She recalled the negotiation of the coded drive; Denny and Cedrick were apparently surprised at the price of 40,000 Simlars. Vely now had a few million Simlars in on her new S-card from the division of profits between the *Gypsy Star* crew. Though she and Liza had never seen numbers like that before in their own possession, their upbringing had caused them to hoard Simlars.

"I think that's the place."

Cedrick pulled Vely from her thoughts. She refocused on the area around them and saw a large building made of Martian bricks, a single metal door breaking apart the bland exterior. There were no windows and no other exits.

"You sure?" she asked. Cedrick nodded. They approached the door, and as they got close, Vely saw a small sign beside the door, hanging from a screw punched through the brick. The sign read 'Ren Para, Antiques.' Vely frowned. *Antiques?*

Cedrick knocked on the door and stepped back. Vely glanced around. The area around the building was devoid of people. The surrounding buildings were silent. The door slid open, and the mass of Ren Pera filled the doorway. He smiled down at Vely and Cedrick, his scarred face stretching. He was bald, and his facial hair was elaborately braided and threaded with beads and shiny, metal objects. Vely wondered if it had some cultural significance.

"Glad you could make it," he said, reaching a hand out to them, shaking their hands in turn. Vely saw the spot on his arm where he'd been hit by a gamma pistol. Denny's death flashed back to her.

"Thank you for replying to my message," Vely said. "I wasn't really sure who else to contact." Ren smiled again.

"Come on in, and we can talk. Then I'll show you what we're working on," he said and stepped aside, allowing room for Cedrick and Vely to enter the building. Inside was chilly, dark, and empty.

"You're an antique dealer?" she asked while she waited for her eyes to adjust to the low light. Ren chuckled.

"No. That's just a cover," Ren said. "Come on."

In the darkness, Vely saw his shadow move towards the rear of the room. Cedrick slipped his hand into Vely's, and they followed behind Ren. He stopped at a door, and a keypad beside it lit up. He punched a couple of numbers, and the door opened. But it wasn't another room. It was a lift. The three crowded into the small space, most of it taken up by Ren's bulk.

"So if you aren't dealing antiques, what are you dealing?" Cedrick asked. Ren patted Cedrick's shoulder, nearly knocking him over.

"You'll see."

Vely blinked, and Cedrick was about to lean to her to say something when the lift doors opened. The room below was much bigger than the building above, and for a moment, Vely thought it was another black market. But upon further inspection, it was not a black market. It looked more like a gathering of pirates.

The room appeared to have been carved out of the ground, as the walls were roughly hewn and crumbling in some spots. The space was full of people, most of them talking and laughing, some collecting and cleaning weapons. Others looked at building layouts on holoprojectors. The general din in the room was loud, but as soon as Ren stepped off the lift with Vely and Cedrick in tow, the chatter stopped. Ren waved to the gathered people.

"Carry on," Ren added. The noise rose in the room once more, and Ren walked along the side of the wall, motioning for them to follow. He led them towards a small alcove, where a woman sat on a low, beat-up couch. She was engrossed in something on a tablet, her boots propped up on a low table. She had short bobbed blonde hair and stunning blue eyes. Vely stared at her, suddenly very aware of her haphazard hair colors and blunt trim job. When Ren approached, she glanced up, set her tablet aside, and rose to her feet.

"This is Maggie Wyse," Ren said, gesturing towards the woman. She had a shock of red lipstick, which stood out brilliantly against her pale skin. "Maggie, this is Vely Strange and Cedrick Sones."

Maggie grinned. "Two of the SSA's most wanted," she commented, her eyes lingering on Vely. "How exciting."

"Maggie and I are the co-leaders of the Cosmic Resistance," Ren said. Vely and Cedrick both frowned.

"The Cosmic Resistance?" Cedrick asked, raising an eyebrow. Ren pointed to the other couch in the alcove.

"Have a seat. First, tell me what I can do for you," Ren said. Vely and Cedrick exchanged a glance and sat down on the couch. Maggie returned to her spot, and Ren sat beside her, the couch groaning under his bulk. Vely tried to read Cedrick's scowling expression. She decided that if he wasn't going to ask for help, she would do it for him.

"I was wondering if you knew anything about Augur sickness," Vely said. Beside her, Cedrick tensed. Ren tapped his chin with his fingers while Maggie glanced up from her tablet.

"I have heard of it," Ren said. "Excessive forcing of visions by an Augur causes violent and excessive visions, resulting in sleeplessness and more visions." His eyes shifted between Vely and Cedrick. "Not many Augurs survive."

"That's what I'm concerned about," Vely said. "Our ship's doctor said Cedrick has Augur sickness."

Ren gave Cedrick a grave look. "I'm sorry to hear that," he

said.

"Do you know anything? Or anyone who might be able to help?" Vely asked. Ren leaned back and rubbed his palms together. He glanced at Maggie, who also appeared to be thinking. She rolled her face towards Ren.

"What about--"

Ren seemed to be reading her thoughts. "Maybe." Vely felt a flush of nervousness wash over her. She wanted to know who they were talking about. "We know someone who might have some insight," Ren said. "But I'd have to reach out to him first. He may not be willing. In the meantime, Vely, have you tried your Tranquility?"

"No..." Vely said. "I didn't know if that would make a difference."

"It's worth a try," Cedrick muttered beside her. Vely nodded, but her usual unwillingness to use her ability swelled in her mind. Every time she'd used it for the pirates, she had anxiety and misgivings, worried that she'd misuse her power. But this was Cedrick, and he needed her help.

"We can try it later, back at the hotel," Vely said. Cedrick nodded. Desperate now to change subjects, she asked, "Can you tell us about the Cosmic Resistance?"

Ren and Maggie both perked up, smiles on their lips. "The Cosmic Resistance is something Maggie and I have been working on for a while and has been gaining speed," Ren said, his large hand gesturing to the space outside of the alcove.

"I've never heard of it," Cedrick said, crossing his arms over his chest, obstinate as ever. Ren smiled.

"That's the point, up until now, anyway. We're almost ready to begin making ourselves known as an entity," Ren said. "Our group is comprised mainly of spies, set in various organizations around the solar system, collecting information. Very soon, we'll implement our plans to take down Walnad and the SSA from the inside. Once we have reduced their power and control over the solar system, we will set up a republic as the form of government for the solar system, where each colony and planet will have a say."

Cedrick laughed. "You really think a few spies will be able to take down a mega-corporation and the most heavily-armed organization in the solar system?" Vely shot Cedrick a dark look.

"Let them talk," she growled. Ren and Maggie smiled.

"We have more up our sleeve, of course," Maggie added. "As you said, the SSA is the only major powerhouse in the solar system, and attempting to use all-out force will not win. That's why we're working from the inside out."

"We recognize the futility of the situation," Ren said. "But that's not going to stop us. The more people we have to join our cause, the better chance we have of taking down both of those organizations."

Vely leaned forward in her seat. "Have you talked to the Galactic Syndicate," she asked. Ren and Maggie shook their heads, both with annoyed expressions on their faces.

"No. There's very little confidence that the Galactic Syndicate would want to *help* someone else. Not to mention, the trade routes they attack frequently include ships of ours that are trying to bring resources to Mars," Ren said. Vely frowned. "Anyway, we tend to disagree on several important points."

"Such as?" Cedrick asked.

"A difference in opinion about laws and rules to govern people. They would rather have the entire solar system descend into anarchy," Maggie said with a snort. "As for the SSA, we have a theory..." Maggie looked to Ren, who nodded. "We have a theory that mind-control tactics are being used on many of the people involved with the SSA and Walnad." At this, Vely perked up.

"They are!" she said, shouted a little too loudly. A few people outside the alcove glanced at her. Ren raised his eyebrows and twisted his goatee.

"How do you know this?" he asked.

Words flew out faster than she could control. "My sister,

Liza, and Cedrick here. She was sold to the SSA because she's a Kathokinetic. She said that while they were there, she underwent a few brainwashing sessions that were used to keep all the Psychogen trainees on the side of the SSA." Vely turned eagerly to Cedrick. "Right?" He nodded to confirm.

"Really?" Maggie asked, her blue eyes lighting up with intense interest. "So if those Psychogens are being brainwashed, who's to say that's not happening all over Walnad and SSA as well?" Ren gave Maggie a playful punch on the arm.

"I told you these two would be helpful."

Vely stared at Ren and Maggie. He had been right in his message. She *was* willing to join this cause. But when she looked at Cedrick, she could see his indecision and uncertainty. Vely forced down her urge to immediately tell Ren and Maggie that she'd help them. Instead, she said, "I think Cedrick and I need to chat about this first."

"Sure," Ren said and rose up from the couch. Maggie picked up her tablet and followed Ren from the alcove, leaving them alone.

"No," Cedrick said, crossing his arms over his chest. Vely scowled.

"Why?"

"There's no way these people can achieve their goals," Cedrick said. "Some of my visions, now that I'm here, are making more sense."

"What do you mean?"

"I have seen constant visions of destruction and death. You, me, Liza, the *Gypsy Star* crew. Nothing good is going to come out of this attempt to take down Walnad and the SSA," Cedrick said.

"Your visions don't always come true," she said, glaring at him.

"They do fairly often," Cedrick replied. "I'm trying to keep you from falling into a pit of denial, Vely. If we join them, we're going to die." Vely rose up from the couch, her hands clenched at her sides.

"We're all going to die anyway," she said. "I'd rather die trying to help people than trying to save my own ass."

She stormed away, leaving Cedrick alone in the alcove. Her earlier compassion for him disappeared in anger.

26

With so many members of the SSA gone, the headquarters was quiet. Usually, Alis could walk the halls and hear training, conversations, plans, construction, and ship repairs. She preferred the silence to the chaos. The remaining SSA employees were busy working on the logistics for her next wave of attacks. The plan was for the Supersensory Agents to take control of the colonies using their TK blasts, allowing the Enforcers a better chance to overthrow whatever pitiful excuse for government existed. And after that, Alis would get rid of Gael Daniels and Dorian Brenton, and Alis Foste would control the entire solar system.

The very thought made her skin tingle with excitement and anticipation.

Lynwood's office door was ajar. As she passed by, Alis saw him talking to a young man in a black outfit. Pausing outside the door, she tilted her head to the side. Lynwood glanced up from his conversation with the man at his desk. "Alis," he said. "Would you like to meet Chip Wilson?" Alis stepped into the office.

"Who is Chip Wilson?" she asked.

The young man turned in the chair to look at her. Alis frowned. He looked slightly familiar, but she couldn't place where she'd seen him.

"I'm hiring him as an assistant," Lynwood said. "General office duties." Alis raised an eyebrow.

"I see. Welcome aboard," she said, nodding to the young man. He smiled.

"Thank you, ma'am. I've been a great admirer of yours

for a long time," Chip Wilson said. "It's an honor to finally meet you." Alis couldn't stop the smile that formed on her face at the compliment. She glanced at Lynwood, composing herself.

"I'll need a status report on the ships later today," she said.

"Of course."

Alis stepped out of Lynwood's office and proceeded towards her own. Inside, she closed the door, locked it, and sat down at her desk. Using her holo screens, she brought up the files she was particularly obsessed with. Liza Strange. Gwen Adan. Cedrick Sones. The three Psychogens who escaped her clutches. More than ever, Alis was determined to find them and bring them back, with more intent to punish than to recalibrate.

Alis opened Gwen's file further and read through the details collected by the Psychosensory Division. Born: Sun Station Alpha, approximately twenty-six years ago. Birth Name: Gwendolyn Daniels. Family: One Brother - Gael Daniels.

Alis smiled to herself. She loved leverage.

27

Becce's voice over the ship's intercom announced that the fleet would be initiating the next FTL jump in a few minutes and that jump would take them through the wormhole. Liza wasn't sure she'd fully recovered from the previous FTL jump. Her stomach was still queasy.

In the medical bay, Gwen and Doctor D leaned over a microscope. Liza stepped inside the room and glanced over their shoulders to see what they doing.

"Figure anything out yet?" she asked. The tiny piece of astarte sat on a glass slide. Doctor D glanced up at her.

"Not yet. This stone has some very unusual properties, but I can't understand why Walnad would want so much of it. Gwen has been searching the Sol Network, but there's no information, like the solar system doesn't even know it exists," Doctor D said. Liza pursed her lips together.

"Nothing happens when you touch it?" Liza asked, and Doctor D shook his head.

"Seems to only affect you two, though I don't know if it would affect other Psychogens. It's too bad we don't have Vely and Cedrick here," he said. Becce's voice came over the intercom again, announcing the next countdown. "Let's go strap in, ladies," Doctor D said. "We'll continue this later."

Doctor D locked the small piece of astarte up in a drawer, and the three of them proceeded to the bridge. Before sitting down, Liza stepped into the cockpit. Becce glanced up at her. From the windshield of the ship, Liza could see the other ships of the fleet. Thane Lezal's ship, the *Astral Empress*, was in the lead.

"Ready?" Becce asked her.

"No," Liza said. "I might puke." Becce chuckled.

"I don't think anyone really gets used to FTL jump," she said. "It's best to not resist the pressure and movement of the jump."

"Thanks," Liza deadpanned. Becce leaned down and pulled something from under the console and handed it back to Liza. It was a waxy brown bag.

"Here. Puke in this," she said, laughing. Liza took the bag, stuck her tongue out at Becce, and retreated from the cockpit. She sat down in a seat beside Gwen and strapped herself to the chair. Liza leaned her head back and closed her eyes, ready for the jump.

The FTL jump through the wormhole was the strangest thing that Liza had ever felt. She kept her eyes closed because when she opened them, it seemed as if everything around her was swirling, like water in a drain. With her eyes closed, she felt like her mind had separated from her body. Strange visions and sounds filled her mind, and she forgot who she was. Her name disappeared, her life and legacy replaced by a blank slate. Just when she felt like her mind would transcend the physical world, the ship shuddered out of the FTL jump. Liza felt her entire life and mind crash back into her consciousness.

She opened her eyes, and everything continued to spin. A headache throbbed at her temples. The rest of the crew had the same reaction, as they struggled from their harnesses, most pulling puke bags from under the seats and heaving. Liza struggled to open the bag, and she managed just in time before her entire stomach contents relocated themselves.

It took a while for the crew to recover from the wormhole FTL jump. When Liza finally stopped dry heaving, she opened her eyes and wiped a sheen of sweat from her forehead. The rest of the crew sat with her heads between their knees, most breathing with deep rasps. Even Dom was pale. Becce stumbled from the cockpit and sank onto one of the chairs, her hair around her face soaked with sweat.

A chime went off on the bridge communication lync. Without looking, Dom accepted the lync connection. Thane Lezal's face appeared, looking as pale and sick as the *Gypsy Star* crew.

"I've confirmed that the entire fleet made it through the wormhole. Good work, everyone. We're going to cluster the ships together and spend some time recovering," he said. "We've located a Walnad fleet heading towards the wormhole, so we'll wait for them to show up. My crew will continue to monitor the fleet, and we'll contact everyone when it's time to strike." The connection terminated.

"Thank the stars," Becce cried out, her hands pressed to her face, a little hysterical. "I don't think I can handle another jump." The rest of the crew grunted in response.

Liza pushed herself to her feet and waited for the ship to stop spinning. She desperately wanted to lie down. The communication lync chimed again. This time, Liza accepted the connection, and Wayne River appeared on the screen.

"Hey *Gypsy Star*, I'm going to hook to you in the cluster. Can you open your connection port?" he asked. Becce groaned, and she stumbled in front of the screen.

"Yeah, just give me a sec," she said. Wayne smiled.

"First wormhole jump for ya?" he asked, glancing around at the crew members he could see.

"Yeah," Becce replied.

"They're a bitch." Becce stumbled back into the cockpit and pressed a button. "Ah, there we go. Thanks!" Wayne cut the connection himself. Becce slumped into a chair in the cockpit and refused to move.

"Go sleep this off," Dom commanded. Liza thought about trying to make it to her room, but like some other crew members, she slumped down to the ground and curled up on her side, her arms tucked under her head. It was as good a place as any.

When Liza woke up sometime later, the crew had removed themselves from the bridge or were still asleep on the ground. Someone had dimmed the lights in the bridge. Liza's head finally felt almost normal, and her stomach cramped. She could feel the hunger pangs gnaw at her. Before heading towards the galley, Liza stepped into the cockpit. Becce was still asleep in the pilot's chair. Liza leaned towards the windshield and looked out. She could see some of the ships of the fleet maintaining their positions around the *Gypsy Star*. Beyond, she could see what looked like a planet. From their distance, the planet looked purple. And it slowly dawned on Liza. She had left her own solar system and was seeing a completely different planet in a different solar system for the first time in her life. A thrill of excitement crawled up her skin, and before she could control it, her power awakened, jumping to Becce. Her eyes popped open.

Becce's hand shot up and grasped Liza's sleeve. "Isn't it beautiful?" Becce asked. Liza nodded, looking back out the window. "Did you ever think you'd be this far from home?"

"No, never," Liza answered.

"Me neither," Becce said. Using Liza, Becce pulled herself to her feet and wiped a hand down her face. Becce slung her arm over Liza's shoulder and leaned into her. "I'm excited to see what'll happen."

"I am, too," Liza said. "Dom showed Gwen and me what we're going to be stealing from the Walnad ships. If we succeed, we're going to make a lot of money."

"Good," Becce said. "It'll make how awful I feel right now completely worth it." Liza laughed. They left the cockpit, Becce still leaning on Liza. "Let's go to the galley," Becce suggested.

"That's the plan," Liza confirmed.

Picking up a few crew members on the way, Liza and Becce made their way to the galley. Corbin was already cooking up a storm. When the crew slumped into seats around the table, he glanced at them and smiled. "Take one of those tablets and drop it in a cup of water," he said, gesturing to a bottle on the end of the table. "It'll help with the FTL sickness."

"Thank goodness," Doctor D said, grabbing at the bottle

first. "I forgot I had made more."

"You made those? Liza asked. "You could have brought them to us sooner," she added with a slight pout. Doctor D chuckled and slapped her shoulder.

"They don't really work until after you're done vomiting," he said. "I haven't been able to make them work any sooner," Liza grunted but took the cup he offered her, and he dropped a small white pill. Inside the cup, the pill began to fizz and bubble. Liza downed the cup and hoped that it would do the trick.

28

Pioneer was about to dock with *Swift* when a secured communication lync from the SSA HQ attempted to connect to the ship. Gael allowed the lync to connect and waited, slowing the speed of his ship. Charles Mann appeared on the screen.

"Ah, Charles!" Gael said, smiling at his assistant. "I take it things are going well?"

"So far. Neither of them recognizes me," Charles said. "You are on your way to meet with them?"

"Yes. I'm nearly at *Swift*," Gael answered. "Have you found anything out?" Charles nodded.

"SSA and Corsair Collab ships are heading towards the wormhole to intercept the pirates," he said. "They have also dispatched their Supersensory Agents out to many different colonies."

"Why?"

"Intimidation, I think. To help their Enforcers," Charles said. "They're sending them to the Sun Stations, too." Gael scratched his chin.

"Interesting," he said. "What is Alis playing at?" Charles shook his head. He didn't know yet. "Keep your ears open. You're doing a great job," Gael said. Charles thanked him, and they terminated the connection. Gael increased *Pioneer's* speed and resumed his short trip to *Swift*. Nearby, Gael could see Dorian's personal ship approaching the docking bay. Alis had called the meeting but neglected to inform them about the purpose or agenda, nor did she disclose why they were meeting on her ship and not the SSA headquarters. Gael wasn't fond of being surprised. And without Charles, he felt like he was missing his right hand.

Pioneer docked on *Swift* alongside Dorian's ship. Gael climbed out of his ship and met Dorian on the catwalk. "Gael! Pleasure to see you again," Dorian said, tapping his chest with his fist and thumb. Gael returned the gesture until Dorian gave him a slap on the back. Gael winced.

"And you, Dorian," he forced himself to reply. Two Enforcer officers in red uniforms met them on the catwalk.

"Director Foste is waiting for you," one officer said. Gael stepped aside to allow Dorian to walk ahead of him. They followed the officers through a set of double doors, where an electric-powered cart waited to take them to Alis's office. Gael and Dorian climbed on, and the cart rolled away.

The ship resembled what Gael remembered about Alis's office. Dark, sleek, and shiny. The ship's crew wore white, deepening the contrast between themselves and the black metal. Dorian leaned closer to Gael and whispered, "Have you been on this ship before?"

"No," Gael whispered back. The officer driving the cart turned and smiled at them, then quickly turned back to the hallway through which he was navigating.

"What did she want to meet us for?" Dorian asked, and Gael shrugged his shoulders. "I'd rather not be blindsided." Rarely did Gael actually agree with Dorian.

The cart made a turn down another corridor, and another, and another, until Gael lost track of where they were. Perhaps this was intentional; he was now reliant on Alis to get him back to his ship. *Devious.*

The cart finally rolled to a stop outside of a lift that could have been made of glass. Gael climbed off the cart and rapt on it, discovering it was only very clean plexiglass. The officer gestured for Gael and Dorian to enter the lift and take it up to the bridge. They did so, leaving the red-clad officers behind.

Alis and Lynwood were waiting for them on the bridge. The cockpit was a few steps down from the bridge, giving the entire area a view of space from the ship's windshield. There were a few other people in the room, Enforcer officers in orange and crewmen in white.

"Welcome," Alis said, arching one of her eyebrows. Gael and Dorian approached her.

"Is there a problem with the SSA HQ?" Dorian asked, his voice concealing his discomfort. Alis shook her head.

"I thought this would be easier. It's closer to you," she said.

"I see," Dorian said. He sank down in an armchair and stretched his feet out in front of him. Gael watched his uncouth behavior. Alis turned to Lynwood.

"Please have the cook bring up refreshments for Dorian and Gael," she said. Lynwood nodded and turned away. "Sit down, Gael." Gael sighed inwardly and took a seat beside Dorian. Alis joined them, leaning forward over her knees. "I'm glad you were able to make it." Gael wanted to ask her why she was lying, but he held back his questions. Lynwood turned away from a communication lync and sat down rigidly beside Alis.

"So?" Gael prompted her. Alis smiled, her narrow lips curling. The amount of trust he had in her quickly diminished.

"My plan is currently underway, gentlemen, and I hope that you will be on board," she said. Dorian chuckled and repeated 'on board' under his breath. Gael tried not to roll his eyes.

"What plan?" Gael asked.

"You may have heard that I am sending factions of my Supersensory Division out to the colonies," she said, eying them.

"What for?"

"I'm sure you recall what Bill Howards said before he met with an untimely demise," Alis said. "The Cosmic Resistance."

"Don't tell me he was truthful," Dorian said. Behind him, the lift door opened, and a crew member stepped into the bridge, carrying a large tray balanced across his arms. He set the tray down on the short table between the four. On it was several decanters and four glasses, along with a tray of frozen stone cubes. Gael, already feeling annoyed, leaned forward immediately, dropped a few stone cubes into his glass, and poured himself a measure of Sun Whiskey.

"Unfortunately, he was," Alis said. "We have discovered evidence of a group called the Cosmic Resistance. Their intent is to take down the SSA and Walnad."

"That's impossible," Gael said with a laugh, the burn of the whiskey calming his nerves.

"Naturally," she said. "There's no way that a small fringe group can have the resources to take us down. I am aware that we shouldn't be paying attention to this, but with the Galactic Syndicate increasing their troublesome activities, I think it best we take care of this resistance problem before they get too large."

"What do you propose?" Dorian asked, also helping himself to a glass of whiskey.

"My Supersensors," Alis said. "They're on their way, in groups of Bloodhounds, Kathokinetics, and Tranquils. They will be creating a new culture on some of the more hostile colonies, a culture of calm and pleasantness, and unwavering loyalty to the SSA and Walnad."

"How does that help Walnad? We're not a police force or a governing body," Gael said.

"Happy people work more, and happy people produce more. And happy people buy more," Alis said. "Your benefits will come naturally."

Gael pressed his lips together, staring down Alis. Dorian glanced between the two. "What if the people find out?" he asked. Alis' gaze shifted to Dorian.

"Then we will bring them under control once more," Alis said. "And with the Kathos will help keep the pirates away, especially from the Rad stations."

"How will the Kathos keep pirates away?" Gael asked.

"Do you know anything of their power?" she replied. Gael shook his head. "They can create walls of willpower, turning ships around and forcing people backward and to do their bidding. A pirate coming in for a raid or fuel will suddenly realize he needs to be elsewhere-- perhaps somewhere out in the middle of open space with no way to return."

"Why not just kill the pirates?" Gael asked, his gaze hardening. Alis smiled.

"We may have other uses for them after they have been sufficiently recalibrated," she answered, her voice flat. Gael tried not to wrinkle his face in disgust. He couldn't understand her need to collect her enemies, and he certainly didn't understand what she meant by 'recalibration.'

"Where is this Cosmic Resistance based?" Dorian asked.

"We believe they're hiding out on a drifter colony," Lynwood interjected. "We are scouting out the location with a few officers to verify."

"And what do you need from us?" Dorian asked, and he turned to look at Gael. "We can't argue with this, right? Alis is already moving forward on this plan." To keep suspicions off of him, Gael nodded. Perhaps it was the whiskey, but his earlier annoyance seemed to be diminishing.

"Yes, we'll go along with this. Dorian is right. What do you want from us?"

"Cooperation. Dorian, when the Sun Stations begin to grumble about increased Enforcers and other Agents, you'll smooth them over. And Gael, we may need you as a spokesperson for the cause, showing your support. Many people look up to you, you know," Alis said.

"Fine," Gael said. He poured himself another glass of Sun Whiskey.

"Excellent." Alis pressed her fingertips together. "We'll keep you both updated with regular reports. Please, feel free to enjoy the whiskey and take a look around the ship. We have some interesting features here, and of course," Alis paused for effect. "If anything were to happen, we'd have plenty of room on our ship to protect both of you."

Gael knew he should feel bristled at her comment, but he didn't. The second glass of whiskey was gone, and he was feeling light-headed. Gael was no stranger to Sun Whiskey, so the buzzing in his body was strange and unfamiliar. He felt himself becoming tired, and he struggled to keep his eyes open. A young man stepped from the cockpit, dressed in a black uniform with blue stripes on the arms. In this complacent state, he couldn't quite remember what that particular uniform stood for. What he did know was that he was more than willing to relax in this chair and drink Sun Whiskey for a long time.

29

Vely returned to the hotel alone that night, and when she woke up the following morning, Cedrick had not reappeared. His bag was still in the room where he'd left it. Vely assumed that he had not come back to the hotel room at all, even while she slept. Rising and stretching from the narrow, uncomfortable bed, Vely saw that the communication lync was blinking with a message. She sat down in the chair and pressed play.

It was another message from Ren Para, sent not long after she'd left. It was another request to return the following night, same time, same place. Vely smiled. Though Cedrick had his misgivings about the Cosmic Resistance, Vely was ready to join. It gave her a better feeling than piracy, knowing that their end goal was to help the entire solar system have more freedom and more government representation. It was a way to get back at the SSA for the things they did to Liza and Cedrick and everyone else that had been kidnapped and forced into training.

Vely used the shower in the room and changed into relatively clean clothes. She wasn't excited about the prospect of staying in the hotel. She'd have to remind herself to talk to Ren about finding a better place to stay.

Leaving the room, she glanced back, wondering if she should do anything with Cedrick's stuff. Perhaps he would come back eventually. Unsure, she left them as they were. She turned away from the room, allowing the door to slide closed behind her.

Without Cedrick, Vely felt free to wander Mars,

understand how the sectors were laid out and what shops, restaurants, and people inhabited the space. She passed through an alleyway that spit her back out onto the main street. With her recently embedded S-chip, she no longer worried about pick-pockets stealing her things. Vely smiled, remembering how Liza balked at the process, which was painless and quick. She had moaned and groaned for days after, as Liza had bruised and Vely had not.

The thought occurred to her that she had not contacted Liza since arriving on Mars. The ship must be through the wormhole by now or at least close. Captain Lezal didn't seem to be wasting much time. Even if Vely could somehow reach the *Gypsy Star*, she doubted her message would come through clear. She'd have to wait and try to establish contact with Liza later.

Down the main stretch of road outside of the docking bay, Vely recognized familiar business signs and storefronts. Like the Moon, there were stands and shops set up all along the street while the owners hawked their wares in loud voices, clashing with the general chatter of the people and the unusual strains of music coming from every direction. The atmosphere was less "party-like" than the last time she had been on Mars. Perhaps there had been some special occasion she missed out on.

Towards the end of the stretch of road, which ended right where the sector's dome met the ground of Mars, Vely saw a small shop wedged in between two pubs. An older woman sat in a chair just inside the door, using a tablet. The word *Salon* was painted above the door. Vely touched her hair— the bad dye job and even worse cut. She remembered one salon existing on the Moon. The owner was murdered by Enforcers, and the shop had been ransacked by Moon. As usual.

Vely turned towards the salon and stepped through the open door. The woman sitting in the chair glanced up from her tablet and smiled through her wrinkles. Her gray hair was pulled back in a knot on the back of her head, and when she stood, she stooped with age. Vely wondered how well this woman could see. Hopefully well enough to fix the atrocities on Vely's head.

"Good morning," the woman said, glancing up at Vely, who was so rarely taller than anyone else. Vely could see that her eyes were a clear brown.

"Good morning," Vely said, inspecting the salon. It was clean and appeared to be well-organized. The salon was even free of the reddish-brown dust that seemed to coat everything on Mars. Vely realized she had been staring and glanced back at the woman, who was staring at her.

"I can take a guess as to why you've come in here today," she said, gesturing to Vely's hair. She blushed and absently touched her hair again.

"I know it's obvious," Vely said. "It had been necessary at the time." The woman smiled and waved Vely over to the chair. Vely sat down, and the woman lowered the chair down almost to the floor and fluffed out Vely's hair with her fingers.

"I'm going to turn your hair back to your natural color," the woman said. "You have lovely hair."

"Thank you."

"And we'll even up these ends. You'll look alright in time. My name is Lynn." Vely watched herself in the mirror as Lynn mixed up a smooth paste that smelled rather chemical and applied it to Vely's hair, covering the brown dye job. Vely knew she'd be more recognizable again, not that her fake brown hair did any good, but she doubted anyone really remembered her face unless they were frequent observers of the SSA Most Wanted. Vely hoped most people were not.

Lynn chattered at Vely, asking random questions about her life. Vely kept her answers vague and answered with lies when necessary. She did not mention the Moon, Psychogens, the pirates, or any of her adventures in the last three months.

Lynn set a timer when her hair was covered in dye and sat down on a stool to continue talking. Vely was absorbed into the world Lynn painted about her own life and the recent happening on Mars. Before long, the timer went off, and Lynn took Vely to a sink, where the dye was washed from her hair, her scalp scrubbed, and her hair coated in something that smelled wonderful. Lynn directed Vely to sit up and led her back to the chair, where Lynn snipped away at Vely's hair.

In the mirror, Vely could see that Lynn had dyed the brown hair to match her white-blonde roots and cut the ends to a consistent length. Little tendrils of hair fell onto her shoulders and collected on the floor. Vely closed her eyes and smiled to herself.

Lynn proclaimed she was finished. Vely opened her eyes to see her new hair reflected back at her. She now had a short blonde bob instead of choppy, two-toned hair. Vely sighed with relief; she felt more like herself.

"Thank you," she breathed to Lynn, who smiled and patted Vely on the shoulder.

Vely returned to the hotel, feeling an extra boost of confidence and energy. She found herself running her fingers through her smooth hair. In the hotel, she passed through the door to her room and was surprised to see Cedrick lying on the bed in the hotel room, one foot hanging off the bed, his arm thrown over his eyes, apparently asleep. A strange chemical smell hung in the air, forcing Vely to cover her nose with her hand. It did little to stop the smell from burning her insides. She marched to Cedrick's side and looked down at him. The dark circles under his eyes were more pronounced now, and he was definitely the cause of the smell. What in the Stars had he been up to?

Vely shook him by the shoulder to try and wake him. He groaned and flinched, but his eyes remained closed, his breathing heavy. She rolled her eyes and turned away from him. She was going to leave the hotel again when she heard him call her name. Vely turned.

Cedrick had opened his eyes and turned his head towards her. His eyes were bloodshot. "Where were you?" he asked her. She planted her hands on her hips and glared down at him.

"Where were *you*?" she retorted. Cedrick didn't answer, and he shifted his eyes away from hers. "I'm going to Ren's," she said and stormed from the room. She expected him to call out her name, to stop her from leaving and explain himself, but he didn't. He remained silent. Vely let the door close behind her.

In the hallway, she paused, a few tears brimming in her eyes. She squeezed her eyes shut and wiped the tears from her lashes, suppressing her feelings as far as she could. She didn't understand what was going on with Cedrick, but if he was going to become dead weight, then she wasn't going to support him. She couldn't shake the feeling that he was purposely allowing himself to sink into this Augur sickness. She could tolerate many things, but that was not one of them. Vely had been taught to survive, never to wallow. Vely took a deep breath and continued down the hallway. She reminded herself that she would need to find a new place to stay.

30

Captain Lezal's announcement broadcast over the fleet without warning. *"Walnad ships are approaching! To your stations!"*

Liza and Gwen glanced at each other and sprang up from the table in their room, where they had been practicing Liza's Kathokinetic fine motor skills. With her willpower still buzzing through her body, Liza grabbed her jacket and boots and struggled into both. Gwen followed suit, pulling on a favorite jacket and a pair of boots she picked up at the Rad station. Liza ran to the door and paused to glance back at Gwen. "You ready?" she asked. Gwen waved her on.

"Go ahead. I'll just be in the bridge," she said. Liza nodded and left the room. She jogged down the hall to the stairs that led her down to the gunner stations. She didn't see Weed or Speed, but their suits were gone, meaning they were already in their stations. Liza grabbed her suit, yanked it on over her clothes, and simultaneously made her way towards the control room. She stuck her lync earpiece in her ear and dropped into the group channel. Her ears flooded with voices.

"Lezal hasn't decided yet if we're going to raid these ships," Dom was saying. "When he decides, then we'll have to send Liza and Gwen over to his ship. He'll be making contact."

"I'll stay nearby," Wayne replied. "I'll reattach the grappling hook, and they can just skim over to my ship. I have that little speeder they can use to hop over to Lezal."

"That's a good plan," Dom replied. "Did you hear that Gwen, Liza?" he asked.

"Aye, Captain," Liza said. There was silence from Gwen.

"Gwen?"

"She's not in the bridge yet," Becce said.

"I left her in our room. She should be there," Liza interjected.

"Oh, here she is," Becce said after a moment of silence on the line. "She's ready, Captain."

"Give her a lync," Dom said. Silence fell on the line. Liza brought up her cameras and surveyed the interior and exterior of the ship. She could see the other ships of the fleet trailing alongside the *Gypsy Star*. Weed and Speed were waiting patiently in their gunner stations. Liza switched to a camera on the bridge and saw Gwen standing in the bridge. Liza frowned. Gwen was standing beside the command console in the bridge, but the way she was standing seemed off. Liza couldn't zoom in further with the camera, so she couldn't get a good close-up view of Gwen. Dom entered into the camera's view, and Gwen turned to him, and it appeared that a conversation passed between them. Liza's concern faded away.

Outside of the ship, *Astral Empress* pulled forward to the head of the fleet. The communication lync buzzed as all the pirates dropped into the same channel from Lezal's ship. "We're boarding the large ship. Wear your lightest suits. We don't have time to do this delicately," Lezal said. "If you're in the boarding party, you know who you are. Either make it to my ship or find a way to the largest blue ship."

Liza took a deep breath and released it. She pulled Weed and Speed into their own lync. "You two gonna be okay without me?" she asked.

"Sure thing, boss," they said together. Liza bumped them back into the group communication lync and stood up from her chair. Her helmet and oxygen tank were stored on a shelf in the command room. She grabbed them and hurried up to the airlock door. Gwen would be meeting her there, and Liza would have a chance to see if something was up with her.

She hurried up the steps and turned towards the airlock door. Gwen beat her there, carrying a helmet under her arm.

"Ready?" Liza asked, attaching her oxygen tank to her suit. Gwen nodded but didn't meet Liza's eyes. As Liza pulled her helmet on over her head, she thought Gwen looked ultra-focused on the task at hand, which was strange. At most, Gwen was merely amused by situations like this. She rarely made herself serious about a raid. The airlock door opened, and Liza and Gwen stepped inside, and the door hissed closed behind them.

"Airlock depressurization beginning now," Becce said over the communication lync. Liza stood beside Gwen, feeling her willpower swell. The airlock hissed as the oxygen was removed from the room. When the process was complete, the outside door opened to space. Liza stepped forward to the cable that was stretched between *Gypsy Star* and *Wasp*. Liza flew through zero gravity and grabbed onto the cable with a push, her legs trailing weightlessly behind her. She glanced back to see that Gwen was right behind her.

The door on Wayne River's ship was already open. Hand over hand, Liza pulled herself along the cable to the other ship. She reached his ship and climbed inside the airlock chamber, Gwen following behind. Inside the airlock, the door closed, and the alarm went off, indicating re-pressurization of the room. Through the window, Liza saw an unfamiliar face watching them. The re-pressurization process was completed, and the door to the interior of the ship opened. Two pirates waited for them on the other side.

Liza removed her helmet and shook out her dreads. "Liza Strange," one of the pirates said, holding out a hand to shake. "I have been anxious to meet you." Liza raised an eyebrow.

"Why?" she asked. The pirate smiled.

"You and your sister are well known among some of us. Your stories and status as SSA Most Wanted make you interesting," he said. Liza shook her head.

"Don't believe things you hear," she said. The pirate grinned and turned to lead them down into *Wasp's* cargo bay.

"Captain Wayne has already prepared the speeder for

you to hop over to Lezal's ship," the pirate said. "Should only take you a few minutes to get there."

"One problem," Liza said. "Neither of us can pilot that thing."

"I can."

Liza halted and turned to Gwen. "Since when?" Liza asked. Gwen shrugged.

"I just do," she answered. Liza frowned, but she turned back to the pirate.

"Let's go then."

The pirate led them down to the cargo bay, where Wayne's speeder was waiting. The small black ship was docked inside the bay, waiting for a pilot. Liza pulled her helmet back on and pulled her communication lync from a pocket on her suit. She changed the lync channel and pulled Dom into a private channel.

"What's wrong?" Dom asked.

"I've got a bad feeling," Liza said, trying to keep some distance between herself and Gwen.

"About what?"

"Gwen is acting weird," Liza said. "She apparently knows how to pilot the speeder, and she's… she's just not herself." Dom was silent for a moment.

"Keep an eye on her, then," Dom said. "If anything happens, contact me immediately."

"Okay." Liza changed back to the public channel. The pirate was waiting beside the speeder with the small door open. Gwen had already crawled inside. Liza climbed in beside her in the passenger seat. The pirate saluted them and hurried away from the cargo bay.

As the cargo bay door opened, Gwen fired up the engines, and the speeder dropped from the belly of the *Wasp*. Gwen hit the engines hard, and the speeder arced upwards and around the ship until they were flying above the other ships. Liza unconsciously clenched the sides of her seat. She hadn't realized how *close* to space they would be inside the speeder.

She trembled slightly from adrenaline.

"Gwen and Liza. Do you see my ship?" It was Captain Lezal.

"Yes, sir," Gwen replied. She pushed the thrusters forward, and their speed increased. It only took a few moments to reach Lezal's ship. *Astral Empress* was impressive up close. Liza had never seen his ship before. The ship was probably a Class B ship, based on its size. That size ship was usually used for transportation, but Lezal had apparently modified it to be a massive weapon. There were gunner stations everywhere, in addition to many smaller laser guns and two ion cannons. Liza let out a breath of appreciation.

"This is nothing," Gwen said. Liza glanced at her.

"What do you mean?" But Gwen shook her head. An unsettled feeling sank over Liza once more.

The speeder ship docked aboard *Astral Empress*, and Liza and Gwen climbed out of the cockpit and were greeted by several pirates. Liza recognized a few from their stop at the Rad station.

"We're heading straight to the airlock," one of the pirates said. "We'll be making contact with the merchant ship soon." Liza and Gwen nodded and followed the pirates.

Liza was amazed at the size of Lezal's ship. There were pirates everywhere, running to their posts, working on panels in the walls, and guarding doors. Each one of Lezal's pirates wore a scrap of purple material around their right bicep, likely to identify themselves as part of the crew.

The walk to the airlock took several minutes, which passed in silence. Liza wavered between wanting to contact Dom again and wanting to wait and see what would happen. He didn't have much to advise her last time, so it was unlikely Dom would have anything else to say. Liza had a strange desire to be comforted.

The group of pirates waiting at the airlock was much larger than Liza anticipated. Before she could get lost in the crowd, she heard her name called. Captain Lezal strode through the crowd, greeting and nodding to his crew members. Liza and Gwen turned towards him.

"Ladies," he said by way of greeting. He held out a hand, in which he held a small device. "I hope Captain Rhyne showed you the astarte." Liza and Gwen nodded. "Excellent." He pressed a button on the device, and a holographic map of the ship appeared. "We believe the astarte is being kept in this room," he said, pointing to a room in the lower part of the ship. "After you board the ship, I'll need the two of you to head to this location and find the astarte. You'll have to be careful, though. Security has likely increased since your crew attacked that other ship." Liza and Gwen nodded. "Grab as much astarte as your can and get back to this ship."

"Got it," Liza said. Lezal closed the holographic map and nodded to them. He disappeared before any questions could be asked. An alarm blared, and the gathered pirates surged towards the airlock door as it opened. Liza and Gwen were caught up with the first wave. They pulled their helmets back on right before the outside door opened, and the whole group flew out of the airlock into space.

31

When Vely arrived at Cosmic Resistance's hideout, she found it to be in a flurry of activity. She descended the lift to the lower level and stepped out into excitement and chatter. Vely looked around, standing on her tiptoes to see over the others' heads. Someone shouted something over the noise, but Vely couldn't make out what they said, followed by a large cheer.

"Vely Strange." Maggie Wyse appeared beside her.

"What's going on here?" Vely asked. Maggie smiled broadly.

"We've received some fantastic news," Maggie said. "One of our spies successfully misdirected the SSA. They're sending their ships right into a trap." Vely blinked in surprise.

"That's amazing," Vely replied, smiling to match Maggie's energy

"Yes. This plan has been in place for a long time," Maggie said. "Everyone is celebrating that it has finally come to fruition."

"What will happen when the SSA arrives in the trap?" Vely asked.

"They will be eliminated." Vely stared at Maggie. "The SSA are dangerous foes, but our people know the dangers. The SSA is sending a group of their Supersensory agents. We have one Katho there, but I believe our brute strength will overcome them."

"You have a Katho," Vely repeated. Maggie nodded.

Ren was across the room, talking to someone Vely did not recognize. He was shorter than Ren, with blonde hair and scruff on his chin. He greeted Vely with a smile and a slap on the shoulder. Ren shook the man's hand and walked away, joining Vely and Maggie.

"Did you tell Vely the news?" he asked Maggie, who grinned.

"Naturally."

"I have a favor to ask," Vely said, feeling very short while standing between both Maggie and Ren. They both looked down at her. "I need a different place to stay. I'm still in that hotel. Can either of you tell me where I can find a place?"

"Of course," Maggie said. "We have a building nearby, sort of like a dormitory. You can take a room there. What about that man you were with?" Vely's face burned with anger.

"I don't know what's wrong with him," Vely said, averting her eyes from Ren and Maggie. "He doesn't want to join you, and when I found him back at our hotel earlier, he smelled... weird."

"How do you mean?" Ren asked.

"Like a very strong chemical," she said. "I know I've smelled it before, but I can't remember where." Ren and Maggie glanced at each other.

"Have you heard of Fultra Dens or a Tranq Dens?" Maggie asked, and Vely shook her head. "Fultra Dens are where people go to get high on Fultraline. Tranq Dens are similar, but instead of the patrons smoking the drug, the Tranqs do, and they release their Tranquility, making the effects of the drug extra potent. They're called tainted Tranqs." Vely's mouth had fallen open in horror.

"People do that?"

"Yes. It sounds like your friend may have found one of those places," Maggie said. "It's a possibility, anyway. They're common here on Mars."

Vely clenched her fists and stared hard at her boots, her emotions welling up inside of her. She couldn't understand why Cedrick would willingly make himself worse. Ren gave her a sympathetic look and rested his hand on Vely's shoulder.

"Come on. I could use some help on a small project," he said, guiding her through the room. Vely said nothing but allowed herself to be led away.

Ren took Vely to a smaller room that held an elaborate setup of holo-screens and control panels. The light in the room was very low, the primary sources coming from the holo-screen. There were a few chairs inside the room and only one other person. The man already inside didn't look up when they entered. Vely could see that he had a set of communication earpieces in his ears and concentrated on something. Ren sat down in a chair and motioned for Vely to follow.

"I'm going to teach you how we help our spies," Ren said. "I think you've got the right brain for this."

"Really?"

"Yeah. It takes a lot of reading and the ability to quickly process information. That guy there," Ren gestured to the other man in the room. "He hacks into the computers of the SSA and Walnad, along with several other organizations that we have our eyes on, and grants us access into their systems. We use that access to find out information, which we can pass on to our spies and other groups of Cosmic Resistance members. But we only have a short amount of time to find information before we have to pull out of the systems; otherwise, we'll leave traces," Ren explained. "Our last member who was good at this left to join a group working on infiltrating the Sun Stations. So we need a replacement if you think you're up for it."

Vely stared at the screens. She couldn't argue that she'd be good at the task. And she'd be helping the Cosmic Resistance.

"I'll do it," Vely said. "I'll help."

"Great. I'll show you everything you need to know."

Vely didn't know how long she sat in that darkened room, reading through pages and pages of reports written by SSA officers in the field. She spent a lot of time checking their reports against the current activities of the Cosmic Resistance. Much of what she read wasn't helpful, which was a point that Ren failed to mention. But she felt her work was worthwhile when the other man in the room thanked her.

When her eyes could remain open no longer, she closed down the information she'd been reading and left the small room. The secret headquarters was nearly empty now. Vely wondered what the remaining people were all waiting for-- perhaps a call to action.

She was about to ride the lift up to the main floor when a man obstructed the way. Vely looked up. It was the man that Ren had been talking to earlier. With a serious expression on his face, he stretched his hand out to Vely. "Sehen Aerni," he said. Vely shook his hand.

"Vely Strange," she said. He nodded.

"I know. I'm happy to meet you, especially someone else from the Moon," he said. His serious expression became friendly.

"Huh? You're from the Moon?" she asked. Sehen nodded.

"I managed to get away several years ago and came here. I met Ren right away and joined him," Sehen said.

"What work do you do for the Cosmic Resistance?" Vely asked.

"I'm a spy," he said. "I just returned from the SSA headquarters, under the guise of an Enforcer."

"The SSA? So you're the one who gave them bad information?"

"No," Sehen said, shaking his head. "There are others still there, doing the work of the Cosmic Resistance." He winked. "I wanted to welcome you. Having another Tranq will help us out."

"Thank you," Vely said, wondering who else in the Resistance was a Psychogen. Liza had met others like her, but Vely had not met another Tranquil. She then remembered what she had to deal with back at the hotel, and her stomach sank. "Thank you," she repeated. "I don't want to be rude, but I need to go take care of some things."

"Of course," Sehen said, taking a step out of her way. "I'll see you around." Vely nodded and hurried to the lift.

Outside the headquarters, Vely pondered what to do next. She wasn't sure if Cedrick would still be at the hotel. She didn't know where she thought she'd find him. She supposed she'd figure it out eventually. Her first task was to retrieve her things from the hotel and check out from the room. Maggie had given her information about the Cosmic Resistance dormitory, and Vely planned to go there as soon as she could.

The streets were still crowded as she made her way back to the hotel. During her walk, she wondered if Sehen was as surprised as she was by the happiness and general demeanor of the people who lived on Mars. It was easy to get lost in the activity and splendor of the atmosphere. Vely followed the path back to the hotel, trying to remain focused on her plan.

At the hotel, she hurried up to her room and unlocked the door. It was empty, and Cedrick's things were gone. Vely's items were still where she'd left them. She gathered these up quickly, stuffing them back inside her bag. The room still held a lingering smell of whatever chemical had come in on Cedrick's clothes. She wrinkled her nose in annoyance. Her bag was packed, and she slung the strap over her shoulder. With one more look around the room, she confirmed that nothing had been left behind. She left the room without another look back.

Down in the lobby, she stopped at the reception desk. Vely slid the key across the counter. "I need to check out," Vely said. The woman picked up the card, tossed it under the desk, then brought up a holo screen and typed in a few commands.

"You're all set," the woman said. Vely thanked her and was about to walk away when she had an idea. It was a bad idea, but an idea all the same. She turned back towards the desk.

"Can you tell me where the nearest Tranq Den is?" Vely asked. The young woman lifted a judgmental eyebrow at Vely.

"Go two alleys that way," the woman said, pointing at

the rear of the hotel, "and go north. You'll smell it." Vely forced a smile and thanked her.

Following the directions from the woman, Vely wandered through two alleys. Each road she came to seemed to be darker and less populated. Some people milled around the streets, peering at her from under hoods as she passed by. Vely wished she had a weapon on her. She wouldn't use it, but she thought it might make her feel safer. Perhaps Ren or Maggie could help her find something. Vely turned down another alley and heard footsteps behind her. Vely glanced back over her shoulder. A group of hooded men had followed her from the previous street.

Vely stopped walking, and the footsteps behind her halted as well. She glanced back again, her skin crawling with unease. The footsteps began again, and the group of men closed in on her. With slow movements, Vely removed her gloves from her hands. She tucked them in a pocket and flexed her bare fingers. If she was going to walk around weaponless, then she'd have to protect herself with what she had. She turned her mind inward and drew on her Tranquility. The cool sensation ran through her veins, pooling in her hands as the men moved closer. Vely released her Tranquility, the mist filling the space around her body. The footsteps moved closer and faster, and Vely radiated more Tranquility.

Just as the men reached her, Vely turned, her palms out. They slowed and passed into the mist of her Tranquility. The first two men caught up to her, and Vely pushed her hands into their faces. She released her power into them and felt the coolness leave her hands and enter into their minds. Their minds went blank, and they froze in place. Vely withdrew her hands, and the two men sank down to their knees. The remaining men slowed as they passed through her Tranquility mist. She left them, turned, and ran from the alley, leaving a trail of Tranquility behind her.

Perhaps she didn't need an additional weapon after all.

32

The force of a blast brought Liza back to reality. She flew through space, surrounded by pirates. Someone blasted a hole in the side of the large blue merchant ship, and in a moment, they would either pass through the hole in the hull or hit the side of the ship. In Liza's case, she was aiming for an intact portion of the hull. She called on her willpower pressed against the ship's hull to slow herself down considerably, which allowed the other pirates to pass by her. Liza saw Gwen do the same. They pushed against the ship and forced themselves into a more favorable spot to pass through the hole.

Gwen and Liza landed side by side in the ship. The pirates were already breaking off in different directions. Liza turned in the direction that Lezal had shown her and pushed herself forward, half-floating through disrupted gravity. Gwen followed behind, her own willpower steadily rising in preparation for any attacks. Liza drew on her willpower, allowing it to crackle and jump around her skin.

"That way," Gwen said, pointing to a door. Liza turned and followed Gwen as she pushed a door open with her willpower. Stairs led down, and with the gravity malfunctioning, Liza and Gwen used the handrails of the stairs to push themselves down and down until the stairs reached the bottom level of the ship. Gwen led the way through a hall. Up ahead were several crew members wearing orange SSA uniforms. The gravity was stronger at the bottom of the ship and allowed Liza and Gwen to run.

"Get ready," Gwen said. Liza pulled her ability, the crackling on her skin amplifying. She ripped off her gloves and pushed a powerful wall of willpower out at the guards. It hit them full force, pushing them back away from the door they were guarding. Gwen followed up with a second blow, knocking the guards even further back.

Liza reached the door first and blasted it open. The door ripped from its frame and crumpled to the ground inside the next room. Liza and Gwen trampled over it and down the next hall, where several more guards were stationed. They were unprepared. The double blasts of willpower knocked them off their feet, eliciting screams from the guards' throats.

"Which room?" Liza asked Gwen.

"Just start blowing down doors," Gwen shouted back.

They split apart, each taking one side of the hallway. Liza drew willpower from the guards, her nose filling with smells. She tried to ignore the distraction and pushed doors from their frames. Some of the rooms had metal crates stacked inside. Liza groaned and forced the lid off a few bins. They were full of rocks but not the ones she wanted. She left the room and moved on to the next, pulling lids from crates, finding other materials. Moving to the next room, she pushed in the door and stepped inside. There was only one crate in the room, and when she reached the center, an alarm began to echo down the hall. Liza rolled her eyes and ripped the lid from the crate. Inside, she found glittering blue stones.

"Found it," Liza said to Gwen through the lync. Staring at the stones, Liza reached down and plucked one from the pile. As soon as the stone touched her bare skin, she felt her willpower expand, stretching against the limits of her control. Liza dropped the stone into a small pocket on the leg of her suit and pulled on her gloves. She snapped the lid of the crate back on and waited for Gwen.

A blast hit Liza, and she flew through the air and hit the wall. Her breath escaped from her lungs, and she crumpled to the ground. When she looked up, she saw Gwen striding across the room.

"Gwen, what the hell?" Liza cried out, pushing herself

back onto her feet. Gwen pushed Liza back down with another blast.

"This will be easier if you just stay down," Gwen said. She lifted the lid up from the crate and checked inside, then pushed the lid back down.

"What's wrong with you?" Liza asked, making it to her feet once more. Gwen held out her hand and forced her up against the wall.

"Nothing," Gwen replied. "If you're going to resist, I'm going to have to kill you." Liza felt a punch in her gut, but it wasn't from Gwen's power.

"W-what?" Gwen stared at her with her dark eyes. Gwen reached down to pick up the crate. Liza pulled herself together and pushed against Gwen's mind, breaking through a moment of weak defense. Gwen flinched and released the bin. She pushed back against Liza's power, breaking through to Liza's own mind. She felt her own will begin to bend, and she could hear Gwen's voice inside her head.

I will not hesitate to kill you. Stay down.

No. I won't. Who are you?

Liza pushed back, trying to force Gwen from her mind. She stole power from Gwen, and a scent filled her nose. But it wasn't right-- the smell she pulled from Gwen was unfamiliar. Liza faltered for a moment, and Gwen took her chance and threw a massive blast of willpower at Liza. She hit the wall hard and crumpled to the ground. Pain exploded through her body. The last thing she heard before darkness enveloped her was Gwen speaking to someone over her lync.

"Returning to headquarters."

33

Vely felt the Tranq Den before she saw it. A heavy, sick feeling weighed on her body, making her mind feel cloudy and sluggish. It was a thick, depressed feeling, and she realized as she walked that she'd felt this before. This feeling had come over her when she and the *Gypsy Star* crew had dropped Warwick and Zimir at the SSA prison. Perhaps the SSA used Tainted Tranqs to keep the prisoners complacent.

She reached the door of the Tranq Den, which was called *Smoking Rock*. Vely noticed that they made a wide berth around the storefront when people walked by, keeping to the far side of the road. With a deep breath, which did nothing to calm her, she pushed open the door and stepped inside.

She was immediately confronted with the chemical smell of Fultraline. The *Smoking Rock* was a large open room filled with cushions, chairs, couches, and pillows. Several people were sitting around the room, using small glass pipes to inhale the Fultraline, leaving the smoke to linger inside the room. Though Vely could not see the other Tranq's mist, she could feel it. The rest of the patrons in the room lounged on couches and cushions, their eyes half-lidded or closed, not moving.

Vely could already feel the drug moving into her body. She covered her mouth and nose with her sleeve. Before she could search for Cedrick, a woman approached her, a glass pipe dangling from between her fingers. Her hair was a tangled mess, and her skin looked pale and unhealthy. This woman must be a Tranquil. Vely shuddered.

"It's two thousand Simlars for an hour," she said.

"No, I'm just looking for someone," Vely said. The woman shrugged and turned away, breathing in on the pipe. Vely took a few more steps into the shop with her sleeve still covering her mouth and nose and looked around.

She spotted Cedrick on the other side of the room. He was lying on his back on a cushion, and two other people were lying beside him, and a Tranq perched on a chair nearby. Vely marched across the room, grabbed Cedrick by the arm, and pulled him up into a sitting position.

"Cedrick, I need to talk to you," Vely said, shaking him by the shoulder. He looked up at her with foggy eyes.

"Vely?" he asked. She rolled her eyes and pulled on him. He'd lost so much weight since before he was taken to the SSA training facility that Vely had no problem pulling him up to his feet. She half-supported, half-pushed him through the door of the den and out into the street. She hoped that the relatively fresher air would clear his mind.

"Cedrick, what are you doing in that place?" she asked, restraining herself from slapping his face to get his attention.

"I have to," he mumbled, not meeting her gaze. He wavered on his feet. Vely gripped his bicep to keep him from falling over.

"Why?" she asked. "Why would this be the best way to take care of yourself?"

"I can't sleep without visions," he said, finally looking up. His eyes were still foggy and bloodshot. "I see your death over and over again. And I see my death. And I relive every other death in my life. Here, I can sleep without visions. No dreams. Just darkness." Vely's mouth fell open, wanting to yell at him more, but the look on Cedrick's face held her tongue.

"There has to be a different way to deal with this," she said, "rather than poisoning yourself. Ren and Maggie said they might know someone who-"

"There's no cure," he interrupted. "I know I did this to myself. After I left the SSA, I kept trying to force visions. I needed to know what was going to happen to me. I made it worse." Vely sighed, her hands clenched as a multitude of emotions coursed through her.

"You're an idiot," Vely said, feeling tears well in her eyes, burning with anger and remorse. Cedrick nodded.

"There's something you need to know, Vely," Cedrick said, meeting her gaze. He reached out to touch her cheek, but Vely pulled away, glaring at him. "It was me."

"What are you talking about?"

"I am the reason that Liza was kidnapped off the Moon. I told Warwick and Zimir where she was and how to catch her."

Vely blinked. A rage she'd never known welled inside of her.

"Why?" she asked through gritted teeth.

"The SSA paid me to find other Psychogens, and Warwick was a double-crosser, working for the SSA," Cedrick said. "It was part of the deal, so the SSA wouldn't kill me. I knew that if Liza was gone, it would be easier to get to you. I knew you'd want to leave the Moon to find her. We'd go off together, and I could make sure my visions came true. But things didn't happen as I envisioned." Vely had no words. She stared at Cedrick, her mouth hanging out. "I had plans, but I tried too hard to make them happen. I wanted to be on the path I saw, but I have never been on the right path. All my plans have failed."

"I can't believe—"

Cedrick shook his head.

"Go on," he said, shooing her with his hands. "You know the truth, and now we'll never see each other again. I had one more vision. I'll die on this planet, in a Tranq den. I intend to see this one through to the end. Now go." Vely watched him disappear into the cloud of smoke that curled from *Smoking Rock* when the door opened. Her body was frozen. Tears ran freely down her cheeks now, soaking into her jacket collar. People talking by stared at her, but no one stopped to talk to her. Perhaps a crying person outside a Tranq Den wasn't an unusual sight.

34

Alis Foste was elated, and for her, it was a strange feeling. Rarely did a combination of news come at such a time that her mood should elevate from passive interest. As it was, she stood on the bridge of *Swift*, waiting. First was the call to come through from Dorian Breton and Gael Daniels, and second, for Commander Jeffry Morre to arrive with his secret weapon.

While she waited, she brought up the footage that was recorded during the destruction of pirate ships. After the pirates limped through the wormhole back into the solar system, SSA and Corsair ships attacked their already weakened fleet. Many of her own ships were lost, along with several Corsair ships, but that was a small sacrifice to make to leave the pirate lord Thane Lezal, and his fleet decimated, far from any resources. She was slightly annoyed that her ships didn't blow the fleet up into tiny pieces, but there was nothing she could do about that now. Her remaining ships were almost back to the SSA headquarters, where they would repair and regroup for the next wave. On the screen, she watched one pirate ship, *Gypsy Star,* go dark as their power systems failed. Thane Lezal's ship, *Astral Empress*, smoked in several locations, and her weapons were all destroyed. Another ship, *Wasp*, was in better shape, but Alis was told the crew was small and ineffective at that point in the battle.

And her favorite piece of news was that her shipment of astarte had made it through the chaos. In a small speeder, stolen from a pirate ship amid the raid, Morre's secret weapon retrieved the small crate and brought it with her. In a moment, Alis would be able to run her hands through the tiny, valuable stones.

The communication lync lit up. Alis received the call, and the screen changed to show both Gael and Dorian, using separate lyncs. Gael looked angry, and Dorian just looked confused.

"What's going on here, Alis?" Gael asked. "You stole my shipment of astarte."

"It was going to end up in my hands anyway," she said. "You'll receive your payment." Gael crossed his arms over his chest, not comforted by her words.

"We received your report," Dorian said. "You really destroyed all those pirates?" He looked nervous, hopeful.

"Mostly destroyed," Alis replied. "They will die soon when their ships fall apart, and their resources run out." Gael snorted.

"That's hardly comforting. Pirates won't be taken down that easily," he said.

"You received the rest of your shipment, did you not?" Alis asked, her anger flaring. "We succeeded in making sure you received your blood resources." Gael's dark face became darker in annoyance.

"You're one to talk," Gael retorted. Alis opened her mouth to respond when the door to the bridge opened, followed by the sound of many voices. Four people entered the room along with several guards in *Swift* uniforms.

"My apologies, Director Foste! These men insisted," one of the guards said, gesturing to Captain Warwick and Zimir Tchesova. Both had furious expressions on their faces. Behind them stood Commander Morre and his secret weapon, the young Kathokinetic woman, Agent Gwen Adan. Agent Adan held a metal crate in her hands.

"Is that my astarte?" Gael called over the lync. Alis waved a dismissive hand towards his screen.

"Captain Warwick, what are you doing here?" Alis asked. Warwick advanced on her, but her guards stepped around to protect her, blocking Warwick's path.

"You said I'd get to kill Liza Strange," he shouted. "I was almost there, and your idiot commander called us back." Morre shrugged his shoulders.

"There's nothing I can do if you were unable to work quickly enough," Alis said. "I'm sure you will get the chance again soon, assuming she's still alive." Her eyes shifted to Agent Adan.

"I left Liza Strange on the transport ship for dead. I cannot say if she survived," Adan said, her voice monotone. Warwick and Zimir both growled.

"She's mine to kill," Zimir said, but Warwick threw a look at him.

"She's mine." The two men glared at each other. Alis turned to her guards.

"Please take them to a cell in the brig. They need to calm down," she said. The guards nodded and converged on Warwick and Zimir. Their arms were restrained behind them with metal cuffs, and with gamma pistols pointed at their heads, they were escorted from the bridge. The restraints and guns did little to keep Warwick from shouting the whole way out of the room and down the lift. Commander Morre and Agent Adan waited patiently. "Now then-" Alis said and stepped towards Agent Adan. She held out her hands for the crate. Agent Adan handed it over, and Alis hugged it to her chest, feeling more affection for the bin than she had for any other living being.

"What else did you want, Alis, other than to flaunt my astarte in front of me," Gael asked.

"Please be patient," she said. Alis set the crate on the control panel surface in the center of the bridge. She pried off the lid. Thousands of tiny astarte stones filled the bin, glittering blue in the light from the bridge. She stuck her hand in the bin and let the cool stones touch her skin. She drew her hand through, stirring the stones.

"Director Foste," Agent Adan said. "May I ask a question?"

Without looking up, Alis replied, "Of course."

"What are those used for?" Alis glanced up, an eyebrow lifted, and a smile on her face.

"They are used for my Psychogenic implants," Alis said. "You are a Katho. Have you touched one?"

"Yes, ma'am."

"And your powers were uncontrollable?" Agent Adan nodded. "We use these stones to create the implants for normal people, which gives them the powers of a Psychogen." Agent Adan nodded, her expression unreadable. Beside her, Commander Morre appeared to be struggling to control himself. Alis smiled to herself. She knew the subject of implants was a touchy subject for the man.

"You're using those to *make* Psychogens?" Dorian asked. Alis had momentarily forgotten about Gael and Dorian. She turned and lifted a stone up for Dorian to see.

"Yes. You see, they're much easier to control when they are implanted, rather than those born with the powers naturally," Alis said. "And Psychogens are much more powerful than normal humans. How do you think we've maintained control all these years?" Dorian said nothing but continued to look concerned. Alis dropped the stone back into the crate and secured the lid.

"Commander Morre, I'm putting you in charge of ensuring this crate arrives at the Supersensory research center," she said. "Take Agent Adan with you. Protect it with your life. I'm tired of the pirates stealing my precious stones."

"Of course, Director Foste," Morre said. Agent Adan stepped forward and took the crate back into her arms. Morre led the way from the bridge, leaving Alis alone with Gael and Dorian.

"I have things to do, Alis. What else do you want?" Gael asked.

Alis watched his face, wondering if he would recognize his sister, the Supersensory agent, but he merely looked annoyed. It had been many years since Gwen had been

153

kidnapped from Sun Station Alpha after revealing her abilities. It seemed that Gael no longer recognized her.

"I wanted to discuss where we move on from here," Alis said, "after dealing with the pirates. I thought we could-"

The door to the bridge opened once more, and Lynwood crashed inside, carrying a tablet in his hand, his face harried. Alis turned towards him, her arms crossed.

"Lynwood. What's going on?" she asked.

"Alis! The ships we sent to flush out the Cosmic Resistance," he said, breathing heavily. Alis nodded. "It was a trap! They've all been destroyed."

Alis' eyes widened in horror. Lynwood was doubled over, trying to catch his breath. Behind her, Alis heard Gael's shout of laughter. Lynwood pushed himself up, tapped his tablet, and held it up to Alis. On the screen was a man, a large man with many scars. He was smiling.

This message is for the Solar System Authority and Walnad Interplanetary Corporation. Your reign of terror is coming to an end. Your ships have been destroyed. You will be met with resistance at all other locations. Pull your agents out from every civilization in the solar system. We are the Cosmic Resistance, and we will destroy you.

Alis' elation melted away. Her body buzzed in anger, which rose the longer she listened to Gael's laughter.

35

"Have you retrieved everything from her room?"

"Yeah. Most of our stuff has been loaded into *Wasp's* cargo hold."

"Are the twins still over there?"

"They are, but I'm not sure what they're doing."

The two voices fell silent for a moment. Liza struggled to open her eyes. She groaned and tried to move, her body heavy and sore.

"Liza?"

She forced her eyes open. Her vision was clouded, and she blinked it away. As her mind registered where she was, she realized she was in an unfamiliar room. With effort, she braced herself on her elbows and sat up. Becce and Dom were sitting beside her bed.

"Where am I?" Liza asked, glancing at her crewmates. She was in what appeared to be a medical bay, and her bed was surrounded by a white curtain. Beyond the curtain, she could hear other voices whispering to each other.

"We're on *Astral Empress*," Dom said, rising from the chair to stand beside the bed. Both Dom and Becce looked worse for wear, bruised and exhausted. Liza pressed a hand to her head.

"What happened?"

Dom and Becce exchanged a glance.

"A lot has happened," Dom said. He took Liza's hand in hers, which she noticed was still gloved. She silently thanked whoever left that barrier on her hands. "The *Gypsy Star* is nearly destroyed."

155

"What?" Liza cried. She winced at the pain from shouting. Dom gave her hand a squeeze.

"It's not an ideal situation," Dom said. "We were already at our limit after attacking the merchant ship. After the wormhole jump, we were blindsided by SSA and Corsairs." Liza felt her stomach sink unpleasantly. Their ship was gone?

"Is everyone okay?"

"Yes. Battered and bruised, but okay." Liza closed her eyes and allowed herself to sink back into her pillows. She closed her eyes, her body still heavy and exhausted. She thought she'd slip back into sleep, but her memory tried to piece back together what happened to her. She jerked herself up, despite the pain.

"Gwen? Where is she," Liza asked in a panic, looking between Becce and Dom. Both had sad expressions on their faces. "Is she dead?" Becce stood from her chair and stood beside Dom at her bedside.

"We have been trying to piece everything together," Becce said. "We know you thought she was acting strange. We're fairly certain that she knocked you out at some point and took the astarte that we were after. She made her way back to *Astral Empress*, telling the others that you were dead. She took Wayne River's speeder and disappeared. It didn't take long for her to get the speeder out of tracking range."

Liza felt a wave of emotion wash over her. She trembled from fear, anger, and confusion. Whipping off the blanket that covered her, Liza tried to push herself up from the bed.

"Hey, hey," Dom said and tried to stop her from getting up. "You're not in any condition to get up yet."

"Something must have happened after I left our room," Liza said, still pushing herself to her feet. "Where are the twins?"

"They're on the ship," Becce said. "Liza, please lay back down." She shook her head.

"No."

The curtain around the bed was pushed aside, and

Doctor D stepped through. His eyebrows rose up at Liza's attempting to get on her feet. Her body was still in pain. On her feet, she doubled over for a moment, her hands pressed against her ribs.

"Liza, what are you doing?" Doctor D asked.

"I need to get to the ship," she said. "I need to talk to the twins." With her eyes closed, she pulled on her willpower, directing it internally. Her arcs of power woke up all along her skin, crawling around her, numbing the pain she felt. She wished Vely were around. "I refuse to believe that Gwen betrayed us. Something else must have happened."

"How, though?" Becce asked. Liza frowned and glanced at her gathered crewmates. Fire burned in her eyes.

"I don't know, but I have a hunch."

It took much bribery and promises for Doctor D to allow Liza out of the medical bay. Only after she vowed to return straight to bed that Liza was allowed to don her spacesuit. One of the pirates of *Astral Empress* gave her a new oxygen tank. Becce and Dom were against her going to the ship but agreed to accompany her. They informed Liza that the life support systems on the ship were destroyed. With the tank hooked up, Liza glanced down at the small pocket on the leg of her suit. She felt along the pocket and detected the small lump of astarte that she took from the crate.

Becce, Dom, and Liza stood in the airlock and waited while the room depressurized. The outer door opened, revealing several cables attached to the ship's exterior, leading out to several other damaged ships. Liza surveyed the wreckage with heavy disappointment

"Second to the left," Becce said over the lync. Liza nodded and stepped forward. She grabbed the cable and pulled herself along, hand over hand, with Becce and Dom behind her. The cable was long and stretched past several other ships. Several minutes passed before she finally saw the *Gypsy Star*. Her heart clenched when she saw how much damage the ship sustained. There were holes in the hull, the ion cannon was gone, and most of the bridge was destroyed. She glanced back at Becce. "It's a sad sight," Becce said. Liza continued on her way.

The cable was attached to *Gypsy Star* by the airlock door, though neither door was closed. Liza pushed herself from the cable into the airlock. Sparking wires and dangling metal sheets surrounded her. The entire ship was dark since the power systems were also destroyed. Liza turned and pushed along the wall, floating to the stairs that led to her room. It was difficult moving in zero gravity.

As they neared her room, Becce pulled the twins into their lync channel. "Where are you two?" Becce asked.

"Removing the ship's identifier," one of the twins said.

"When you're done, meet me in my room," Liza said.

"Liza!" their voices said together. Liza smiled to herself.

"I'm alright," she said. They cheered into the lync and agreed to meet them in her room.

At the door to Liza's room, she found that it had already been forced open. She pushed inside. The room was dark until Becce and Dom arrived with flashlights. They shone the beams around the room, lighting it up. "Where's my stuff?" Liza asked.

"Everything was packed up and moved to *Wasp*," Becce said. "He's going to take us back to the Cove."

"We're going to be there until we can acquire a new ship," Dom explained. Liza frowned, feeling sad about the loss of the ship. It had only been her home for a short time, but it had been more of a home than the Moon ever was. "So, what's your hunch?" Dom asked after a moment.

Liza pointed to the communication lync. "That's the only way anyone from the outside could contact us," she said. "I have been suspicious about how easily Gwen and I were able to escape, and I wouldn't put it past Morre to have some other motives." Liza crossed her arms and tapped her fingers. She raked her memory to the month she spent with the SSA and every interaction with Gwen that she could remember. As her agitation grew, her willpower woke up along her skin, buzzing in her body.

Liza remembered when she and Gwen squared off on the merchant ship. Gwen had been acting strange, and when Liza borrowed power from her, Gwen's willpower smelled different than it had before. It was as if Liza had drawn willpower from someone else.

She remembered the brainwashing sessions and how Gwen was able to resist their brainwashing, time after time. Liza fought it as well, but she'd only been subjected a handful of times. Gwen only remembered the training facility as if she'd been there her entire life. Gwen could have been brainwashed but didn't realize it. Gwen might have been further in Morre's pocket than Liza realized.

Two beams of light appeared outside the door, followed by the twins. They floated into the room, pulling a small crate along with that, which held several different electronic components.

"What do you-"

"Need help with?"

Liza pointed to the communication lync. "Is there any way you can see what communications came through?" The twins nodded and approached the lync. Liza floated beside them as Weed pulled apart the panel below the link, exposing wires and components. Speed pulled a small device from the crate they left floating in the air and attached several wires to a box inside the panel, then attached a cord from his own suit into the device. Speed turned the device on.

"Audio only," Speed said and looked up at Weed, who nodded. The touch panel of the communication lync turned on, but the light was dim. Weed began to tap on the screen. Liza could hear static over the lync from whatever they were doing.

"Only one message survived, the last one to come through," Weed said.

A voice that belonged to none of them spoke into Liza's

ear.

"Gwen Adan. Pandora, Galatea, Hydra, Carpo." Liza's lands clenched into fits. It was a voice she recognized. Jeffry Morre. *"Agent Adan. Find the astarte and return to Swift."*

The message ended. Liza could feel the gazes of Dom, Becce and the twins lingering on her.

"What does this mean?" Becce asked. Liza dropped her chin, trying to force back the overwhelming emotions that threatened to turn into tears.

"This is my fault," Liza said. She called her room from Jeffry Morre's office to tell Vely that she was escaping. She gave him the lync code without him even asking. He knew that by Liza fleeing with Gwen, he could track them wherever they went.

The tears fell from her eyes and lifted up, forming small balls of moisture in zero gravity.

36

It was late, but no one in the Cosmic Resistance's dormitory building was asleep. The building had once been an office building and renovated into small apartments. Maggie Wyse and Ren Para claimed the building for themselves. Ren bought the property and allowed the homeless Cosmic Resistance members to stay in the many rooms. Most rooms had some furniture in them, and the members made do with what they could find in other abandoned buildings.

Vely sat on her bed in her tiny room, flipping through one of her books. The musty smell of the paper wafted up to her nose as she read the old pages. The scent reminded her of Liza and her home back on the Moon. Outside her room, she could hear other men and women of the Resistance talking and laughing. There was a wide range of ages among the Resistance members, from very young to very old. Many of the people she'd met so far came from poor drifter colonies, some from the Moon, and a few who grew up on Mars and lost their families.

Down the hall from her room, a large open area held several couches and chairs, holo-screens, and projection screens. Many of her neighbors hung out in this area well into the night, talking and laughing.

Vely wanted to join them; she usually did, but this particular evening, she had a bad feeling gnawing at her insides. She felt like something was wrong somewhere, and she couldn't help but think that it had something to do with Liza.

That would be like her-- getting into trouble.

The noise outside her room diminished. Vely glanced up from her book. She could hear someone pounding up the steps to their floor. A voice shouted down, "Everyone! Come downstairs!"

A trail of members jogged past Vely's room. She set aside her book and followed them into the hall and down the steps.

"What's going on?"

"Ren and Maggie are here."

"Must be something important."

At the bottom of the stairs on the first floor, the dorm residents crowded into the lobby. Near the door stood Ren, Maggie, and Sehen. Vely hadn't seen them for a few days, and no one had mentioned where they'd been. A fourth man stood beside them whom Vely didn't recognize. He had a grim expression on his face, which didn't match the smiles on the faces of the others.

Someone in the crowd shouted, "What's going on, Ren?"

The large man smiled and motioned for everyone to be quiet. "We have good news!" The crowd responded by becoming silent and waited for Ren to elaborate. Instead of saying anything, he reached into a bag and pulled out a red uniform. He held it up over his head like a flag. "We captured and imprisoned entire squads of SSA officers and enforcers."

Maggie held up a brown striped black uniform. "And Supersensory Agents."

A cheer rose from the crowd. Vely cheered along with them. Their last good news concluded that they had successfully led the SSA to believe that the Cosmic Resistance resided on a drifter colony.

"Where's the crew?" someone else shouted.

"They're being debriefed at HQ. You can celebrate with them tomorrow," Ren said. "I know you all want to celebrate tonight, but you need to get some rest. We have a busy day tomorrow, and I need everyone in top form."

The crowd cheered again and dispersed obediently. Vely was about to turn away when Ren called her name over the heads of the people around her. She turned and stood on her tip-toes. He motioned for her to join him.

"What is it?" she asked. Ren pulled her aside, away from Maggie and Sehen.

"What ship was your sister on?" he asked. Vely blinked.

"What ship? The *Gypsy Star*," she said. "Why?" Ren flipped a tablet from his coat pocket and handed it over. He pulled up an article from the Sol Network. Vely took the tablet and read the report, and her heart sank to her navel.

The *Gypsy Star* had been destroyed in a joint effort between the SSA and the Corsair Collaboration. Several other ships, including the *Astral Empress*, took large amounts of damage and were left in deep space for dead. The SSA took no prisoners.

Vely handed the tablet back to Ren. He stared at her with a heavy frown. She avoided making eye contact and turned away. There was a room of communication lyncs off the lobby. Without a word to Ren, she hurried off towards that room. It was thankfully empty. Vely sat down at one of the lyncs and quickly tapped in the number for Liza's room on the *Gypsy Star*. Anxiously, she waited until the screen said *Unable to Establish Connection*.

Vely couldn't help the tears that fell down her cheeks. Her body curled over itself, and her tears fell from her cheeks and landed on her knees. Her breath hitched in her chest as sobs escaped.

"Vely?"

She groaned to herself. Peeking from between her fingers, she saw Sehen standing in the doorway to the room. He sat down in the seat beside her, his knees almost touching hers. "What's wrong?" He took her hands away from her eyes, his fingers wrapping around her wrists. She wiped her cheeks with her fingers.

"Just uh, got some bad news," she said. Her voice cracked. Sehen looked at her with sympathy.

"What is it?" Vely tried to meet his green eyes, but they

were too intense. She looked away and explained to him the news that Ren had just shown her. "So you don't know if your sister is still alive?" Vely twisted her fingers together. She tried to feel her sister, find the connection she always felt when they were together, and how it felt when they were apart. She felt herself calm a bit as if she used her Tranquility on herself.

"No," she said. "I think she's alive. But I don't think she's well. And maybe it's silly, but I'm sad that the *Gypsy Star* was destroyed."

"Is that where you were before you came here?" Sehen asked.

"Yeah. It was my home for a short time." He looked impressed. "What?"

"I've never actually met anyone who was a pirate," Sehen said. Vely ducked her head and smiled.

"It wasn't exactly a choice. It just sort of happened." Sehen laughed.

"I want to hear this story sometime," he said. With a finger, he reached out and wiped a lingering tear from her eyelashes. Vely tried not to flinch, and her face burned. "Come on. As Ren said, we have a lot to do tomorrow."

Vely nodded and rose from the chair. She followed Sehen from the room and into the lobby, where he said goodnight to her. Sehen left through the door of the building. Vely tried to force her blush to go away, but it remained spread across her cheeks. As she made her way up to her room, she hoped no one could see the mixture of emotions colliding in her eyes.

37

Supersensory Agents peppered the streets of Sun Station Alpha. Though he knew Alis was behind it, their presence didn't make Gael comfortable. Agents in black uniforms with blue, gray, or brown stripes on the sleeves stood on busy street corners, surveying the bustling activity. Gael was surprised that most people barely paid them any attention. At first, he thought maybe the Tranquils weren't directing their Tranquility towards him, but that theory ended when he passed by too close to one. He felt a strange coolness envelope his body, and he thought that if he stopped moving, he might just sit on the street and go to sleep.

That was what some people were choosing to do under the Tranquility influence. When this happened, SSA Enforcers showed up in their garish orange uniforms and swept them away. Gael had no idea where those Tranq-ed out people ended up.

In his office, Gael read the most recent report from Charles Mann, working under the alias of Chip Wilson. As far as Alis and Lynwood knew, 'Chip' was just a capable assistant from Sun Station Alpha interested in working for the SSA. Gael almost couldn't believe his luck.

According to Charles' report, the confirmed loss of SSA and Supersensory Agents from the mishap with the Cosmic Resistance totaled four hundred and fifty-three along with twelve ships. The colony residents stripped the Enforcers of their uniforms and left for dead. The ships were blown up or left for the colony to dismantle and re-purposed for other ships or repair their homes and buildings. The others, the more valuable ones, were captured. The report stated that no one knew where the captured ended up.

Gael couldn't help but laugh. It was rare that Alis messed up on something and such a large scale. He hoped to lord it over her for a long time.

At the end of the report, Charles included an exciting piece of information. According to Lynwood, the Corsairs were not working out as the SSA had hoped. The Corsairs who joined the SSA were hungry for pirate blood, but they weren't keen on listening to the SSA. Not to mention, the pirates were not used to sharing their spoils with anyone other than their crew. If Charles' information was correct, then Alis was not aware of this potential disaster. Gael wouldn't say anything. He would enjoy watching her plans fall apart.

For his part, he did receive his latest shipment from the Hestia II solar system, though he never got to see his crate of astarte in person. Alis had kept that to herself, but she did make sure that he received his money. Gael found it unnatural to use those implants to make fake Psychogens. Did the solar system need more people with power beyond what the average human could do? Gael didn't understand how the implants even worked, and frankly, he didn't want to know.

Gael closed the report from Charles and turned away from his desk to look out the large windows of his office. Below on the corner, he could see a Supersensory Agent peering out at pedestrians from the shadows of the building. It dawned on Gael that he had seen those uniforms before— back on Alis' ship, hiding in the shadows while he sipped his whiskey. He recalled the last time he was on Swift and how Alis had fed Dorian and himself Sun Whiskey with a frown. Had Alis intentionally used a Tranq against him to make him agree to her plans? He wouldn't put it past her. As it was, his distrust of her continued to grow, and Gael knew he'd have to play with his cards even closer to his chest.

38

Liza hated being useless while the rest of the crew worked to transport their belongings from the *Gypsy Star* and *Astral Empress* over to *Wasp*. Lezal had decided to split up some of the pirates between the most in-tact ships to save their numbers should they be attacked again.

After her return from the decimated ship, all Liza wanted to work to keep her mind off her various problems, but she had promised Doctor D that she would return to bed until he deemed her healthy enough to get up again.

She didn't tell anyone, but the trip to the *Gypsy Star* and back had aggravated whatever injuries she had received from her fight with Gwen. Doctor D mentioned something about her ribs again, which likely hadn't fully healed from the beatings she took at the SSA training facility. Not to mention, she was bruised in several places and sore everywhere else. There was a large bump on the back of her head that was tender to touch.

According to Dom, she had passed out for a few days, which had worried the crew. Liza figured it was her over-exertion of using her willpower, especially when she tried to steal willpower from others. In the heat of the moment, she hadn't realized just how much willpower she was using to try and stop Gwen from attacking. And yet, Liza couldn't help but think it wasn't enough. She should have been able to stop Gwen and figure out what was wrong with her, but Gwen had gotten away, and who knows where she ended up.

Brooding didn't do Liza any good. When she was in the depths of negative feelings, her willpower took on a mind of its own; objects tossed around the room, and her skin crawled with little arcs. To keep her mind occupied while lying in the medical bay of *Astral Empress*, Liza sent her arcs across the room to move objects around and tease the staff.

She was in the middle of flicking the curtains around her bed back and forth when Dom appeared. He wore a spacesuit with his helmet tucked under his arm. Liza flashed him a grin. "Doctor D says you're clear to transfer to *Wasp*," he said.

Liza breathed out in relief. "Thank goodness." She threw the blankets off her and slid out onto the floor. The impact of her feet on the floor jarred her body, and she winced. Dom rested his arm around her shoulders and led her from the medical bay into the corridor.

"Becce has your spacesuit," Dom said.

"And we have to go back to the Cove?" she asked. Dom nodded. "What are we supposed to do there?"

"We have to get a new ship. *How* we're going to get a new ship is up for debate," Dom explained. Liza crossed her arms over her chest.

"Steal one?"

Dom shrugged. "It's a possibility but comes with challenges. We'll most likely have to buy one and fix it up," he said.

"That could be fun," Liza commented, but her heart wasn't in it.

"Just time-consuming," he replied. "Lezal will probably help us find something. Many of the junk ships floating around the area get snatched up by drifter colonies and used for building."

They rounded a corner and arrived at the airlock. The rest of the crew was waiting there, already dressed in spacesuits. Liza nodded to the others. Corbin slapped her on the shoulder in greeting. Liza could have sworn that her bones shifted under her skin.

"Glad to see you on your feet," he said. Liza gave him a grin.

"Barely, if you ask Doctor D," she commented. Corbin

laughed. Becce appeared and handed over Liza's spacesuit. With Becce's help, Liza pulled the suit on over her clothes. As she fastened the suit closed over her chest, Thane Lezal tromped down the hall. He stood beside Dom.

"You may arrive back at the Cove before me," he said. "When I arrive, we'll get a ship for you. In the meantime, get your crew well. We're going to need all the healthy pirates we can get." Dom raised an eyebrow, and even Liza thought Lezal sounded more severe than she would have expected.

"Captain?" Dom asked.

"We have a new problem," Lezal said, his gaze sweeping over the crew. "A new force in the solar system has cropped up, and I think they're going to get in our way."

"Who?" Liza asked. Lezal scoffed and shook his head.

"The Cosmic Resistance," he said. "We don't know where they're operating from, but they took out a fleet of SSA ships, with many Supersensory Agents on board." Liza leaned her hip into a hand.

"Isn't that a good thing?" she asked.

"It is good, in a way," Lezal said. "But they don't much care for pirates either."

"We don't know anything else about them?" Becce asked. Lezal shook his head.

"Our discussions will continue back on the Cove. Hopefully, by then, I will have uncovered more information," Lezal said. He nodded to the crew. "Safe travels." He nodded his head and swept away down the hall. Dom turned back to the crew.

"Let's go," he said. Tsuto stood beside the airlock control panel and pressed a button with his long, green appendage, and the door to the airlock opened. The crew crowded inside and waited.

Wayne River waited for them on the other side of *Wasp's* airlock. He smiled and held his arms out to the crew. "Welcome to the *Wasp*," he said. "I do hope you'll enjoy your stay." Dom held out a hand to shake Wayne's.

"Thank you for taking us on," Dom said. Wayne nodded and grinned.

"This feels a little more like what I'm used to--transporting cargo and people," he said. "I'm afraid due to limited quarters, most of you will be bunking together."

"No problem," Dom said. "We'll make due." Wayne nodded and turned towards one of his crew members.

"Show them to the bunks," Wayne said. The man nodded and motioned for the crew to follow. Before Liza could join then, Wayne stopped her. He gripped her shoulder.

"Liza, I want to talk to you about Gwen," he said. Liza shook her head.

"I don't think I know any more than you."

"Dom told me what you learned from your excursion to the *Gypsy Star*," Wayne said. "It doesn't surprise me that Morre would do something like that."

"What do you mean?" Liza asked.

"Plant a sleeper agent," Wayne said. "I've seen it happen a few times." Liza grabbed the front of his jacket.

"A sleeper agent? What are you talking about?"

"You didn't figure that out?" he asked. "Those four words he said? They were her activation phrase."

Liza's eyes widened, and her mouth dropped open. Gwen, a sleeper agent? It couldn't be true. Wayne slung an arm around her shoulders, and Liza was in too much shock to pull away. In a small voice, Liza asked, "Did Dom know this?" Wayne thought for a moment.

"Maybe not," he replied. "He didn't mention it, anyway. He just told me what you guys heard Morre say. You didn't realize that's what happened?" Liza shook her head. "I'm willing to bet she's got a tracking device in her too if she's a sleeper agent. That could be how they found us." Liza pressed a hand to her forehead, trying to process this information.

"We have to get her back," Liza said, glancing up at Wayne, who still had an arm around her. "I don't care what it takes. We have to bring her back."

"That would be incredibly dangerous," Wayne said. "She could be more powerful now than she was before. Not to mention, the SSA will protect her."

"I don't care!" Liza slipped out from under Wayne's arm. "I'm not going to let the SSA take away another person I care about!" Her chest heaved with anger. Wayne smiled.

"If you're that determined, then I will help you," he said. "For now, go get some rest. You're still injured, and we can't do anything until we regroup at the Cove."

Liza sighed heavily, trying to release her built-up anger. But it was difficult. Her mind raced, trying to perceive how Gwen could be a sleeper agent and how Liza never noticed. But that was the point, wasn't it? For her to blend into society until needed? She thought of every interaction she ever had with Gwen and tried to remember how Morre treated Gwen. Did he treat her any differently than everyone else? Morre knew, during their final confrontation, that Liza was escaping with Gwen. And he just let them go-- because he knew.

Wayne prodded her in the direction of the living quarters while her power crackled over her skin.

39

Alis paced her office aboard *Swift*. The room was almost a replica of her office at the SSA headquarters, with dark tiles, straight lines, and minimal decor. She enjoyed her office, but she was a little stir crazy from being stuck on her ship. Her penthouse-like apartment at the headquarters afforded her more room and more luxury than her rooms on *Swift*, and she was ready to move back.

Lynwood advised her against it, however, and he wouldn't tell her why. She was still waiting patiently for that explanation but trusted him enough to take him at his word. His response, when questioned, was that he was still gathering information about the Corsairs, and he was afraid for her safety.

Alis tried to remember whose idea it was to bring in pirates to the SSA. She was reasonably sure that it was not her idea.

The communication lync on Alis' desk chirped. She halted her pacing and returned to her desk, seating herself in her large chair. The call was from Lynwood. She answered it.

"Alis!" Lynwood's face appeared, looking haggard and stressed.

"What's going on?" she asked.

"Warwick and the other Corsairs are revolting!"

"What?" Alis rose from her chair, her hands planted on her desk. Lynwood nodded and glanced back over his shoulder, then he turned back.

"Warwick talked the other Corsairs into a rampage. They're destroying a part of the headquarters and talking about stealing their ships and returning to the Syndicate," Lynwood said.

"What do they want?" Alis asked, feeling her anger rise. Lynwood just shook his head.

"They haven't made any demands," he answered. "I think they just want to cause trouble and destruction."

"I'm coming back there," Alis said.

"No. You should stay where you are. It's safer."

Alis laughed. "I'm not afraid of them." She cut off the call and stepped away from her desk. Lynwood tried to call back, but she ignored him. From her hidden closet in her office, she pulled out a long jacket and her holster, which held a gamma pistol and a laser pistol. She strapped the holster around her waist and drew her jacket up over her shoulders.

When Alis stormed from her office and down the hall, several guards and other officers stopped and stared at her. One officer stopped and called out to her.

"Is something wrong, Director Foste?"

"Get a speeder ready for me," she snapped. "I need to go back to headquarters." The man snapped into a salute.

"Yes, ma'am." The officer burst into action, running ahead of Alis to make a call to the hanger. Alis' anger grew as she walked, and she itched to put Warwick in his place or kill him. Whichever came first. He was nothing but a problem for her when he should have been a successful member of the Corsair Collaboration. His ultra focus on that Liza Strange girl was too much of a distraction, it seemed.

When Alis strode into the hanger, the crew there had a speeder fueled and ready to depart. She nodded to them and slipped inside the small ship. The trip to headquarters would be short, thankfully. Alis did not enjoy cramped speeder ships.

The conveyor brought her ship to the hanger airlock, and the large door closed. Alis started the speeder's engines and waited. The platform rotated the speeder towards the external door, which opened to outer space. She pushed the thruster forward, and the speeder shot forward and away from

Swift. Alis turned the speeder in a tight circle and pointed it in the direction of headquarters.

The first sign that told Alis something was wrong was the lack of response from the docking port. She was able to fly right into a bay and attach her speeder. She climbed out and headed down the catwalks. There were many ships docked, but there were no other people around. No pirates and no SSA. The lone sound of her boots on the metal catwalks was eerie.

She passed through a doorway into the main hallway that ran most of the length of the headquarters. This hallway was silent as well. Alis frowned. Where was this chaos Lynwood mentioned?

Breaking into a run, she ran down the hall towards the lifts. When she got there, she found that the lifts' emergency lights were blinking. She pressed the button to go 'Up,' but nothing happened. Turning away, she pushed the button for the door to the stairwell and raced up the steps. She halted when she heard the noise coming from below, where the officers and Enforcers had their living quarters. Alis changed directions and headed down the steps towards the noise. As she neared the lower levels of the headquarters, she could hear shouts and voices calling to each other, screams and cries of agony. She increased her speed and hit the bottom of the stairwell.

Bodies filled the hallway, some moving, some lying still in puddles of blood. Alis stepped around the bodies, her boots leaving prints in the blood. Up ahead, she could hear more shouting and sounds of discharging gamma pistols. Metallic rings echoed down the hallway from the gamma pistols' impacts against the walls. As she passed by the mess hall, she stopped and looked inside the large room.

Warwick stood on a table, laughing as other pirates attacked and beat down the Enforcers. He looked as if he'd gone insane. Alis stepped into the room and pulled her gamma pistol from her holster.

"It's Director Foste!" someone shouted. The chaos in the

room halted for a moment as all eyes turned to stare at her.

"Why are you destroying my headquarters and killing my people?" she asked, arching one eyebrow. Warwick stepped down from the table. Blood dripped from his hands, in which he clutched a gamma pistol.

"We grew tired of your deal," Warwick said. Zimir emerged from the crowd in the mess hall and joined Warwick at his side.

"Well, that didn't take long," Alis commented. "You've only been an official Corsair for a few weeks."

"The promised money hasn't come, and the thirst for blood has not been satiated," Warwick growled low. Now that he was closer, Alis could see the bloodshot veins in his eyes and the slight haze that obscured his iris and pupil. Drug use?

"Money will be provided when it has been earned," Alis said. "And the SSA certainly didn't promise for your blood thirst to be satiated, either. I believe the deal was that you would receive ships and crews, and you assist us in taking down the pirates with your intimate knowledge of the Galactic Syndicate. However, the only useful information you could provide-- the location of the Cove — was wrong. So really, you are no use to me." Warwick growled low and stepped closer to her; his gamma pistol raised to her chest. "This was merely a volunteer opportunity."

The crowd behind Warwick erupted in violent shouts, many calling for her death. They closed in on her, their foul stench overwhelming her nose. "I can kill you now, and our troubles would be over," Warwick said. Alis smiled.

"You could kill me now, but your troubles would be far from over," she replied. This sent a wave of murmurs through the crowd. "If you kill me, you will certainly *never* receive any money. And you will all be dead."

"Liar," Zimir growled. Alis shrugged her shoulders.

"I will offer you a new deal," she said, directing her gaze at Warwick, who lowered his gamma pistol towards the floor. "And this time, I'll make sure you can get your hands on Liza

Strange."

40

The Cosmic Resistance headquarters was quiet. Many people trained as spies had been sent off through the solar system to take up their posts. Some had places that were already expecting them as employees or laborers, while others had to try and finesse their way into Walnad and the SSA. Because of the vast losses the SSA had sustained when the Cosmic Resistance tricked them, they were desperate for new Enforcers.

Vely was not one of those people. Given a choice, she would have turned it down anyway. She wasn't sure her acting abilities were strong enough to pretend to be someone else or keep her Tranquility a secret from others. Since hearing about Liza and the *Gypsy Star*, Vely developed a problem controlling her ability. She called it 'leaking.' When her stress, sadness, or loneliness rose, she'd release Tranquility in the area. She hadn't even noticed she was doing it until Maggie pointed it out to her, having almost knocked the woman out with her power.

She locked herself in the small room with the computer terminals and searched endlessly for information through the Walnad and SSA systems to keep everyone else safe. Not much had happened that she could find-- both were excited about what they deemed a success in attacking the pirates at the TRAN67 wormhole. Reading this made Vely upset, and she noticed that her blue mist seeped into the room. With a sigh, Vely closed down her access into the SSA system, pushed herself away from the terminal, and stood up.

Outside the room, the headquarters was pretty empty. A few people still sat around, talking and discussing plans.

Maggie and a few other people Vely didn't know stood around the table, pointing and talking.

Vely stretched her arms above her head and walked to the small kitchenette. She wouldn't say she was *addicted* to imitation coffee, but she had been drinking a lot of it lately. She noticed that the hacker who sometimes appeared in the terminal room often left his cups at his station, some empty, some half-full, and stone cold. She cleaned up after him, though he never thanked her or said anything to her. Ever.

After filling a cup with hot water, another thing she'd never had on the Moon, she dumped a packet of the black powder into the water and stirred it with a bit of a spoon. The powder dissolved, creating instant imitation coffee. Vely inhaled the heavy, slightly burnt smell and sighed.

A figure appeared in the doorway of the kitchenette. It was Ren. Vely smiled at him as she sipped her coffee. "We received some intel you'll be interested in," Ren said, leaning against the doorframe. Vely lowered her cup.

"What is it?"

"Not all the pirate ships were destroyed in the attack by the SSA and Corsairs," Ren said, unable to contain a smile. "I have it on good authority that the crew of the *Gypsy Star* made it out alive."

A wash of relief escaped from Vely, and she nearly crumpled when her muscles gave way. She set her cup down on the counter and wrapped her arms around her body, steadying herself.

"They're alive?" Vely asked. "How do you know?"

"I have a contact on the *Astral Empress*," Ren said. "It's-"

"Captain Lezal's ship," Vely finished, nodding her head. "So they're alive." She thought she might cry, but she held back the tears. There was no need to cry in happiness.

"They're going back to their hideout. But that's all my contact told me," Ren said. "Even though I've known him for a long time, he knows the divide between the Resistance and the Syndicate." Vely chuckled a little too wildly. Ren smiled at her, his scar stretching across his face.

"Thank you, Ren." He nodded to her and was about to turn away when she called out to him. "Wait, I've been wondering something," Vely added. He raised an eyebrow. "Who was the person you thought might have been able to help Cedrick?"

Ren's gaze drifted away to look up at the ceiling. His large shoulders shrugged under his heavy coat. "It's better not to say much," Ren said. "But he is, what we consider, the father of the Resistance."

"Why isn't he here, then?"

"He's ancient and very frail. He set the plan in motion, and he would prefer to live his days out in relative peace," Ren explained. Vely frowned, not satisfied, but perhaps someone else would know more and be more willing to talk.

"I see."

Ren nodded to her once more and excused himself. He turned from the doorway and disappeared. Vely picked up her coffee once more and sipped on it, thinking, trying to put pieces together that didn't quite fit. There had to be a way that Walnad, the SSA, the Galactic Syndicate, and the Cosmic Resistance all work together-- somewhere in history, they must have converged and broken apart. There was too much hatred between the groups for this to be a normal rivalry for total solar system control.

Vely left the kitchenette to wander headquarters, deep in thought, her Tranquility under control for the first time in several days.

41

Aboard the *Wasp*, Liza was anxious, constantly pacing her room that she shared with Becce, toying with her power, and begging Wayne for something to do. But he refused to give her any work, based on Doctor D's orders. Liza couldn't deny that she could feel the pain and exhaustion mounting in her body, but as soon as she tried to lay down and sleep, her mind would whirl once more, her body would fidget, and her muscles would demand activity.

Becce watched Liza pace across their room, an amused smile on her face. "Why don't you help me research these Cosmic Resistance people?" Becce offered, picking Liza's tablet up from the small table where she'd left it. Liza shook her head.

"I'm no good at that," she said. "That's Vely's thing." Becce snorted.

"It can be your thing, too," she said, but Liza shook her head.

"I feel like I'm going to explode," Liza confessed, coming to a halt for a moment before she resumed her pacing. "My willpower is all over the place, trying to escape."

"Is it usually like that?" Becce asked.

"No. When Vely is around, she keeps it calm, but since she'd gone, and with Gwen--" Liza said, stopping short. Anger and frustration welled inside of her once again, and her willpower buzzed against her skin. From the expression in Becce's eyes, she understood what Liza meant to say. "I don't want to be stuck on this ship." Becce released a sigh and rose from the table. She planted her hands on Liza's shoulders to still her for a moment.

"You know that you're dangerous when you're agitated," Becce said. "You've got to calm down. Or at least try." Liza sighed and closed her eyes, tilting her chin to the ground. She tried to slow her breathing, as Gwen had taught her, and to think of something peaceful.

Becce released her hold on Liza's shoulders while Liza drifted back into memory.

"Hurry! Get up!"

At the insistence of her little sister, Liza rolled from her bed, pulling her blankets along with her. Vely bounced impatiently from foot to foot.

"We're gonna miss it!" Liza waved a hand dismissively.

"It happens every two weeks, Vely."

"Come on! You know mom won't let me go unless you come, too!"

Vely dashed from the room, eliciting a shout from their mother. Liza shook her head, wiped her face with a pale hand, and pulled on a sweater over her pajamas. When she stepped out of the bedroom, her mother was already making some soybean concoction for breakfast.

"You know I don't like you girls going up there," their mother said, leveling a stare at her daughters.

"We'll be safe. Come on!" the younger girl whined, tugging on Liza's sleeve. Rolling her eyes, she allowed Vely to pull her along outside to the rickety ladder that led to the roof of the apartment building.

Their neighborhood was dark-- just before the sunrise, all the outdoor lights turned off automatically. Despite the dark, Liza followed Vely up the metal ladder, which creaked with age, all the way up to the roof. Sliding on the smooth metal plating, they shifted down to a flat area, where they could sit and watch the sun rise over the horizon of the moon. Liza could see silhouettes of other kids on their roofs; they waved at the Strange sisters.

Vely bounced, waiting in anticipation for the sunrise.

"Seriously, Vely, it's nothing special," Liza insisted. Vely

ignored her, as usual.

The chatter and shouting between roofs quieted. Through the domed glass of the colony, they could see the curve of the moon's surface, and on the edge where the emptiness of space met the ground, the sun rose, quickly lighting the area with its rays. Vely squealed in delight at the sight, as usual.

Liza could remember when the sight was exciting, but it had since become a boring tradition. Glancing at her sister, who was staring at the sun with her hands clasped against her chest, Liza wondered if perhaps she shouldn't let go of childlike wonder. Liza smiled and looked back at the sun rising above the Moon colonies, ready to flood the area with light for the next two weeks.

Liza opened her eyes and found that Becce had gone back to whatever she'd been doing on her tablet. She still stood in the middle of the room, her shoulders and arms hanging limp. Her willpower was calm, and her body no longer felt like she might explode into a million pieces. A smile trailed across Liza's lips, remembering Vely's face atop the roof every two weeks.

"Better?" Becce asked without looking up.

"Yeah..." she trailed off and sank back into her bed. When her head hit the pillow, she drifted off into sleep.

The crews of the *Gypsy Star* and *Wasp* crowded around the table in the galley, eating. The chatter was a low rumble, different from the conversations back on the *Star*. Liza drifted from conversation to conversation as if searching for something that would interest her. She picked at her plate of food. She could feel Corbin eying her from across the table.

"Something wrong, missy?" he asked. Liza glanced up and shook her head.

"It's perfect, as always," she said, trying to force a smile but failing miserably. Corbin gave her a stern look but followed quickly with a smile.

"You need to eat more," he chided gently. Liza nodded to placate him, and he went back to his meal and conversation.

She pushed the food around her plate, wishing she felt hungry. She caught Corbin glancing at her again, so she lifted a few bites to her mouth and forced them down, where they landed in her stomach, only making her feel bloated and over-full. Finally, when some crew members rose from the table, Liza joined them, dumping her plate into the bin for dirty dishes. She tried to escape from the galley, but Wayne called her back.

"Hang on there, Liza," he said and turned to address the rest of the crew. He had been in quiet conversation with Dom during the entire meal. "We have a slight problem," Wayne said, his voice commanding the attention of both crews. "We need to stop for fuel, but the SSA heavily guards the nearest Rad station along our course. We will barely make it to the Rad station as it is, so I need some volunteers to perform a moderately dangerous task." The crews glanced around at each other. Liza threw her hand up in the air.

"What do you need done?" she cried out, far too eagerly. She saw Dom give her an exasperated look.

"We need to remove the name of the ship from the exterior paint job," Wayne said. "Meanwhile, Weed and Speed are going to change out our ship identifier with one that we… found." He winked.

"I'll do it," Liza said. Wayne nodded to her. He waved his hands, dismissing the crews. Dom approached Liza, but before he could speak, she said, "I need to do *something*."

"I know," he said, smiling at her with fondness in his eyes. It was an expression Liza had come to enjoy. "I'll help you. Come on."

He placed his hand between her shoulder blades and guided her from the galley. They walked side-by-side to the airlock, where lockers along the walls contained space suits. One of the *Wasp* crew members appeared with two thin metal tools.

"These will scrape off the paint, but it'll be a tough job," he said. Dom took the tools from him and thanked him. The crew member disappeared down the hall. Liza and Dom donned their spacesuits, and as Liza secured her helmet, she saw Dom staring at her with a slight grin on his face.

"What?" she asked via the in-suit communicator.

"Nothing." She leveled a stare at him, but he said nothing more. Instead, he pulled her along into the airlock and tapped the button to close the door behind them. The countdown began, and the lights flashed, indicating that the airlock was depressurizing. Liza noticed that Dom was staring at her the entire time, and she desperately wanted to know why. Did she have something on her face?

The second door opened when the process was complete, and the two drifted out into space. Dom secured both of them to the ship's hull using a reel of cable just outside of the airlock door. Together, they floated through space towards the front of the ship, where *Wasp* was painted.

"Why do you keep staring at me?" Liza asked after they'd begun to scrape the paint off the hull.

"Why not?" Dom asked, and Liza gave him a skeptical look. He smiled. "I've been doing a lot of thinking," he finally said after a few moments of silence.

"About what?"

"A lot of things," he said. "About you, specifically." Underneath her helmet, Liza blushed a furious shade of red. She was grateful that Dom couldn't see her. When Liza said nothing, Dom continued. "I think when we get a new ship, I want you to be my first mate."

"What?"

"I think you'd do well at it. The crew respects you, and you are quite the natural at this whole-- pirating lifestyle. I mean, you would rank third on the crew, under Becce, but that's only because--"

"I don't care where I rank," Liza blurted out and quickly realized her words didn't come out quite the way she meant them. "I just mean, I'm happy to be a part of the crew, no matter what."

"That's good to hear," Dom said. "I'll still want you to be

Master Gunner, of course, if you don't mind."

"I can do that," Liza said. A calm settled itself in Liza's chest, and for once since Vely left, Liza didn't feel like her kathokinesis would explode. Her mind retreated inward, and she began to feel like she had found a place in life. Back on the Moon, she didn't fit in. She knew she never would, but she thought she would be a junker for the rest of her life. But the *Gypsy Star* had afforded her a new, unexpected purpose, and she was more than willing to embrace it. And with the confidence from Dom and Becce about her kathokinesis and pirating ability, she felt like this was something she could do for the rest of her life. Maybe even one day, she'd be the captain of her ship.

"Liza?"

"Hmm?" She didn't realize that she'd stopped scraping at the paint on the hull. "Sorry."

"You disappeared for a minute," he said.

"I was just thinking about my future," she said. "How, maybe someday, I'll have my ship." Dom let out a chuckle.

"That's a distinct possibility," he said, nodding his head. "And you'd be one hell of a captain."

Liza chuckled. "Thanks, Dom."

42

Gael read report after report. He felt as though it was the only thing he did anymore. Mining operations, intelligence operations, the building of the new greenhouse for the Sun Stations. He was bored and didn't care much about these reports. It was the reports from Charles Mann that he coveted as he watched Alis' plans seemingly fail over and over again.

He leaned back in his chair, smoking a cigar, waiting. He had a scheduled recon call with Charles soon, and there was nothing he preferred more than smoking a cigar and drinking Sun Whiskey while he waited.

Finally, the communication lync chirped. Gael leaned

forward and pressed the button to receive the call, and Charles' appeared, dressed in a white SSA uniform. Gael was proud of his assistant's ability to blend in with the SSA.

"Sir," Charles said, giving him a quick salute.

"Charles! Or, Chip, rather. I hope all is well?"

"Yes, sir. At least, from your perspective." Gael raised an eyebrow.

"What do you mean?"

"Alis had a revolt at the SSA headquarters. The Corsairs killed fifteen Enforcers and injured five," Charles said. Gael burst out laughing.

"I knew that pirate nonsense wouldn't work," Gael said through his laughter.

"Indeed, sir. We tried to keep Alis from coming back to the headquarters, but she insisted. She got the situation under control before Lynwood could and offered the pirates a new deal."

Gael frowned. "What kind of deal?" Charles shook his head.

"I'm not sure yet. I don't think it has anything to do with money, this time," he said.

"Well, good. Dorian's people are already taxing the Sun Station populations enough as it is, just to support her operations," Gael said. "We can't have *another* revolt on our hands if we have to increase the taxes." Charles nodded his head. "Well, see if you can find out what the deal is that Alis offered the Corsairs, and let me know. And if you can, try to stop whatever it is she's planning."

"Two steps ahead of you, sir," Charles said, giving Gael another salute. "I have to go. I will report out again soon."

"Thank you, Charles," Gael said. Charles nodded once and cut the connection. Gael leaned back in his chair and tapped the tips of his fingers together. His cigar sat in the ashtray, still smoldering. He picked it up and took a long draw of smoke. It filled his lungs until he exhaled the smoke out through his nose and mouth. He stared at the cigar, wondering what *real* cigars were like back on Earth. They must have tasted infinitely better than the stuff they grew on the Sun Stations, though probably less potent. Gael sighed and set the cigar back in the ashtray.

Lost in thought, he almost didn't hear his door slid open. Gael leaned forward, clearing the fog in his mind. He blinked several times. A young man had entered the office, wearing the uniform of a pilot of the Walnad fleet. He leaned his hands on his knees, his lungs huffing air in rapid bursts. Gael rose from the chair and walked around the desk.

"What is it?" he asked, hoping it was an emergency. Otherwise, why else would someone burst into his office unannounced? The young man nodded his head and stood up straight.

"I only just arrived back," he said, his breath gasping through his lungs. "Barely made it back."

"Why?" Gael asked, feeling more annoyed as he waited for an explanation. He needed a replacement assistant, someone to keep people from just waltzing into his office.

"Our ship was attacked on our way back from the mining colony!" the man gasped out. Gael froze, his hands balled into fists at his sides.

"Pirates?" Gael asked through clenched teeth. The man shook his head.

"I think it was that new division of the SSA. The Corsair... something," the man said. Gael closed his eyes for a moment and tried to slow his breath.

"The Corsair Collaboration," he muttered. "Alis' brain-child. Are you positive it was them?" The man nodded his head.

"They declared themselves, demanding that we had over all our valuable cargo. We resisted, and they attacked," the man said. "The ship is in bad shape, and we lost some of our cargo to the Corsairs. I thought, sir... I thought they were on *our* side."

Gael released a heavy breath and nodded. "That was the intention," he growled. "This is not to be tolerated. I will talk with Alis immediately. Go back to the ship and salvage what you can. I'll send Charles- no..." Gael sighed. "I will join you soon, and we'll write up the report for the insurance on the ship."

The man nodded, saluted Gael, and turned to leave the room. Gael watched him go, anger fluttering in his chest. Who did Alis think she was, allowing her filthy pirate squad to attack *his* ships? He knew he was too angry to have that conversation now, so he sat back down in his chair, back rigid, and waited for the tide of fury to ebb before making the call.

43

Alis looked up from her screens when Lynwood entered her office. She hadn't called him in, and the grim expression on his face told her something was wrong. She raised an eyebrow and waited as he crossed the expanse of her office and stopped before her desk.

"We have a problem," Lynwood said. Alis motioned for him to go on. "One of the Corsair ships attacked one of Gael's ships and looted their cargo."

Alis burst out laughing. Lynwood stared at her, his mouth slightly open in surprise. She reined in her laughter and folded her hands together, and looked up to meet his eyes.

"Do we know which ship?" she asked, trying to school her features into one of concern. Lynwood pressed his lips together and nodded.

"The ship *Sequoia*," he answered.

"That is not Warwick and Zimir's ship, correct?" she asked. Lynwood shook his head. "Hmm."

"I've sent you the report. Gael is not happy," Lynwood said. Alis chuckled.

"I imagine that is an understatement." Lynwood gave a slight nod.

"He's asking for restitution."

Alis sighed. She brought up one of her screens and tapped away on the keyboard for a moment. She brought up the report that Lynwood sent and scanned it over.

"Alright. We'll compensate him for the trouble," she said. "Have the ship that attacked them give back the cargo." Lynwood nodded and turned to leave, but Alis called him back.

"Have a seat. I have some other things to discuss." Lynwood turned back and sat down in one of the chairs opposite Alis. She pushed her screen to the side and leaned forward, resting her elbows on the table.

"I believe it's time for me to make my move," she said. Lynwood raised his eyebrows.

"Move? What move?"

Alis smiled, baring her teeth. "I'm going to take over control of the Sun Stations."

Lynwood blinked, his mouth opening slightly. "Director..." She waved a hand at him.

"You are likely surprised that I haven't informed you of this plan," she said, smiling at him. "I haven't informed anyone of this plan. I think things are more exciting that way."

"But how?" Lynwood asked. "You can't just waltz in there and--"

"That's exactly what I plan to do," Alis said. "I've had Lieutenant Commanders Carte and Morre working on a technique." Lynwood stared at her, waiting. "They have been devising a way to simultaneously Tranq and bend the will of a person or group of people, to give a double dose of command over a person."

"That sounds dangerous," Lynwood said. Alis shrugged.

"There have been a few mishaps, but I believe they've figured it out. Either way, it will work, and the current leaders will come to believe that I, Alis Foste, am the most suitable person to run the SSA and the Sun Stations. And perhaps, if Morre and Carte do their job properly, I can take control of Walnad as well."

"Are you afraid of reaching too far?" Lynwood asked.

"Of course not. I am confident that you and I can exert control over everyone and become the supreme ruler of the solar system."

Alis watched Lynwood shift in his seat. He looked nervous, and it was a reaction that she had not expected to see from him. She thought he'd be elated at the idea of controlling the solar system. Naturally, he'd be her right-hand man.

"Is there a problem, Lynwood?" she asked, staring him down. Lynwood shook his head.

"I am surprised at your goals," he said. "I simply am afraid of potential failure."

"I will not fail," she said. "There's nothing to stop me from taking over. And after I become the head of the Sun Stations, I will convince them to allow an all-out attack on the pirate syndicate and finally eradicate those menaces, along with that joke of a cosmic resistance."

"Couldn't you do that without the Sun Stations' approval?"

"Perhaps, but I will need more money, and as you know, we receive most of our financial backing from the Sun Stations. And from Gael."

"Naturally."

"I plan to make the Solar System Authority the true police force of the solar system. We will officially have that power, and the tax dollars from the Sun Stations and the rest of the solar system will fund our efforts."

"I can still see how things could go wrong," Alis shook her head.

"Don't you worry about that," she said. "Let me lead the way, and you do what I tell you. We'll be the most powerful duo in the solar system."

"So you've said," Lynwood mumbled. Alis grinned.

"Have faith, my friend." She waved a hand. "You're dismissed. And of course, this is all between us."

"Of course." Lynwood rose and crossed the office to the door, and let himself out. Alis watched him go with a grin. Perhaps Lynwood didn't believe her now, but soon he would see how much control they would have, and soon he would reap the benefits of her plan. A small part of her could understand his consternation-- he had not been privy to her thoughts and plans for several months. To him, the plan was out of the blue. But soon, she knew, he would understand, and he would join her, whether he wanted to or not.

And as for Warwick and his ilk, Alis would give him what he wanted: a chance to bring in Liza Strange. Alis had heard enough about the girl from Morre, and she was determined to bring the girl onto her side and use her power for Alis' own gain. Alis knew that Morre was reluctant to admit it, but the Strange girl was a powerful Katho, having defeated Morre once already. With proper mind-control and programming, Liza Strange girl would become one of the top Kathos in the SSA.

44

The *Wasp*, disguised as a trading ship called *Titan*, drifted into the docking bay at the R24 Rad Station. The thrusters used the last fuel to dock, and the ship shuddered as the docking bay arms clamped onto the ship. The gangway extended out to the platform, and the exhausted crew spilled out into the Rad station. Wayne River split off from the group to have his ship refueled as quickly as possible to avoid staying on the Rad Station for very long. The rest of the crew needed a few minutes to stretch their legs and once again feel a sense of personal space.

Liza glanced around the Rad Station. It was smaller than the one she'd been to a few times, with far fewer travelers, but there appeared to be an influx of Enforcers, as Wayne had predicted. Liza kept her head down as she wandered towards the shops, Becce and Dom trailing behind her.

Her body still ached as she moved, partially from the attack by Gwen and partly from the work of scraping the name *Wasp* from the side of the ship. Even Dom had confessed to being sore. But nothing physical could compare to the ache in Liza's heart. Every moment when Liza wasn't distracted by something else, she thought of Gwen and how they'd all been betrayed. Unknowingly, but still betrayed. All Liza wanted to do was invade the SSA headquarters and get her friend back from their clutches. But she didn't know when that would be possible, if at all. Gwen would likely be guarded by Morre and maybe other Kathos, and that was a confrontation that Liza did not look forward to.

"Liza?"

Liza stopped walking and turned at the sound of Becce's voice. She and Dom hurried to catch up with her. "What's wrong? You look angry," Becce said. Liza shook her head.

"Just thinking," she replied and glanced away. Becce and Dom exchanged glances. Dom stepped closer to her and laced his arm around her shoulders, pulling her into his side.

"We'll figure out a way to save Gwen. I promise," he said. Liza pressed her lips together in a thin line and nodded, wanting to believe him. At the very least, he approved of her decision to go after the other Katho, even if it meant diving head-first into danger.

Becce motioned for the two to follow her. "Come on. Let's get something to eat." Liza nodded and allowed herself to be pulled along by Dom, who kept his arm slung around her shoulders. Becce led the way to a small cantina, boasting the most Earth-like food in the solar system. Liza doubted that claim but joined Becce and Dom inside.

The cantina was dim inside, with scattered tables and chairs. A few of the tables were filled with shady-looking characters. Becce led the way to a table in the back and sat down, Liza and Dom following suit. A young man approached the table and set down three stiff cards. Liza picked one up and glanced over the menu. All the items had words like "earthling," "ocean," "ozone," and "sunlight" to describe the food. The descriptions did little to increase Liza's appetite, but she picked an item at random, anyway. She knew most of the food would be soy-based, and the thought made her cringe inwardly.

Liza glanced around the cantina, taking in the sights and smells, realizing how few times she'd actually sat in a place that resembled a restaurant that wasn't exclusively for drinking.

A nearby table was surrounded by a few boisterous men, who laughed and pounded the table with their fists, trying to speak through the laughter. Liza trained her ears on them, listening for what was so funny. By the expressions on Dom and Becce's faces, they were doing the same.

"Then, when the Enforcers arrived, they were cut down by those Resistance fellows," the man said, and the others bellowed in laughter. "I've never seen such terror in a man's eyes as I did that day. The Enforcers had no idea what was happening!" More laugher, including the man who was speaking.

"I have half a mind to go join them," another man said after taking a long swig of his drink. The others chuckled. "I'm not joking. If they want to get rid of the Enforcers, then I'm all for them."

"No one even knows where they're located," the third man said. "They're impossible to find."

"Nothing is impossible."

Liza glanced back to Dom and Becce. Dom rolled his eyes. "They're talking about that Cosmic Resistance," he said. "They're just going to cause us more trouble."

"But don't they want to get rid of the SSA? Wouldn't that be good for us?" Liza asked. Dom shook his head.

"Hypothetically, if they were to succeed, they would create their own solar system police force, and *that* would cause us trouble. We don't need more ships and people out wanting to interfere with our operations. We have enough trouble as it is," Dom explained.

Liza thought about this for a moment, and all she could hear was Vely's voice in her head. She spoke the words that Vely would say. "Doesn't that mean we're in the wrong?"

Becce and Dom glanced at each other, then back to Liza. She shrugged her shoulders and looked away, embarrassed.

"It's not about being right or wrong," Becce said. "It's about fighting back against the people who oppressed you your entire life. It's about taking what those rich people want and taking it for ourselves." Liza smiled.

"That's an awfully noble way to describe pirating," she said with a laugh. Dom and Becce were silent. Liza shifted uncomfortably. "I'm not against the pirates. I just wondered how we fit in with all this chaos in the solar system."

"We exist to cause the chaos," Dom said with a smile. Liza laughed.

"I can get behind that."

The waiter brought their food, and Liza poked at it with her fork. It didn't look very appetizing, but she knew she needed to eat. If she wanted to confront Morre and Gwen, she needed all the strength she could get. She took a forkful and brought it to her mouth, chewing slowly. The flavors weren't terrible, but the texture was unappetizing. And as she expected, it was all soy. Soy. Soy. Soy.

After the meal, the three returned to the ship. Wayne was waiting for everyone to return to the ship. He waved to the trio as they approached.

"Any issues?" Dom asked.

"None. The fake identity worked to fool the Enforcers who control this Rad station," Wayne said, lowering his voice.

"Good."

"I'm just waiting for Lezal to send the coordinates of the Cove, and we'll be on our way," Wayne said.

"For once, I'm glad nothing happened," Dom said, allowing his shoulders to droop. Liza pressed her hands to her aching ribs.

"You're telling me."

45

Vely was reading reports from the SSA and drinking imitation coffee when Ren and Maggie found her. They motioned for her to follow them. Vely shut down her access and stood, drained the dregs of her coffee, and followed them from the room.

Outside, Ren and Maggie pressed close to avoid being overheard by others in the headquarters.

"I have gained an audience for you with Dalton Saldek," Ren said.

"Who is that?" Vely asked.

"The father of the Resistance," Maggie replied. "He's interested in meeting you."

"Why the secrecy?"

"Some who have been here longer might be jealous of your admittance to see him," Ren said. Vely pressed her lips together but said nothing. "Come on, we need to leave now."

Ren and Maggie started off, and Vely brought up the rear. Excitement and nervousness fluttered through her body, and she had to fight to control her Tranquility from leaking out. They walked through the lower level of the headquarters and into the lift, which brought them into the abandoned-looking "antiques" store. They left the building and stepped out into the Mars streets.

"What's this man like?" Vely asked once they were a fair distance from the headquarters.

"He was once a powerful man, but age and circumstance have withered him away," Ren said.

"Why he doesn't want to be a part of the Resistance

anymore," Vely said. Ren and Maggie both shrugged their shoulders.

"He put his heart and soul into the things he did when he was younger. You'll find out more once you meet him. Once he started the Resistance, there was little left of him to keep going," Ren said.

"Literally," Maggie quipped.

"What do you mean?" Vely asked.

"You'll see."

They continued on their way in silence. Though Vely was unfamiliar with the Mars streets, it seemed to her that they were moving further and further away from the city. The buildings were shorter, further apart, and more dilapidated. Finally, after what felt like an hour, they arrived at a small hovel. It was positioned behind a larger abandoned building. The hovel used one of the building's walls as a wall of its own. Ren and Maggie led Vely around to the door of the hovel and knocked.

Vely took a deep breath and released it slowly, trying to control her nerves. What would she see on the other side of that door?

When the door finally opened, Vely had to control her gasp. She stifled it with a cough.

Dalton Saldek was hardly a man. He appeared to be missing his left leg and his right arm, both replaced by cybernetic limbs. A chunk of his shoulder was missing as well, also replaced by machinery. The human parts left of him were withered with age, and he stooped as he stood in the doorway. His hair was completely white. Blue eyes shone out from underneath heavy eyebrows. He held a cane in one hand that he leaned on heavily.

"Ren. Maggie," he said, his voice soft and crumbling. Ren and Maggie both bowed their heads in reverence to this man. Vely stood still, unsure of what to do. When his blue eyes pierced into her, she straightened her back and linked her hands in front of her. "And you must be Vely Strange." She nodded. "Welcome."

Dalton stepped back from the door and held it open for the three to duck inside the hovel. Once inside, Vely looked around. It was dark inside, but she could see that it was a one-room home, with a bed in one area and a small kitchenette along one wall. The whole room seemed to be filled with parts of machines, and Vely thought Liza would have a field day going through all the bits that lay inside Dalton's home.

Dalton waved for them to sit at the small table in the center of the room. Vely perched on the chair, following Maggie and Ren, while Dalton sat down on his bed, resting his cane between his legs.

"Thank you for agreeing to see me," Vely said. Dalton smiled, but it didn't reach his eyes.

"It's not every day the Resistance gains another supersensor," Dalton said, staring at Vely. She blushed.

"Are you a psychogen, too?" she asked. The man shook his head.

"Don't degrade yourself with that word," he said. "The appropriate term is 'supersensor.'"

"Oh."

"Tell me about yourself, Miss Vely Strange the Tranq."

Vely told him a brief account of how she came from the Moon to the pirates to the Cosmic Resistance. Dalton said nothing while she spoke, only nodded at various times.

"I had another psycho- uh, supersensor, with me," Vely said. "An Augur. But he got sick."

"Sick how?" Dalton asked.

"Augur sickness."

Dalton pressed his lips together and nodded.

"Augurs like to act like they're the top-tier supersensor because they can see glimpses of the future," Dalton said. "But they're not very useful because their visions don't always come true. Once an Augur realizes that he can't really control the future with his visions, he starts to try and force visions to come to him. This disrupts the brain, and they become Augur

Sick. There's no known cure. It can be managed by not forcing visions, avoiding contact with others, and avoiding any other situation that typically causes the visions. Those with Augur Sickness can try and finish out their lives, but it becomes more difficult every day."

Vely frowned and lowered her head. Then, it was no wonder that Cedrick turned to the Tranq Den to deal with his sickness. He would probably never be the same. He had been so sure about how successful they could be as a trio-- himself, Liza, and Vely-- but he couldn't stop trying to see his own future. If only he could have just let it go.

"Thank you for explaining," Vely said. Dalton nodded, though he looked grim.

"There's a chance your Augur friend could be saved, but it would come at a great personal sacrifice. It is difficult for someone who has visions all their lives to no longer have them and to actively avoid visions."

"He's already succumbed to a Tranq Den. I don't think there's any saving him now," Vely muttered. Dalton nodded once. He seemed to understand.

A moment of silence passed until Ren spoke up.

"You said you had something important to tell us," Ren said. Dalton nodded. He rested his hands on the top of his cane and leaned forward.

"There is a part of my history you don't know about," Dalton said, his gaze shifting between Maggie and Ren. "It's a part of history that goes beyond the Great Migration into space. It began on Earth."

"Earth," Vely breathed.

"We called ourselves The Temple of the Black Moon."

46

Gael Daniels piloted *Pioneer* towards the SSA headquarters. His hands gripped the controls so tight that his knuckles turned white. His chest heaved with the effort of keeping himself calm enough not to crash his ship into one of the many SSA and Corsair ships that hung around the vicinity of the SSA headquarters.

His ship's identity was scanned, and he was permitted entry into the docking bay. He used all his self-control to pilot the ship into a docking station. Once docked, he jumped from *Pioneer* and stormed into the headquarters lobby.

News of his arrival had been communicated to Lynwood, as the young man stood waiting for Gael when he emerged from the docking bay. Lynwood bowed slightly to Gael.

"Excellent to see you again, sir," Lynwood said, ever the polite one. Gael tried not to snarl at Lynwood.

"Take me to your boss," he clipped. Lynwood pressed his lips together in a line and nodded. He turned and led the way towards the lift. Gael followed, his fists balled into tight balls. If only he could lay his hands on Alis Foste, perhaps strangle her...

Inside the lift, the duration of the trip lasted in awkward silence. Gael knew Lynwood was aware of his visit and the purpose, and Gael could imagine the young man had little to say. Of course, he would let Alis deal with Gael.

Gael stormed out and followed the hallway towards her office when the lift halted on Alis' floor. "Just go right in," Lynwood called after him, hustling to keep up with Gael's stride.

"I plan on it," Gael mumbled to himself. He reached the doors at the end of the hallway and threw them open, stepping into the blackness that was Alis Foste's office.

She looked up from her screens. Her eyebrows rose, but she smiled. Gael crossed her office in several quick strides and slammed his hands down on the desk. Alis pushed her screens to the side and folded her hands together.

"What can I do for you?" she asked, her voice sarcastically sweet.

"Call off your damn Corsairs!"

Alis' raised an eyebrow. "I don't know what you mean."

"Bullshit."

"Really, Gael. I don't appreciate you storming into my office, accusing me of--"

"You know very well what I'm angry about!" Gael shouted though it had little influence on Alis. She remained impassive, "Your dirty Corsairs are still attacking my merchant ships and stealing their cargo. Not only *that,* but I'm finding my cargo being sold on the black market. You said you'd control then! This is not what I signed up for when you hired those damn pirates. If they can't tell the difference between a Walnad merchant ship and a pirate ship, they shouldn't be out there patrolling."

Alis rose from her chair and leaned forward over the desk. "I understand why you're angry--" she began to say, but Gael cut her off.

"I highly doubt that."

"I will send a message to the Corsairs to do a better job of determining who is a pirate and who is not," Alis said, though there was tension in her voice. Gael knew she didn't mean it. He had started to suspect that Alis fooled everyone with her evil, wicked ways. But Gael wouldn't stand for it.

"Shut down that Corsair program and send them all back to the pirates," Gael demanded. At this, Alis let out a laugh.

"Certainly not," she answered.

"Why? What good are they doing?"

"Well, if you must know, I made them a promise, and I, as a woman of my word, intend to keep that promise."

"A woman of your word? Hardly. Your pirates are attacking *my* ships," Gael protested. Alis shrugged her shoulders.

"I told you I would do something about that. Can you not be satisfied with my word?"

"Not anymore, Alis," Gael growled. "Not anymore." Alis tilted her head to the side, an expression of anger and confusion mixed on her face. "I need guarantees and results."

"Fine," she spat. "I'll get your results."

"Don't forget who helps fund this operation of yours, Alis. Without my influence, the SSA would cease to exist."

This gave Alis pause. Her mouth opened as if she wanted to speak again, but she clamped it shut. Gael had her backed into a corner now.

"I understand," she said through gritted teeth. "Your merchant ships will not be bothered any longer."

"Good." Gael lifted his hands from the surface of the desk and let them fall to his sides. With a whirl on his heel, he stormed from her office, allowing the doors to slam closed behind him. Lynwood stood waiting outside the door, his hands folded in front of him.

"Take me back to my ship," Gael growled. Lynwood nodded.

"Certainly, sir."

Lynwood led the way back through the SSA headquarters towards the docking bay. Gael followed behind, staring a hole through Lynwood's head, wondering just how loyal that man was to Alis. And Chip. He had not seen Chip this time, though perhaps Lynwood had set him on some task.

"How is your new man, Chip, doing?" Gael asked, squashing his anger enough to have a civil conversation. Lynwood glanced over his shoulder.

"Oh, excellent," Lynwood said. "His work seems to please

Alis as well."

Gael grunted. "That's good to hear."

Lynwood fell silent, and a short time later, they arrived at the docking bay. Lynwood gave him a bow and waved his hand.

"Good to see you again, Mr. Daniels," Lynwood said. Gael nodded to the man, turned, and walked through the doors into the docking bay, traversing the catwalks towards *Pioneer*. He was glad to leave. The SSA headquarters gave him bad feelings. But without a formidable assistant, he had to take care of these tasks himself. He was feeling the impact of sending Charles on his secret mission.

Gael climbed inside the cockpit of Pioneer and started up the engines. He piloted the ship out of the docking bay and back towards Sun Station Alpha.

47

An FTL jump and a short trip brought the *Wasp* to the new location of the Cove. With the conflict between the Syndicate and the Corsairs heating up, moving the Cove a second time was thought best. The amount of fuel used last time meant it would be a while before the Cove could move again.

Wayne docked the ship with a shudder, lined up next to the *Astral Empress*. The crew disembarked and followed the sloping tunnel down to the main level of the Cove.

Liza breathed in the scent of the Cove, like alcohol, sweat, body odor, and some attempt at a cleaning solution. She looked around and remembered the last time she was here, how she was dragged off by some brute and brought into the hands of the SSA. And she remembered how she only had her sister by her side for a moment before they were split apart again. Those months of searching and following, escaping and pillaging felt so long ago. Enmeshed as she was into the pirates' lifestyle, time seemed to speed up. It was hardly believable that so much could have happened in just a few months.

Liza followed the rest of the crew towards a table, at which they sat down. Dom and Becce bypassed the table, likely instead going to find Lezal. Liza settled beside the twins and waited for a waitress to come to their table.

"I sure miss the *Star*," Corbin said. Dr. D looked glum.

"You're telling me. I lost a lot of equipment. I couldn't bring everything with me," he said.

"You can buy it again," Corbin said, slapping his cousin on the shoulder. Dr. D shrugged his shoulders and grunted.

"We lost--"

"A lot, too." The twins said together. The group glanced at the twins, who shrugged their shoulders. "Lots of gadgets."

"You saved the communication devices, right?" Liza asked. The twins nodded their heads.

"Where's Wayne?" Corbin asked, looking around. Wayne's crew sat at the other end of the table, chatting amongst themselves. The others looked around as well, but Wayne was nowhere to be seen.

"He went off to meet with someone," one of his crew said, having heard Corbin speak up.

"Do you know who?" Liza asked, but the crew member shook his head. She wondered if he was doing something to try and find Gwen. She had a feeling that his interest in her went beyond simple friendship. Liza wasn't great at picking up signals, but she noticed the tension between the two. She smiled to herself.

A waitress arrived at the table, took their orders for drinks and food, and whisked away, back to the bar and kitchen. The crew fell into silence, everyone in their own thoughts. Liza sighed and leaned back, glancing around the Cove. There weren't very many ships there, so the main level was pretty empty. Everyone must be out doing jobs or terrorizing the SSA. She wondered how many ships betrayed the Syndicate and joined the Corsairs. That must have cut their numbers down by a lot.

Liza's fists clenched on the table. She couldn't even imagine going to join the Corsairs and working for the SSA. Not after how they treated the Moon citizens, letting them all die like they did.

Drinks and food arrived at their table a little later, and everyone dug into their food. Corbin had tried to feed both the crews on the *Wasp*, but he found it difficult to cook for so many people and make it taste good. He lost a lot of his equipment and spices when they abandoned the *Gypsy Star*, and Wayne's kitchen was severely lacking. The food on the Cove was okay, but it was obvious to Liza that the cooks didn't care very much about their customers.

Instead, she focused on her drink, some concoction she picked at random from the menu. It was a fluorescent pink color and tasted like faux strawberries, a delicacy she never experienced until joining the pirate crew. Corbin and Dr. D eyed her drink with suspicion, but Liza wasn't a fan of straight Sun Whiskey. It burned too much going down, and its only effect was to make her sleepy.

Halfway through the meal, Becce and Dom returned from wherever they had been. The crew shifted on the benches to make room for Dom and Becce, who sat down at the table.

"What's the word, Captain?" Dr. D asked.

"I talked with Lezal. We have a ship," Dom said, half-smiling. The crew cheered.

"That was fast," Corbin commented.

"Well, I don't think we'll be moving in any time soon," Dom said. "It's not quite set up for a crew like ours, and the ship lacks major weapons for defense. Seems to have been more of a travel ship than a fighting ship."

"Where'd it come from?" Liza asked.

"Well, that's another thing," Dom said. "It was left here after the raid a few months ago. It's just been sitting on the docking bay, and no one has tried to claim it. It's currently registered under the name *Neptune*, but that ship was destroyed a long time ago. So they must have gotten the identity box from somewhere and changed the ship over."

The crew frowned, wondering who would have owned the ship that would be left behind. Was someone killed?

"Wait," Becce said, looking up from the table. "I seem to remember someone being gamma blasted during the raid. He arrived here with Vely and Cedrick." The crew made noises of remembrance.

"Oh right," Dom said. "He may have been the Captain."

The crew fell silent for a moment in reverence to the dead.

"Well, I hope he's okay with us taking over his ship

because Lezal has deemed it ours now," Dom said.

The crew gave a half-hearted cheer, which died down when Wayne appeared beside the table. He was smiling.

"I got some intel you'll be interested in, Liza," he said. Liza stood up from the table.

"You do? What is it?" she asked, stumbling over her words.

"I know where Gwen is."

48

Swift docked on Sun Station Alpha. Alis disembarked and traversed the catwalks into the colony, followed by Lynwood and Chip Wilson. Jeffry Morre trailed behind them, along with Gwen Adan and two Supersensor Tranqs. Two electric cars waited outside the shuttle port. A white-uniformed employee of Swift sat in the front seat of Alis' car. She slipped into the backseat of the first car with Lynwood and Chip, while the Supersensors climbed into the second car.

"Welcome to Sun Station Alpha," the man said, glancing over his shoulder at Alis and the others. "Ready to go?"

"Yes," she clipped. The man turned to face forward and started up the car. Alis leaned back against the seat and smiled to herself. Soon, she would enact her plan.

The driver pulled the car up to the front of the Sun Station Governmental building. Alis glanced out the window at the Government building. It was an imposing structure, made to look like it had been built with marble blocks, with grand columns holding up the precipice. Alis had been the one to call the meeting with the Sun Station's leaders, along with Dorian Breton and Gael Daniels. Soon, everything would all be hers.

Alis climbed from the car and met her entourage on the sidewalk. Two uniformed Kathos met her outside the building, and they joined the group as Alis led the way into the building, passing through the front doors into the air-conditioned building, the cool air brushing her bare skin. Alis looked around, having never been inside the building before. She had always performed her business from her own turf. The main hallway was grand, though far too colorful for her tastes.

A man in a black suit approached and greeted Alis at the door.

"Miss Foste," he said, bowing halfway to her. "This way." Alis followed with her contingency. They walked down the main hall, took a left turn down another hallway, and stopped at a set of double doors. Alis couldn't tell if the doors were made of real wood or not. Based on the wealth of the Sun Stations, she was confident it was real. The man in the suit opened the doors and stepped to the side to allow Alis inside. She strode past him, her chin held up high.

As she entered the room, she was overwhelmed by the amount of wood. Did the Sun Stations have people going back to Earth to harvest wood? Gael had never mentioned such a thing. Perhaps he was not involved. That slight detail annoyed Alis; she wanted to know everything that was going on.

Alis moved to stand in the center of the room, fanned out on either side by her Supersensors, Lynwood, and Chip. From the dais at the front of the room, the Sun Station leaders, Gael, and Dorian all looked down on her. It was unfavorable, but soon, she would be the only one sitting upon that dais.

"Hello, Alis," Dorian chirped from his spot near the center of the dais. "Welcome!"

Alis bowed her head in thanks. The other Sun Station leaders stared down at her, their faces grim. They were waiting for her to explain herself.

"Thank you for agreeing to meet with me," Alis said, cringing at her own words. "I wanted to discuss a crucial topic with all of you."

Gwen, Jeffry, and the Tranqs stepped forward beyond where Alis stood. Skilled as they were, Alis was not worried about feeling the effects of their powers. She stood and waited. The Supersensors went to work. Though Alis was not sensitive to Supersensor power, at this moment, she could feel slight pressure coming from the Kathos and the coolness from the Tranqs.

"What is the meaning of this?" Gael asked, rising from his chair, but one of the Kathos pushed him back into his seat. Alis watched as the expressions of the gathered leaders slackened as the willpower bending of the Kathos, and Tranquils' Tranquility took effect. Alis folded her hands together and began to speak.

"I have asked you here today to discuss an important matter," she began. "We are in turbulent times, though I'm sure you may not have noticed from inside your perfect colonies. We are up against two factions of evil: the Galactic Syndicate of pirates and the Cosmic Resistance of betrayers and troublemakers. Between these two factions, they are causing immense problems within our solar system. They're ransacking ships, they're killing our Enforcers, and they're trying to disrupt *your* very way of life by bringing in a new government to control the entire population of the solar system. We cannot allow this to happen, and I need your help."

Alis paused and glanced around the room. The Sun Station leaders were nodding, as were Gael and Dorian. They agreed with her words through the influence of Supersensor powers. She smiled.

"As you all know, I am the director of the Solar System Authority, and we have been protecting your way of life for many, many years. I have dedicated my life to building the best force for protecting our people from those who wish to harm others. In this turbulent time, I believe that I, Alis Foste, would be the best person to take over the leadership of the Sun Stations, in addition to the SSA, to better protect your way of life and to build a better future for us all."

Silence fell in the room as Alis' words died away. She watched as the Sun Station leaders glanced at each other. Her eyes fell on Gael, who looked particularly Tranqed out. Dorian was looking around the room as if he'd never seen it before.

In a dull voice, one of the Sun Station leaders spoke.

"We agree with you, Alis Foste. We shall relinquish our control of the Sun Stations and put that control in your hands.

We will entrust you to keep us safe and to eliminate the threats in the solar system that are a danger to our way of life."

Alis bowed low in front of them, and when she rose up, she pressed her hands together in front of her face and smiled.

"I promise to bring peace and prosperity to us all," she said. The Sun Station leaders, Dorian, and Gael all nodded, their gazes fogged over by the effects of the Tranq and Katho blast they'd just endured.

Alis glanced at Lynwood, who nodded his head. *It has been done*, his eyes said to her. She smiled again and watched as the Sun Station leaders filed from the room, leaving Gael and Dorian behind. Gael rose up and descended the dais, nodding his head in greeting to Alis. For a brief moment, she thought she saw clarity in his eyes, but it could have been nothing. Alis looked to Gwen, who stood imposingly in the room, her eyes staring at the Sun Station leaders.

She had put brother and sister together in a room, and they did not recognize each other. Gael did not know that his own sister was under the control of the SSA, and Gwen was too far under Alis's control to recognize Gael. Alis wondered where he thought his sister had disappeared to, or perhaps he assumed she was dead. But it was no matter. Alis wasn't in a hurry to use her leverage against Gael. She was going to need it.

49

Maggie, Ren, and Vely stared at Dalton. "The Temple of the Black Moon?" Ren asked. "I've never heard of it."

"Me neither," Maggie said. Dalton shook his head.

"You wouldn't," he said. "First off, you don't live on the Sun Stations, and second, they're a secret society. They don't make themselves known to the general public because of their control over most of what happens these days."

"You mean, they could be behind what happened on the Moon?" Vely asked. Dalton shook his head.

"That was all SSA if my information is correct," Dalton said. Ren narrowed his eyes at Dalton.

"I didn't think you knew what was going on outside of your own home," he said somewhat bitterly. Dalton laughed.

"I may have pulled myself from the Resistance, but I still keep up with the movement within the solar system. I always knew at some point I'd have to show myself again, and when you contacted me, I knew it was time to come out of the shadows," Dalton explained. He nodded to Vely. "I have to give this girl a place in our organization."

"What do you mean?" Vely asked, nerves clenching in her stomach. He held out a hand and waved it.

"In due time, my dear."

"So then, what does the Temple of the Black Moon have to do with anything? Who do they back? The SSA? The pirates?" Ren asked. His agitation at not knowing this information was apparent, and Vely felt a little sorry for him.

"None of them," Dalton said. "They exist for their own purposes."

"Which is what?" Maggie asked.

"The Temple was formed back on Earth, back when the planet was losing its ability to support life. Crops were dying, and people were starving. To try and solve the world's problems, scientists from all over the planet joined forces to find new ways to try and keep the population fed. They would meet during every black moon to discuss their findings. But they had to remain secret. Governments in those days were desperate and would have gone to extreme lengths to control those scientists and their knowledge, to keep it for themselves. The governments didn't care about the human race as a whole. When it was clear that the planet could no longer support life, the members of the Temple were the first ones off Earth and into space."

"They don't sound like bad guys," Vely commented.

"They weren't, at first. Once life support systems in space were stabilized, the Temple changed. But before long, the Temple was only interested in their own affairs, and now, they exist to further themselves in society," Dalton explained. "It wasn't long after when I tried to speak up against them, I was excommunicated from the Temple. Knowing my chances of survival on the Sun Stations was slim, I moved out here to Mars and began the Cosmic Resistance."

"Forgive me, but what does this have to do with our current situation?" Ren asked. His expression was dubious. Vely felt the same way, but perhaps this was the missing link for which she'd been searching. Dalton rose and shuffled to a computer terminal. He tapped a few keys, and some information flashed up on the transparent monitor. Vely squinted and could just barely read the words.

It was the same information that Dalton had just explained. After a few more taps and a moment's wait, Dalton removed a small chip from the computer and handed it over to Ren.

"This contains all the information I've been able to find about the current activities of Temple, along with my own

214

information and musings. I believe, and you'll have to trust me, that the key to bringing down the SSA and ending this conflict lies with the Temple," Dalton said. "I've given this much thought, and it's the only thing I can think of."

"So we infiltrate the Temple," Maggie suggested.

"When I heard you had a Tranquil in your midst, I knew she must be the one to go," Dalton said.

All eyes snapped to Vely. She stared back, open-mouthed.

"I'm not special or anything," she stuttered. Dalton crossed the room and dropped a hand on Vely's shoulder.

"You are. You have the power to sway people to your way of thinking. It just takes more finesse than a Katho's ability," Dalton explained.

"Really?"

"You just need practice," Dalton said.

"Does this mean you're rejoining our cause?" Ren asked. Dalton smiled and returned to his seat.

"For now, I must. You'll need me to navigate the Temple without being discovered," Dalton said.

"But how will I get into the Temple? Sounds like I can't just walk in and sign up for membership," Vely commented. Dalton tapped his cane on the floor.

"I'm sure Ren and Maggie can put some of their spies on the job of figuring that out. Vely Strange, you should leave here as soon as possible and make your way to the Sun Stations."

"But how?"

"We'll send someone with her," Maggie cut in. "Someone who knows the Sun Stations and can help her out. Vely's never been there and will need full documentation to even step foot on the colony."

"She'll get it," Ren said. "And you're right. We have to send someone. I think Sehen Aerni would be the perfect person." Vely's head snapped up, and she blushed, hoping no one noticed.

"Then it's settled. Vely will go to Sun Station Alpha and

infiltrate the Temple of the Black Moon."

Nods all around. Vely's stomach clenched with something akin to fear and excitement. Never in her life would she have dreamed of the current scenario in which she found herself. She was now a spy for the Cosmic Resistance.

50

Gael Daniels left the Sun Station Alpha government building with Dorian Breton at his side. On the steps leading down to the street, the two men turned to each other, tapped their fists to their breast bone, and parted ways. Gael walked to his waiting car, feeling like his head was in a daze. Perhaps he was coming down with some illness, which is practically unheard of on the Sun Stations. Their air quality was too regimented. Gael slipped into the back of the car and settled into the seat.

"Back to the office, please," he called, who nodded and pulled the car from the curb. Gael glanced out the window and thought about the meeting he'd just left. Really, Alis was the best person for the job of leading the Sun Stations. She'd be able to use her police power to protect all the innocent lives who would be caught in the crossfire between the three factions that were currently pitted against each other. Too many pirate raids, too much merchandise stolen and sold on the black market. This was a better alternative.

The trip to the Walnad headquarters was a short one. The car pulled up to the main entrance, and Gael climbed out of the backseat of the car. He climbed the steps and passed into the cool air of the building. The receptionist hailed him in greeting, which he happily returned as he approached the lifts. He jammed the button to go UP and waited a moment for the lift to arrive on the main floor. Gael glanced around. He felt pleased about the meeting and the decision the group came made. And Gael was delighted that the Sun Station leaders, former anyway, had wanted his opinion on the matter. After all, his opinion should matter, considering how important Walnad was to the survival of the Sun Stations.

The lift arrived, and Gael stepped inside. He waited as the lift carried him up to the top floor of the building and arrived with a soft *ding*. He headed for his office. The desk in front of his door was empty, and for a moment, he felt sad. Charles had been at the meeting as well, but they couldn't acknowledge each other. He was working for Alis now, and he needed to remain under cover. Gael would have liked a moment to speak with Charles about a potential replacement.

Gael sat down at his desk and opened a cabinet. Inside was a crystal bottle of Sun Whiskey, which he grabbed, along with a crystal glass. He poured himself a measure of whiskey and leaned back in his chair, content.

He sat for a few minutes in silence, sipping his whiskey, when there was a knock at his door. He leaned forward and pressed the button to open the door.

To Gael's immense surprise, Charles Mann stepped inside. He hurried across the office to Gael's desk and leaned over it, his hands pressed into the surface.

"I don't have much time," he sputtered. Gael set down his glass and leaned forward in his chair.

"What is it?"

"You have to snap out of it," Charles said. "They Tranq-Katho blasted you in that meeting to make you think Alis was the best person for the job." Gael blinked, not understanding. But he always thought Alis was the best person for the job; it was just something he'd never considered heavily before. "You have to remember who you are and what you're doing. You have to pull through the blast, sir."

Gael frowned and thought for a moment. A Tranq-Katho blast? He'd never heard of such a thing. But then, Alis had brought some Supersensors with her into the room. For whatever reason, their faces were hazy to him, like they hadn't been there at all.

"Remember, Mr. Daniels," Charles pressed, becoming

more frantic. Gael couldn't understand his urgency. He tried to remember whatever Charles wanted him to remember. Alis. Those damn corsairs attacking his ships.

A headache exploded in Gael's head. He cried out and pressed his hands to his temples, feeling his heartbeat throb. He closed his eyes, and the meeting flashed before his eyes. Right after Alis began to talk, he remembered his mind going hazy, and everything Alis said was the correct thing to say. But it wasn't.

It wasn't the correct thing to say at all. Alis would never be the best person to run the Sun Stations and the SSA. She was too corrupt.

Gael looked up at Charles through the blinding pain in his head.

"I remember," he whispered. Charles breathed a sigh of relief.

"Thank goodness, sir. I couldn't sit by while you suffered from a blast like that. You have to remain yourself if we're ever going to take down Alis Foste," Charles said. But then Charles did something strange. He clamped his mouth shut, and a hand flew over his lips as if he'd said something he should not have. Gael stared at him but allowed the slip to pass. He wasn't exactly trying to take down Alis, but the thought was certainly pleasant enough. If Gael could get his own people to be the head of the SSA, a merger could take place. And that would benefit Gael immensely.

"I like where your head's at," Gael said. Charles smiled.

"I have to go. Be careful in the future if you see Alis and her Supersensors. They're dangerous," Charles said, already stepping away from Gael's desk.

"I will. Thank you, Charles," Gael said. Charles nodded and spun away, nearly running for the door. He disappeared through it. Gael leaned back in his chair, the lingering effects of the headache fading away. Anger and frustration replaced the pain of the headache. How could Alis do such a thing?

Because she *was* corrupt. Gael would have to work extra

hard to bring her down off her pedestal. He pressed the tips of his fingers together and spun his chair around to face out the windows, taking in the view of the Sun Station from his office. Yes, he knew what needed to be done now. He would need allies and would need to work in secret. And he knew just the people to help.

51

"How do you know where Gwen is? How did you find out?" Liza asked Wayne, grabbing him by the shirt. He chuckled and released her hands from him.

"I have a… friend… who works on *Swift*, which is the ship that belongs to Alis Foste," Wayne said.

"Who is that?" Liza asked.

"She's the director of the SSA," Dom interjected. "Probably one of the most powerful women in the solar system." Liza wrinkled her nose.

"My friend said that they flew Alis Foste, her minions, and a few Supersensors to Sun Station Alpha for some meeting with the heads of the colony governments. Gwen Adan was one of them," Wayne explained.

"So, she's definitely with the SSA. We just need to go to their headquarters then and bring her back," Liza said. Dom and Wayne exchanged glances.

"It's not going to be *that* easy, Liza," Dom said. "You can't just walk onto the SSA headquarters."

Liza pulled at her sleeve, revealing the barcode tattooed into her skin. "Maybe you wouldn't be able to, but I might."

"Bad idea, girl," Wayne said. "Going alone would be dangerous." Liza looked to Dom, whose eyebrows rose in surprise. He shook his head.

"It's dangerous, Liza. We'll have to find a different way to bring her back," Dom said. Liza felt anger and frustration rise within her. She wasn't afraid of the SSA or some director woman. Gwen didn't deserve to be under their control, and Liza was determined to break her out of their control. Besides, she was a powerful Katho, even if Jeffry Morre claimed she wasn't. After all, she was the one who blew the chip out of that Fake's neck. And she defeated Morre in his office, even though she was injured from the repeated beatings. She was stronger now and more in control, and Liza knew she could take Morre on again, given a chance.

"If you won't come with me, I'll find a way to go alone," Liza said, glancing between the two men. "I'm sure someone on this rock has a small ship they would loan out."

"You don't know how to pilot one," Dom said. Liza shrugged her shoulders.

"Then I'll learn," she said. "It can't be that hard."

Dom sighed and looked at Wayne, who shrugged his shoulders. Liza raised her eyebrows and waited. One of them was going to cave. She knew it.

"Alright, fine. I'll go with you to talk to Lezal," Dom said. Liza squeezed her fist in triumph.

"Thank you, Dom. You won't regret this," she said, impulsively grabbing his hand. A small smile formed on his face.

"I might."

Later, after eating a meal and having several drinks, Liza and Dom excused themselves from the group and searched for Captain Lezal. Dom thought that Lezal might have a speeder that would suit their needs. After all, his ship was large enough to house several speeders in the ship's internal bay.

They found him in his pseudo-office, a small room near the top of the Cove. He kept nothing of value in the room but regularly conducted affairs and dealt with disputes from the small room. When Liza and Dom entered the room, they found him talking to two pirates who seemed to have a rift between them.

"I don't care who started the argument," Lezal said as they entered the room. "I don't tolerate problems of this nature, and if you can't get along, you can forget about being a part of the Syndicate."

"The Syndicate is barely an organized group," one of the pirates said. Lezal chuckled.

"Perhaps not, but if you're ever in trouble, you won't count on our help," he said. Neither pirate had anything to say about that threat, so instead of arguing further, the two men turned to each other and shook hands, though they didn't look too happy. Lezal dismissed them with a wave of his hand, and the two pirates turned, shoving each other slightly as they squeezed past Liza and Dom without acknowledging their presence. Dom and Liza approached Lezal.

"Ah, Captain Rhyne. And Liza. What can I do for you?" he asked.

"We have a favor to ask," Dom began.

"Or pay for," Liza added. Lezal chuckled and motioned for them to continue.

"We need a small speeder to go on a short mission to attempt to rescue one of our crew members. We discovered she was a sleeper agent for the SSA, and our crew would like to try and retrieve her," Dom explained. Lezal stroked his beard.

"A sleeper agent for the SSA? Sounds inconvenient," he said. Liza frowned and tightened her fists at her sides. "Is that how they found us so easily?"

Liza's stomach dropped. She glanced up at Dom, who looked resigned. He sighed.

"It's a possibility I had considered," he said. Liza frowned deeper. He'd never mentioned those thoughts to her. Lezal tapped his fingers together at the tips and waited for someone else to speak.

"We can try to find the tracker and remove it from her," Liza said. "We'll do anything!" Even this was too much for Dom. His hand closed around her upper arm and gave her a little tug.

"I told you, it's too dangerous," Dom said.

"It's a fool's errand, Liza," Lezal said. Dom nodded in agreement. "If this crew member is the reason the SSA found us so easily and attacked us after we'd already been in a fight, then she's a danger to us all. You can't guarantee that you'll be able to break her of whatever brainwashing she's received at the hands of the SSA. As head of the Syndicate, I can't take that chance. I'm sorry, Liza."

Liza glanced between Lezal and Dom, and without a word, stormed from the room. Anger bloomed inside of her. The door slid closed behind her, and she stomped her way through the hall back into the main seating area of the Cove. She bypassed the table filled with her crewmates and continued on her way to the docking bay.

If no one was going to help her, she'd have to help herself.

52

The first decision Alis made as head of the Sun Stations was to increase the SSA budget. Using that money, she made plans to enhance the Corsair Collaboration by ordering more ships from Walnad Interplanetary Corporation. To Alis' annoyance, the massive order would help Gael make more money, but that couldn't be helped. His company was already equipped to produce the resources she needed to continue her plan. Besides, if he made more money, he could use it to hire more SSA ships to protect his deliveries.

From *Swift*, she made a call to Captain Warwick. His figure appeared on the holographic projector, and judging from his body posture, he wasn't happy. Alis smirked at him, and he glowered back.

"You've been keeping us on a leash for too long," Warwick said, not waiting for Alis to speak first.

"Well, I'm releasing you," she said. From her pocket, she lifted up a vial. She waved it in front of Warwick's projection. "This is Liza Strange's blood. Come pick it up from my ship and use it to find her." A wicked smile crossed Warwick's face and his arms uncrossed.

"Finally," he muttered. "We'll be there soon. Zimir will be pleased."

"When you find her, bring her back to me, first. I would like a chance to speak with her," Alis said. Warwick snarled but nodded his head.

"If that's what you want," he said. Alis nodded.

"Soon, I will have new ships for the Corsairs. No more ships cobbled together with parts from other ships," Alis said.

"How did you manage that?" Warwick asked. Alis raised an eyebrow. She didn't feel like she should tell Warwick anything about her plan, but he would find out soon anyway.

"I am now the leader of the Sun Stations, and I now have control over their money," Alis said. "I *convinced* the previous government that I would be the best person to do the job, especially during this *tumultuous* time." Warwick released a laugh.

"Genius," he commented.

"Indeed," Alis replied. "I'll be waiting near the SSA headquarters on my ship. Come pick up the blood sample as soon as possible." Warwick bobbed his head and terminated the connection. His holographic figure disappeared. Alis tapped the tips of her fingers together and smiled. She turned away from the holoprojector and sat down at a computer terminal. She brought up a report sent to her by Lieutenant Carte from the Supersensor Division. Her eyes scanned the document, dated a few months ago, regarding the behavior of Lieutenant Jeffry Morre and his *relationship* with Liza Strange.

Carte noted increased attentions, suspicious alone time, and frequent discussions regarding the young Katho. Lieutenant Howards corroborated Carte's story, having noticed that Morre seemed to have a strange attachment to the girl despite his insistence to the contrary. Alis' hope was to dangle the girl in front of Morre and use her as blackmail for another phase of her plan. After that, she would let Warwick and Zimir do whatever they wanted with the girl.

Alis closed the report and leaned back in her chair. Everything was going according to plan, and so far, she could not foresee any hiccups that would interfere. Gael was the only wild card; she wondered if perhaps she should plant one of her people in his office, to spy on him. She wouldn't be surprised if he did the same thing to her, though she didn't believe he had the wherewithal to do something like that.

But she did.

Alis picked up her communicator and pressed the

button.

"Lynwood. I need you," she said into the device. Lynwood's voice came over in reply.

"One moment, ma'am."

She waited in her office until the door opened, and Lynwood stepped inside. He made a quick bow to her and crossed the office. Alis stood up from her chair and crossed her arms over her chest.

"I have a question," she said. Lynwood blinked and nodded his head. "Should I have a spy among Gael's people?"

Lynwood froze for a moment, then shook his head.

"I don't think that's necessary, ma'am," he said. "Now that you control the Sun Stations' government, you control Gael and what he does. He can only operate as you allow him to."

Alis tapped a finger against her chin and thought about his words. "That's a perfectly excellent point."

"You control the entire deck," Lynwood added. "It's up to you which cards you play." Alis smiled and uncrossed her arms. She reached out a hand to Lynwood, which he shook. It was a gesture she only reserved for special occasions and those she trusted, of which there were few.

"Thank you for your advice, Lynwood. That is all."

Lynwood nodded to her, saluted, and turned to leave the room. Alis watched him go, thinking and wondering.

53

When Vely returned from her visit to Dalton Saldek, she expected to see Sehen right away, so she could tell him the news. But he was nowhere to be found. Even Ren and Maggie weren't sure where he was. Several days passed before anyone saw him.

Vely sat on a chair at one of the many tables in the lower level of the Cosmic Resistance headquarters. She practiced her Tranquility, releasing some into the air and concentrating on directing the blue mist to where she wanted it to go. It was something she had found out by accident one night when she released too much Tranquility in a crowd of people, and she was able to direct the mist up towards the ceiling where it wouldn't affect anyone around her. The effort had exhausted her. But as she practiced, she found she could control her Tranquility better and without losing too much energy. She knew that Liza sometimes lost energy when using her Kathokinesis, so Vely's energy loss was no surprise.

Vely released more Tranquility into the air and concentrated until the mist curled into spirals above her head. A hand dropped on her shoulder, and Vely jumped, losing control of her Tranquility for a moment. She spun around and saw Sehen standing behind her, smiling.

"Where have you been?" Vely asked after her heartbeat settled down. Sehen took a seat at the table beside her and leaned his elbows on the table.

"I had some business to take care of," he said, smiling at her. "Just some family things."

"You're family is on Mars?" Vely asked. Sehen nodded.

"My parents do not know that I'm a part of the Cosmic Resistance," Sehen said. "They'd never let me leave home if they knew."

Vely bit her lip. "Well, things are about to become more complicated for you," she said. Sehen raised an eyebrow.

"What do you mean?"

"Sehen! There you are!" Ren appeared beside the table. He slapped a large hand against Sehen's back.

"Ren."

"We've been wondering where you were. We have some news," Ren said.

"I think Vely was just about to tell me," Sehen said. Vely shrugged her shoulders and motioned for Ren to keep talking. "We're sending you to Sun Station Alpha with Vely. Her job is to infiltrate something called the Temple of the Black Moon." A skeptical look came over Sehen's face.

"What is that?" Ren nodded to Vely.

"She'll explain everything to you on the way there. You need to leave right away," he said. Sehen glanced at Vely.

"So she's a new spy, huh?" Sehen asked, flashing a smile at Vely. She blushed and nodded.

"Not that I know what I'm doing," she mumbled.

"That's why Sehen is going with you. He's got experience," Ren said. Vely squeezed her hands together and glanced back at Sehen, who was still smiling at her. A blush crept up onto her cheeks.

"Well, when are we leaving?" Sehen asked.

"As soon as possible," Ren said. "Pack up your things and get ready. Maggie is already working on the documentation that will allow you onto the Sun Station."

"Tomorrow, then?"

"Tomorrow. First flight out."

Vely blinked. It was so sudden. She wasn't sure if she was ready for her mission, but there wasn't much she could do about it now. Ren nodded to the two of them and turned away, walking through the headquarters. Sehen sat down at the table with Vely.

"Nervous?"

"A little," she confessed. "I just don't know what I'm doing." Sehen waved a hand.

"I have some friends in the area that can help us out," he said. "We'll be alright." Sehen smiled brightly at her, and Vely felt her heart flutter.

Early the following morning, Vely awoke to Maggie shaking her shoulder. Vely sat up in bed and rubbed her eyes. She pushed back the blankets and slipped her feet over the edge of the bed.

"I've got your documentation right here," Maggie said, handing over a slim, semi-transparent card. Vely took it and looked at it. An image of her face was etched into the plastic, along with a barcode. The name on the card was not Vely's but a fake name that would get her onto the Sun Station. Karina Malik. She slipped it into her pocket and glanced up at Maggie.

"Thanks," she said. Maggie smiled. "Maggie, can I ask you something?"

"Sure, of course."

"What if I screw it all up?" Vely asked. Maggie sat down beside Vely on the bed.

"You won't screw up," Maggie said. "We all have faith in you. That's why we're sending you. Dalton believes you to be the right person for the job, and he... well sometimes he just knows things."

"What do you mean?"

Maggie sighed and tilted her head to the side.

"He says he's not an Augur, but he knows things," Maggie said. "I don't know how or where he gets his information, but he's always been that way. It's like he's controlling everything we do, even though he stopped being involved with the Resistance. Pulling the strings, so to speak."

"But he's not an Augur?" Vely wondered. Maggie shook her head.

"He's very mysterious, but I think he likes being that way. Now, we need to go before you miss the flight out of here," Maggie said, rising from the bed. Vely nodded and stood up beside her. She stuck the card from Maggie in her pocket and grabbed her bag off the floor. She had to leave some things behind, which made her a bit sad, but she held onto the hope that she'd be back on Mars someday and would be able to retrieve her belongings, like her precious books that she'd brought along with her from the *Gypsy Star*. Those she hid underneath the bed, where she hoped they would not be disturbed.

Vely followed Maggie from the room and down to the first floor of the Resistance dormitory. When they reached the front doors, they found Ren and Sehen already waiting. Sehen smiled at Vely as she approached, picked up his bag, and slung it over his shoulder. Ren nodded to Vely and slapped a hand on her shoulder, giving her a little shake.

"You know you can contact us anytime you need help," Ren said. "You'll be just fine." Vely tried to smile but only ended up chewing on her lower lip. Ren removed his hand from her shoulder and pushed open the door to the outside. Vely and Sehen filed past him. A vehicle waited outside, a Resistance member behind the controls. Vely remembered seeing him around the headquarters a few times. Vely and Sehen climbed into the backseat and shut the door, and the driver pulled away from the curb.

Vely looked around the car, curious. She hadn't seen many on Mars in her few weeks of living there.

"Why don't I see more of these around?" she asked, leaning forward to the driver, whose name she couldn't remember.

"Personal preferences, really," the driver said. "Plus, they're pretty expensive to own, considering we are further from the sun, so charging them is more difficult and costly."

"Huh," Vely grunted and settled back in the seat. She looked to Sehen, who was rummaging through his bag. He glanced up and closed his bag, dropping it to the floorboards between his feet.

"Ready?" he asked.

"As I'll ever be."

54

Liza returned to her room on *Wasp* and dug around in her possessions. She managed to find what she was looking for: her ID badge from the SSA Supersensory Division. She threw on her favorite jacket and clipped the ID badge to the hem. Whirling around, she left the room and disembarked from *Wasp*. Her next stop was the *Astral Empress*.

As Liza walked down the catwalk towards Lezal's ship, she wondered how she would get to the SSA headquarters. She knew little about ship navigation and even less about piloting a ship, even just a speeder. Perhaps it wouldn't be that hard. She always considered herself somewhat mechanically inclined, anyway.

She boarded *Astral Empress* and traversed the ship's hallways until she came to the interior bay where Lezal kept his small speeders. A few of his crew members milled around near a workbench. Liza waved to them, trying to act casual.

"Need something?" one of them called. Liza gestured towards one of the speeders.

"Lezal said I could take one of the speeders out," she said. The crew members glanced at each other and shrugged. What reason would she give to lie? One of the crew members broke away from the group and approached one of the smaller speeders. Liza joined him.

"You know how to fly this thing?" he asked.

"I might need a refresher." The pirate shrugged his shoulders and stepped forward. He gave her a quick rundown of how to operate the speeder. Liza listened intently and felt that it wasn't that difficult of a process. At the very least, no one would be around to see her fumble until she got the hang of it. The problem, she knew, would be locating the SSA headquarters. She should have learned more from Becce about a ship's navigational systems.

"All set?" the pirate asked, pulling her from her thoughts. Liza nodded and thanked the man. He gave her a mock salute, turned on his heel, and rejoined a group of *Astral Empress* crew members who milled about nearby. A few of them glanced her way, but no one bothered her.

Liza had one foot in the cockpit when she heard a voice behind her.

"I thought I'd find you here." She stopped and turned. Dom had followed her.

"You can't stop me," Liza said, glaring at him. She was still angry from before and hadn't forgiven him for not taking her side. But here he was...

"I wasn't going to," Dom said. He reached towards her and placed a hand on her shoulder. "I thought I'd come along. I know you don't know how to pilot this thing." He gestured towards the small ship. Liza felt a blush creep onto her cheek. She shook her head.

"It'll be dangerous for you," she said. "At least I can pass myself off an as SSA supersensor. You could be killed." Dom smiled and gripped her shoulder tighter.

"I'm not afraid." Liza stared up at him, into his eyes. He truly wasn't afraid. And Liza knew, deep down, and despite her constant questioning of their relationship, that he would follow her to the edge of the universe. Finally, she nodded.

"Okay, I could use the help anyway," she said, attempting a dismissive tone. Dom knew her better than that. He leaned forward and pressed a light kiss to her lips, released his hold on her shoulder, and stepped around her towards the small ship.

"Let's hurry before Lezal knows we've gone," he said, climbing into the ship. Liza followed behind and slipped into the passenger seat.

Dom worked at the controls until the engine of the small

ship sprang to life. Liza watched the group of pirates exit the bay while one of them opened the docking bay doors for them. Dom undocked the ship, and it dropped out into space, hurtling into nothingness until Dom punched the engines. The ship lurched forward, speeding away from the Cove.

"How will we find the SSA headquarters?" Liza asked. Dom waved a hand.

"I know where it is. They don't make their location a secret at all," he said. "I think the SSA director likes it that way. She likes to flaunt her power. I've never seen her in person, but I've heard many things about her, particularly from Warwick. Now that I know he was working for her that whole time, I am not surprised he knew so much about her."

Liza frowned. She hoped she wouldn't have to confront the director of the SSA. She would much rather deal with Morre, who she already knew she could beat. But how hard would it be to find Gwen? *Would* they even find her?

Thoughts tumbled through Liza's brain, and she was suddenly thrilled that she didn't have to try and pilot an unfamiliar ship. Reaching out with a gloved hand, she wrapped her fingers around Dom's free hand and gave it a squeeze. He turned his head to look at her, and he gave her a dazzling smile that made Liza's stomach flip flop. She tore her eyes away from his face and stared out into space, nervousness, and excitement gripping at her stomach.

55

Charles Mann's warnings rang in Gael's mind. Sipping his Sun Whiskey, he thought about how he could fight back against Alis. He wished Charles was around so they could brainstorm ideas. He knew he needed to ask the help of his *friends*, but he couldn't be too overt about needing their help. There was the chance that they would refuse. Gael tapped his fingernails against the crystal glass.

He needed a new assistant, that was for sure. And he needed someone that could protect him from Alis and her ways. His own Supersensor would be the ideal situation, but how could he find someone like that without Alis finding out?

Gael hovered a finger over a button on his communication lync, wondering if he should try to contact Charles Mann to ask him for help. But that would be too obvious. Plus, he didn't know a direct lync number to Charles; he only knew how to get in touch with Lynwood. And Gael didn't exactly trust Lynwood. An idea sparked in his mind, and he touched the button and dialed up Lynwood's lync number. He waited, feeling a slight nervous twinge in his stomach.

Lynwood's face appeared on the screen. For a moment, he looked confused, but he schooled his features into passive interest. Gael smiled.

"Hello, Lynwood. I was looking to get a hold of Chip Wilson. I have some questions about a report he sent me," Gael said. Lynwood's eyebrows raised.

"I don't know of any report," he said. Gael shrugged.

"Perhaps it was something Alis asked him to do?"

"Maybe."

236

"Either way, I'd like to speak with him," Gael said, trying to keep his frustration from showing. Lynwood was silent for a moment, then finally nodded.

"I'll transfer you," he said and pressed a button. The screen darkened, and a moment later, Charles Mann's face appeared. He smiled at Gael through the screen.

"What can I do for you, sir?" he asked.

"Are you alone?" Gael asked. Charles nodded.

"Of course."

"I need your help. I need a new assistant, and I want my own Supersensor. I was hoping you had some connections somewhere," Gael explained. Charles thought for a moment, then turned away from the screen. Gael could hear the clicking of the keyboard as Charles typed something. Finally, he turned back to Gael.

"I know of someone. I'll schedule an interview for tomorrow. But you'll have to keep quiet about her. Don't tell anyone she's a Supersensor," Charles said.

"Naturally. Who is she?"

"She's a Tranquil, I believe. A friend of mine said she was looking for a job."

"What's her name?"

"Karina Malik."

56

Vely's mouth dropped open at the sight of the Sun Stations. She'd heard rumors of their beauty but had never experienced one in person before. They were sleek, shining colonies with agricultural domes extended towards the sun-catching rays to grow their food. SSA ships lingered around the perimeter, likely watching for pirate ships. Other smaller ships zipped between the two Sun Stations, entering and leaving the docking bay at an alarming rate. Vely looked down at her hands, clenched together in her lap. She was nervous.

Sehen glanced at her from the pilot's seat. "You'll be fine," he said. "Maggie, Ren, and Dalton... they wouldn't have chosen you if they didn't think you could handle this."

"I just don't understand how I'm supposed to do anything," she said, looking away from the gleaming Sun Stations.

"Just be yourself," he said. "You'll figure it out as you go. That's how we've all learned to be spies. Besides, you've already got an interview to be someone's assistant and Supersensor bodyguard."

"When did that happen?" Vely asked.

"While you were asleep. Someone back at headquarters had put your name out there on the Black Hole as an available Supersensor. We got a hit, and it's a big one."

"What's the Black Hole? And who will I be working for?" Vely asked. She could feel her anxiety spreading from her stomach into her limbs. She was shaking slightly.

"The Black Hole is our secret Network. Only certain people have access to it." Vely shrugged her shoulders, only sort of understanding. Sehen went on. "And the person you're interviewing with is Gael Daniels, the CEO of Walnad." Vely stared at Sehen, her mouth falling open.

"What?" Sehen smiled, tight-lipped.

"He's your ticket into the Temple of the Black Moon," Sehen said. "Once you've earned his trust, he's sure to bring you into the fold."

"How can you be so sure he's going to trust me?" Vely asked, chewing on her lip. Sehen waved a hand.

"You're a trustworthy person. Plus, you have your Tranquility," he said. She exhaled a breath but kept her rampaging thoughts to herself.

The small ship approached closer and closer to Sun Station Alpha, and Vely felt more and more nervous. She looked into her bag once more, replaced the tablet, and rifled around until her hands closed on her forged documents. Lifting them from her bag, she flipped through, noting her name and her false birth location that read Sun Station Beta. She hoped no one would ask her about growing up there, or she'd surely be found out as an impostor. Vely already knew what the Sun Stations did to people they didn't want in their colonies. She shuddered to think of the possibilities.

Sehen pulled a headset from the control panel and placed it over his ears, adjusting the microphone in front of his mouth. Vely wrung her hands together while Sehen got permission to dock at Sun Station Alpha, stating their business for being there and providing them with the ID numbers printed at the top of their forged papers. Vely's leg bounced up and down rapidly as heavy anxiety settled into her bones. Sehen glanced at her and rested a hand on her arm.

"Don't worry. I'll be here to help you," he said, giving her a smile. Vely forced a smile back and turned away to cover the blush rising over her cheeks.

Sehen navigated the ship into the docking bay of Sun Station Alpha. The small ship shuddered as it settled into the docking arms, and Sehen cut the engines. He looked at Vely, who reached down and picked up her bag. He grabbed her shoulder and squeezed gently. His grip on her shoulder calmed her, and she felt like she could at least exit the ship without falling on her face. After that, though, Vely wasn't sure how she was going to make it. Sehen released her. They scrambled from the speeder and headed into the spaceport.

Vely took this chance to look around. Beautiful ships, the likes of which she'd never seen, were docked all in a neat row. They gleamed in the ultra-bright lights above, their names shining in paint along the hulls, some of them declaring the immense wealth of their owners, though some were tacky and made Vely smile. *Gold Swan, Richest Memory, Siren of Desire.* Vely snorted, forgetting her anxiety for a moment.

Together, Vely and Sehen followed the catwalks until they reached the entrance to the Sun Station, which was heavily guarded by SSA Enforcers. Their orange uniforms brought back unpleasant memories of her time on the Moon. But now was not the time to be weak. Vely squared her shoulders and calmly, as calm as she could muster, handed her ID card to the SSA Enforcer. The man stared hard at her face for a long moment, as if scrutinizing every detail. Vely tried to keep herself from shaking. Finally, he swiped the card, handed it back, and motioned for Vely to step into the swirling turnstile that separated the docking bay from the rest of the Sun Station. She stepped through and emerged on the other side.

She had arrived.

57

Alis wondered why pirates couldn't bathe more often. The stench emanating off Warwick and Zimir was overpowering and awful. She was tempted to close her nose and wave off the stench, but they carried gamma pistols. Although, anything they would try would be prevented by the two Kathos standing behind her. They were *her* weapons.

"Well?" Warwick asked, holding his hand out. Alis slipped the vial from her pocket and held it in front of her. The blood gleamed in the light, protected by the vial's temperature-controlled interior. Zimir reached a hand out, desperate for the smell.

"Here," she said, tossing the vial to Zimir. He caught it and held it possessively against his chest for a moment, then removed the stopper and lifted the vial up to his nose. He inhaled deeply as if he were sniff-testing a glass of Sun Whiskey. His eyes lit up and a cruel smile formed over his lips. Alis shuddered at the display.

Zimir turned to Warwick.

"She's on her way here," he said.

Alis lifted an eyebrow. "Is she?" Zimir nodded his head and sniffed again.

"She's not far off, and she's definitely on her way here. I can smell her intentions."

"What are they?" Alis asked, hating and loving this ritual.

"She's after someone," Zimir said, taking another whiff. Alis grinned. The girl, Gwen. So, the little pirate girl was going to come after Alis' sleeper agent after all. She'd begun to wonder when the Strange girl would show her face.

"Well, then, why don't you two go out and make sure you give her a nice welcome," Alis said. Zimir replaced the stopper on the blood and slipped it inside his pocket. Warwick nodded to Alis and turned to Zimir.

"Let's go," he said. The two men turned and left the room, leaving their stench behind. Alis rolled her eyes and turned to the Kathos behind her.

"Get the cleaning crew in here and have them get rid of the smell," she said. Both Kathos nodded. One of them stepped forward.

"Gladly, miss."

Alis turned away from the Kathos and sat down in front of the computer terminal. She hadn't heard from Gael in a while, and she wondered what he was up to. Perhaps she should pay him a visit or send Lynwood and Chip Wilson to see him. She was expecting some report on his plan for providing more ships for her Corsairs. Alis pulled up her messages and looked through the new ones, but there was nothing from Gael. She frowned.

Alis Foste rarely got nervous, and she hated waiting. She needed her fleet to enact the next phase of her plan, and she needed it soon. She didn't know how long the people of the Sun Stations would stay duped to her way of thinking. All of the governing power needed to rest solely in her hands before she'd feel comfortable.

Alis stood up from the computer terminal and walked from the room, the remaining Katho following her out into the hall. She walked in the direction of her office, and along the way, she ran into Jeffry Morre. Gwen Adan trailed behind him, stoic as ever.

"Lieutenant Morre," Alis said, nodding her head in his direction.

"I was just coming to see you," Morre said, bowing his head and clasping his hands behind his back.

"And I have information for *you*," Alis said. She

motioned for him to speak.

"We have reason to believe the pirates are hiding out at the Cove," Morre said. "We lost the tracker when the *Gypsy Star* went down, but we've been tracking their movements until they went into an FTL jump. It makes sense they'd try to regroup at the Cove."

Alis waved a hand.

"I'm not concerned about the other pirates. Let the Corsairs deal with them," she said. Morre, for a brief moment, appeared dejected. Alis pressed on. "I received information that might be of interest to you," Alis said.

"What's that?"

"Liza Strange is on her way here." Morre's eyes grew wide, while Gwen's face remained stony. She had no memory of her time with Liza Strange; it had been suppressed through extensive recalibration after she'd arrived back at the SSA headquarters. "We believe she's coming here to try and save Gwen."

"Then I shall meet her and send her away," Morre said.

"No," Alis said sharply. "I want her here. Warwick and Zimir are already going to intercept her. I want her brought to me, alive."

"And you sent those two? They'll just kill her," Morre said. Alis frowned deeply, her eyes narrowed into slits.

"Then do better," she growled. Morre snapped to attention and saluted Alis. He spun on his heel and marched away, with Gwen following behind at a brisk pace. Alis watched them leave, a smile on her face. Let Warwick, Zimir, and Morre destroy each other over Liza Strange. Soon, the girl would be in her clutches, and she would find out just what made the girl tick.

58

Nerves and anxiety twisted in Liza's gut. She pressed her hands against her stomach to try and dull the pain. She didn't speak of the pain to Dom. He'd only just worry more than he already was. Sure, he put on a calm demeanor, but every so often, he'd bite his lip or chew his fingernail. She knew it was a risky move, putting themselves directly in the hands of the SSA. But Liza was determined to bring back Gwen, no matter what.

Before long, the SSA headquarters came into view. Ships branded with the SSA logo sped around the enormous colony, flitting from one place to another. Larger ships orbited the headquarters. Docked on the headquarters was a long, sleek black ship that blended seamlessly with outer space beyond. The name *Swift* was emblazoned across the side in white. The ship was far too regal to be just anyone's ship. Perhaps the Director's?

"Uh oh," Dom said. "We've got a visitor."

Another ship had appeared beside them, this one older and, in Liza's opinion, looked like it was held together with welding, bolts, and scraps of metal. Painted on the side was the name *Belenus*.

"Do you know that ship?" Liza asked, her body shifting as Dom pulled the small speeder in a tight circle to face *Belenus*. Dom shook his head. The speeder's comm lync lit up with an incoming message. Dom answered the call.

"We're taking you aboard," a familiar voice said over the lync. Liza and Dom cringed.

"Warwick," they said together.

"Do not try to resist."

Dom gripped the controls and spun the speeder away from *Belenus*, heading straight for the SSA headquarters. He punched the engines, and the speeder jumped forward, increasing speed faster than *Belenus* could ever hope to achieve. Another ship appeared. This one was painted blue, and the name *Solstice* was painted in black and white. *Solstice* headed straight for their speeder, flanking them from the opposite side of *Belenus*.

"This is quite the welcome party," Dom muttered, maneuvering out of the way. The comm lync beeped again, but this time, the voice was only familiar to Liza.

"Liza Strange, surrender now, and you'll get a chance to live."

A shudder ran through Liza's body, her hair standing on end. The voice belonged to Jeffry Morre. Liza wasn't particularly keen on having to see Morre again. She knew he'd try to make up for what she did to him last time they were together.

"Well, do we go with the pirates or with the SSA?" Dom asked, glancing at Liza.

"Neither would be preferable," she said. "I imagine Warwick would just kill us both."

"Who is the other guy?" Dom asked.

"Jeffry Morre. He's part of the SSA's Supersensory Division," Liza explained. "He's a katho." Dom pressed his lips together in a thin line. "I bet that Gwen is with him. We should go there."

"Whatever you say," Dom said. He turned the speeder towards *Solstice* and urged it forward. Warwick's voice came over the comm lync, yelling about their movement, so Dom shut off the lync. They were almost to *Solstice's* cargo bay when their speeder veered off course, shuddering from an attack. Liza and Dom whipped their heads around and saw through the hatch that the backside of the speeder had been hit by a laser shot. The speeder's control panel sparked, and Liza could hear pops coming from the back of the speeder. She climbed out of her seat and wedged her way towards the back.

"Liza, what are you doing?" Dom cried out. Liza waved a hand at him and reached for the safety pull. She gripped the lever and pulled down, sealing off the cockpit from the damaged area. She inched her way back into her seat and flopped back down. Dom sighed in relief, but he gave Liza a stern look anyway.

"We've got to reach that ship before Warwick blows us into space," Liza said, pointing at *Solstice*.

"I have a bad feeling about us going straight into danger," Dom muttered.

"Where's your sense of adventure, pirate?" Liza asked. Dom stared at her but couldn't repress a smile. He pushed the speeder forward and closed the distance between themselves and *Solstice*. The cargo bay doors opened, and Dom flew the ship up into the belly of the ship. The doors closed behind them, and Dom settled the speeder down and cut the engines. Liza popped the hatch, and they climbed out of the speeder, gently landing on the floor of the ship. There was only partial gravity, so Liza had to focus on keeping her feet on the ground and not float away. Dom grabbed her hand, and together, they bounded towards the catwalk steps.

Before they could reach the door, it opened, revealing Jeffry Morre. He looked tired and worn out and much older than he appeared the last time Liza saw him. His hair had grayed slightly around the temples, and he had the shadow of a beard. Morre tilted his head up, a motion of recognition. He stepped forward onto the catwalk, and another person appeared behind him. Her eyes were strangely blank as she stared down at Liza and Dom, malice etched around her mouth.

It was Gwen.

59

Gael sat in a conference room with a tablet in front of him. On it was a profile of Karina Malik, Tranquil. The more he read the profile, the less it made sense like someone had made up parts of her life and just stuck it on the form. But Gael wasn't going to say anything about that. He didn't care where she was born, just what kind of person she'd be. He needed someone strong and intelligent who could help him stand up against Alis and her minions. Gael had hope that she would be the one he needed.

The door to the room opened, and a young woman stepped inside, followed by the front lobby receptionist. Gael rose, towering over the shorter woman. He reached out his hand, and they shook. Gael noticed that the girl wore black gloves on her hands. He wondered why. The temperatures on the Sun Stations were always pleasant.

"Thank you," Gael said to the receptionist, nodding to her. She smiled nervously and escaped from the room, the door closing behind her.

"Thank you for coming. My name is Gael Daniels," he said, still looking down at the girl. She managed a smile.

"I'm Karina Malik," she replied. Gael nodded, biting back a smile at the way she stumbled over her own name. He motioned towards the table.

"Please, have a seat."

Gael sat down in his chair and watched as the woman scurried around the table and dropped into the chair opposite him. She stuck her hands in her lap and sat up, rigid and unmoving. Her lips were fixed in a nervous smile.

"So, Karina Malik. You are interested in becoming my assistant," Gael said, and she gave him a curt nod. "It also says here that you're a Tranquil." At this, he saw her flinch. Gael smiled. "Don't worry. I got that information from someone I trust. We'll keep that a secret for now. The reason I need someone like you is to protect me against Alis Foste. Do you know who that is?"

Karina shook her head.

"She's the director of the SSA, and she's up to some sinister things," Gael said, folding his fingers together. He leaned back in his chair, wishing he had a glass of Sun Whiskey with him. "She's already given me a TK blast."

"Sorry," Karina interjected. "I don't know what that is."

"It's when a Tranquil and a Katho both exert their ability at the same time on the same person," Gael explained. "Luckily, my former assistant shook me out of it, but for a little while, I thought Alis' plan was flawless. Sure, let's allow her to take over control of the Sun Stations, along with the SSA."

He knew he was rambling, but he felt his frustrations build. He glanced her over, noting her fidgeting hands. He looked down at the paperwork in front of him, outlining her supposed life story. Something didn't feel right.

"I'm afraid I don't follow you," Karina said. Gael waved a hand.

"I apologize. Tell me about yourself," he said. Karina opened her mouth, closed it, and opened it again to speak. She punctuated the end of her sentences as if she were asking a question. Her words sounded rehearsed, and the way her eyes glanced around the room made him wonder if she was lying.

"My dear," Gael said, interrupting her flow. "Tell me the truth." She hesitated. "You can tell me. I can protect you." He watched her struggle with indecision for a moment. Her fingers twitched her in lap, still clad in those black gloves.

"I'm terrible at this," she muttered. Gael was about to question her further, but she spoke first. "My name is not Karina Malik. My name is Vely Strange, and I'm from the

Moon," she said. Gael's eyes widened, and he leaned back in his chair. *The* Vely Strange was sitting across from him. The young woman from the SSA's most wanted list. He would never forget that name. Alis had a hell of a time covering up the mass murder of an entire colony system, all to stifle the revolution that this young woman started.

"How did you end up here?"

"Some... friends helped me," she said. Gael lifted an eyebrow. Charles Mann had recommended this young woman to him. Did Charles *know* who she really was? What part was he playing in all this? Could Gael still trust his right-hand man?

"Do you know Charles Mann?" Gael asked. She shook her head.

"I don't." This situation didn't make much sense. Why would Charles send him Vely Strange, of all people in the solar system?

"I know there's more you're not telling me. I think we can help each other. Whatever it is, your secrets are safe with me. Now tell me, who sent you here?"

Vely took a deep breath, closed her eyes, and shook her head. When she opened her eyes again, she leaned forward over her knees.

"The Cosmic Resistance."

60

"Gwen!"

Liza jumped forward, her body sailing through the low gravity. She reached the steps and pushed herself up towards the catwalk where Morre and Gwen stood. Before she could reach them, a blast hit her in the chest, and she flew backward. Pain radiated from her ribs, which had never fully healed. The force of the blast pushed her into the hull of the ship, her body screwed up in a painful position. After bouncing back towards the ground, she saw Dom run to her. He grabbed her and pulled her back to the ground. Liza looked up and saw Morre laughing.

"She doesn't know who you are," he called down. "You are the enemy."

"What?"

"She's been Blanked."

Liza was unfamiliar with the term but could guess its meaning. Liza rose to her feet, somewhat heavily, and pushed her will against Gwen's. She felt a slight bend before she was thrust backward, out of Gwen's mind. Liza tried again, this time calling for her.

"Gwen! It's me, Liza!"

But Gwen threw up a wall and pushed Liza back out. For the brief moment that Liza was inside Gwen's mind, she couldn't find a trace of their friendship. It had been eradicated.

A lump formed in Liza's throat, and tears welled in her eyes. But she pushed it down. Deep down while she filled with anger. Anger towards Morre, towards the SSA, towards that Alis woman. She clenched her fist and drew on the energy around her, preparing to blast at Morre. Scents filled her nose, and she could discern each individual one-- Morre, Dom, sleeper agent-Gwen. She shook her head to dispel the smells, but they remained inside her nose. She could feel the willpower flowing through her veins and could feel the sparks emitting from her fingers, ready to take on her target. She looked up at Morre, held out her hand, and blasted as much willpower at him as she could.

He flew back and hit the wall, knocking Gwen aside in the process. A wave of exhaustion flowed through Liza, and she dropped to one knee.

"Liza!" Dom cried from beside her. He placed one hand on her shoulder, and Liza saw his gamma pistol in the other hand. He lifted his arm and aimed at Morre.

"Don't," Liza said. "You'll kill us."

"Not if I'm careful."

Liza watched Morre pick himself back up. His scent still filled her nose as though she was still drawing willpower from him.

"You haven't changed at all, have you?" he asked, taking a flying leap and landing on the floor at the base of the steps. Gwen followed behind and landed beside him. "You're still reckless with your ability. You should have let me train you properly. You could have been as powerful as Gwen."

Liza scoffed. "What? And end up as a slave to you? Not likely," she spat. Morre shook his head.

"Gwen performed just as she was programmed to do. But if you had just listened to me, you could be out on your own, tracking down those so-called pirates that you run around with. You could have been great."

"I don't care much for your plans," Liza said, pushing herself into a standing position. She pushed against Morre's willpower, but he threw up his own wall and pushed her back.

"You're still untrained, Liza Strange. You will never truly defeat me," Morre said.

"Prove it. Kill me."

"Stop it, Liza," Dom cried out, throwing his arm in front

of her, his gamma pistol still trained on Morre.

"Alas, my superior wants you alive, though, for what reason, I am not sure. I imagine she'll want to experiment on you, to find out where your reckless and excessive powers come from," Morre said. He held out his own hand, and a blast hit Liza in the ribs and closed around her like a thick blanket. Her arms lay flat against her sides, and she found she could no longer move. Beside her, Dom struggled against the same force.

Fury escalated inside Liza, and something broke in her mind. It felt like a wall in her mind finally shattered. She pushed back against the force around her, and it fell away. She looked up and saw surprise in Morre's face. Liza forced a blast against Gwen, which distracted her enough to release Dom. Liza drew on the power and energy around her. It swelled in her veins, under her skin, and through her hair. Darkness edged at her vision. A new smell came into her nose; it was sharp, like metal cutting the inside of her nose. She reached for the scent, drew it closer to herself. It filled her with a power she'd never imagined she could wield.

"Whatever you're doing, stop it now!" Morre called out. "You're going to kill us all."

Liza could barely hear him. A distant noise filled her ears, a thrumming sound that seemed to come from outer space itself.

"Liza, what's going on?" Dom asked. He'd lowered his gamma pistol and was staring at her. "What are you doing?"

"She's drawing on some other energy," Morre shouted. "Liza, stop!"

But she couldn't stop. The wall had come down, and she could see the infinite possibilities of power. Her body went cold. She drew the power in, closer and closer, until it filled her. Her anger subsided, and all she could feel was calm. Her gaze came to rest on Morre. Her power wanted to attack him. She released her hold. A power blast erupted from her, crackling along her skin as it escaped. The force struck Morre in the chest, and he flew backward into the steps, his body crooked and prone. Gwen jumped out of the way at the last moment. Liza collapsed. Voices rang in her ears, but she couldn't understand anything they were saying. Hands grabbed her arms and legs, tugged on her, but she couldn't move. The power dissipated from her body, and her vision went black.

"Liza!"

61

Alis sat at her desk, scouring the Sol Network. Alis knew that Liza Strange had a sister, and she had started the revolt on the Moon. However, Alis could find nothing on the Sol Network. Alis switched over to the SSA internal network. When she brought up her most-wanted list, it was one person short. Vely's information was gone.

Alis fumed.

Someone must have hacked the system and removed Vely Strange from her list, and culled the Sol Network of any mention of her name. But for what purpose? She had hoped to use the sister as leverage against Liza Strange. But it seemed Alis would have to alter her plans.

She shut down her computer terminal and leaned back in her chair, fingertips pressed together. She thought for a moment, then opened a drawer. Inside lay a black case, which she picked up and opened. A relatively large piece of astarte sat nestled among the cloth. She wanted to try the stone on Liza Strange and see the effects it would have. She knew what happened to Kathos when the stone touched her skin, but she had never seen the effects in person. She was not the direction of the SSA when Morre was experimented on. So naturally, she was curious. And if this experiment killed the girl, then so be it.

A hurried knock sounded at her door. She pressed a button to open it, and an SSA officer burst into the room, gasping for breath. He stopped in front of her desk and doubled over. Alis searched her memory but couldn't remember this particular officer's name. But she knew he was a member of

Morre's crew. The black piping on his uniform denoted him as a Bloodhound. Alis waited while he caught his breath. Finally, he rose up to his full height and saluted her.

"Forgive me for barging in, Director Foste, but I have some terrible news," he said. Alis raised an eyebrow.

"Go on," she said.

"Lieutenant Morre is dead."

Alis stared at the officer and lifted one eyebrow. Morre was dead?

"By whose hand?"

"Liza Strange."

Alis stood up abruptly and slammed her hands on the desktop, louder than she meant to. "Did you catch her?" she cried out. The officer flinched and nodded.

"We've captured her and the pirate that was with her," the officer said. Alis waved a hand.

"I wish to see her," Alis instructed. "Dock Morre's ship, if you haven't already." The officer swallowed hard and nodded his head.

"The Strange girl is in and out of consciousness," the officer said.

"Bring her to me, anyway."

The officer saluted and turned towards the door. He threw a look at Alis before leaving the room. She nodded to him and turned back to her contemplation of the astarte.

So, Alis thought. *Morre is dead, and Liza Strange killed him. I knew she must be stronger than he, after what happened several months ago. But just how strong?*

Alis held the astarte in her hand and rolled it around in her palm. She felt nothing from the stone, no fluctuation of power within. Alis knew she was 'normal,' and that was one thing that frustrated her. Many things did not bother Alis, but knowing she was an average human was one of them. If she were a Kathokinetic or even a Tranquil, she'd have extra power to wield over mere humans. Alis had considered becoming a Synth-gen, but the idea of an implant in her own neck was appalling. She would not degrade herself that way, although she had forced a few hundred people to receive that very implant. She had a small army of Synth-gens out controlling the populations of the colonies. And if she could learn what made Liza Strange so powerful, she could use that ability to make her Synth-gens even stronger.

Another knock sounded at her door. She pressed the door release button admitting the visitors. This time two Enforcers entered, carrying Liza Strange between them. Gwen Adan followed them inside. Alis rose from her chair and stepped around her desk until she was standing in the middle of the room. The Enforcers dropped a semi-conscious Liza Strange to the ground, where she landed slumped over her knees. Gwen stood behind Liza, her fingers twitching with unseen power.

Alis stepped forward and reached down. She grabbed a fistful of dreadlocks and pulled backward, revealing the girl's face. Her eyes were half-lidded, her breathing shallow. She barely moved when Alis pulled on her hair.

"Wake up, girl," she said, staring down at Liza, who lifted her chin and tried to look at Alis in the eye. Liza struggled against the holds on her arms until the Enforcers released her. Her arms fell to her sides, and she pressed her palms into the smooth floor.

"What do you want?" Liza grumbled from her place on the floor. Alis smiled.

"Though he is now deceased, I have been wondering why Lieutenant Morre took such an interest in you," Alis said. Liza's head shot up.

"He's dead?"

"Yes, and you killed him," Alis said, lacing her fingers behind her back. "You murdered my Lieutenant, and that's a crime, Liza Strange. Now you have to pay the price." She waved at the Enforcers, who reached down and gripped Liza tightly by the arms. They yanked her back up onto her feet, but her knees buckled under her own weight. Whatever she'd done had left her weakened. Perhaps this was the perfect time to experiment on her. But no. If Alis wanted to see the girl's true power, she should wait until the girl had recovered. Alis waved a hand, dismissing the Enforcers.

"Take her and lock her up. See that no one bothers her. I want her well before I start my experiments," Alis said, trying to suppress a laugh. The Enforcers nodded and dragged Liza from the room. Gwen hovered for a moment; she seemed unsure of what to do. Alis stared at her.

"Where is the other pirate?" Alis asked.

"Locked in a cell," Gwen answered, her voice dead.

"Leave him there. Perhaps I can use him," she said. Gwen nodded but didn't move. "You may leave."

Gwen nodded, saluted, and walked to the door of the office. She glanced at Alis once before she disappeared. Alis frowned as the door closed behind Gwen. Her behavior was strange. Although, perhaps it had something to do with being Blanked. It was new technology, and they hadn't thoroughly studied the long-term effects of such a procedure. Or perhaps Gwen was confused without Morre telling her what to do. After all, she was programmed to follow his orders. For all Alis knew, she could be standing right outside the office, waiting for another direct order.

Alis returned to her chair and sat down. She brought up Liza Strange's profile on the SSA network. She studied the profile, smiling to herself.

62

Vely sat in Gael Daniel's office. And she was talking. While she spoke, she could feel the plans of the Cosmic Resistance break and fall away. It was possible, as she kept replaying in her mind, that she was ruining everything. But for some reason, she could not stop talking. Word vomit fell from her mouth.

"They took me to see Dalton Saldek," Vely said. Gael's eyebrows rose, and he leaned back in his chair.

"I know that name," Gael said. "I thought he was long dead."

"He's alive but barely human," Vely said. "He's mostly made up of mechanical parts."

"What did he have to say?" Vely hesitated. Gael waited patiently.

"Well, he said that the Temple of the Black Moon used to be a good organization, but then they fled Earth and became selfish. Now they are only concerned about themselves," Vely said, paraphrasing what she'd heard back on Mars. Gael smirked.

"You're not wrong. The Temple of the Black Moon is made up of wealthy individuals whose primary goal is to preserve their money. But I believe we can convince them to join our cause," Gael said.

"Our" cause?

"You mean, you agree with the Cosmic Resistance?" Vely asked.

"The Resistance will have a tough time changing the minds of the Sun Stations, and the only way to accomplish anything is to take down Alis Foste and the SSA. And I'm willing to help bring her down." Vely stared at him in surprise. "I've done a lot of regrettable things and have allowed things to happen that are terrible. Those things weigh on me every day, and I'm ready to make amends."

"So you won't send the SSA after my friends?"

"No, of course not," he said. "But to take Alis down, we'll need the help of the Temple. But you'll have to be initiated. That way, you can be my second set of ears." Vely felt a rush through her body. Whether it was excitement or fear, she wasn't sure. "We'll need all the help we can get. Another wrench in the situation is Alis' Supersensor army. She's got authentic supersensors, and she's got those Synth-gens. I hope the Resistance has enough of their own supersensors to fight back against them."

Vely shrugged her shoulders. She knew that the Resistance had people all over the Solar System, spying and gathering intel, but she didn't know the extent of their reach. As far as she knew, she was the only Cosmic Resistance member to be a part of the Walnad Corporation. What could she do on her own? Considering how easily she spilled out everything to Gael, it was probably best that she did not know who else was in the Cosmic Resistance. It was a safety measure for herself and for them. Who knew what else Gael would draw from her.

Gael leaned back in his chair. "We have a lot to think about," he said. "Why don't you go home for now, and we'll reconvene tomorrow morning."

"Okay," Vely said, rising from her chair. Gael smiled at her, rose, and reached out a hand. She shook it. Vely turned and walked towards the door, expecting Gael to say something else to her before she left, but he had sat down in his chair and spun around, so he was looking out the large window over the Sun Station city. Vely slipped from the room and headed back down to the street.

When she arrived back at the rented apartment, Vely

found that Sehen had already set up a computer terminal and was working away at something. He turned when she entered.

"You're back! How did it go?" he asked.

"I got the job," she replied, hesitating at the door. How much should she tell him? After all, she was supposed to spy on Gael, not divulging all the secrets of the Cosmic Resistance. But perhaps she could do both. Gael would never know that she was spying on him if they thought they were helping each other. And besides, the goal was to get into the Temple, and he would help her. That was the plan after all, right?

"Excellent work, Vely!" Sehen rose from the chair and wrapped her in a hug, which startled her. She leaked some Tranquility into the room, the fine blue mist swirling lazily around their bodies. Sehen must have noticed because he pulled away blushing, his eyelids heavy. "Sorry about that."

"It's alright," Vely said, mustering up a smile. Vely took control of her ability and restrained it, stuffing it down inside of her. Sehen gazed at her, the same smile on his face. She smiled up at him and thought of Cedrick. Was he still alive?

Vely shook her head and sidestepped Sehen. Something was growing between them; she could feel it. But she didn't feel ready to move on just yet. Cedrick was the first person to ever kiss her, to show her that he cared for her more deeply than just a friend. And that was a place she held in high regard within her heart. Could she so easily shove him aside for another man? Did that make her heartless?

Vely's chest tightened at the thought of Cedrick, likely killing himself on fultraline and Tranquility. He'd been too ambitious to try and make his futures a reality. He sacrificed his mental state to achieve greatness. He probably didn't know that forcing visions would cause Augur sickness, but he didn't stop even after discovering why he was sick. He couldn't stop.

And then there was Sehen, who seemed more stable than Cedrick. And he obviously liked her, for whatever reason, or he wouldn't have accompanied her to the Sun Stations. Although, perhaps she was mistaking his attentions-- maybe he was only mildly interested in how she could do as a Cosmic Resistance spy. Though, he *had* hugged her just now.

Vely pushed these thoughts away and retreated to the small alcove that held her bed. She stretched out on the mattress and kicked off her boots. Tomorrow, she would start officially as Gael Daniels' assistant, and she would have to try and keep the Cosmic Resistance plan from failing.

63

Liza opened her eyes and immediately regretted it. Pain radiated from her ribs and from around her eyes. Her limbs were heavy with fatigue. She tried to move her hand, but her fingers and palms felt detached from the rest of her body. Lifting her head, she made sure that all four limbs were still intact. Satisfied that they were all there, she let her head drop back to the thin pillow on which she rested.

Staring up at the ceiling, Liza determined that she was in a cell of some kind, lying on a cot. From her vantage point, she could see the cell door, locked and barred. She could hear quiet chatter and laughter coming from the other side of the door.

Liza tried again to sit up, pushing hard against the heaviness in her body. Once she was in a sitting position, she slumped over her legs. Her hair hung down over her shoulders. She looked at her gloved hands, lying limply in her lap.

Then she remembered. She killed Morre. But how? How had she drawn on so much additional energy, so much that her body felt like it might be ripped at the seams? What was that energy? She knew she should feel something like guilt or sadness, but she didn't feel anything. It didn't feel real. Besides, he was the enemy. Right?

And where was Dom? He couldn't be dead, too. Perhaps he was nearby, in another cell. She hoped he was alright, that they weren't hurting him or torturing him. She had an insane thought that perhaps she would instinctively know if he were harmed or dead. But that was crazy, wasn't it?

Liza struggled and pushed herself so that her legs hung over the edges of the cot, her boots touching the floor. Her chest heaved with effort. The voices outside of the room went quiet, and a face appeared in the window. A nasty grin formed on the guard's face.

"You're finally awake," he said, rather mockingly. Liza ignored him, pushing herself to a standing position. Her shoulders hunched over, and her knees buckled.

"Where's my friend?" Liza asked, lifting her chin to look at the guard through the bars.

"We don't have to tell you anything," the guard said, laughing. He turned away from the bars, and his face disappeared. Liza hobbled towards the door and grabbed at the bars, trying to pull herself up to look through, but they were too high, and she was too weak.

"Dom!" she cried out, but the guard whirled around and slammed the butt of his gamma pistol against the bars.

"Shut up!"

Liza stumbled backward and tripped, landing painfully on her tail bone. A shock wave of pain rode up into her ribs. She rubbed at her back, grumbling to herself, gritting her teeth against the pain.

Liza had no idea how much time had passed. She'd managed to drag herself back onto the cot, where she slipped in and out of consciousness. Eventually, a rattling sound pulled her from sleep. Eyes half-lidded, she stared at the door as it swung open, and two men stepped inside the room.

"Hello, Liza Strange," the first man said, the taller of the two. He wore a black SSA uniform with silver piping. "Welcome to the SSA headquarters."

"Quite the reception," she muttered, gesturing around the room. The man smiled.

"My name is Lynwood Gammon, and this is Chip Wilson," he went on. "I am the assistant director of the SSA and Chip is my assistant." Liza stared at them, wondering why she should care who these two men were.

Liza watched as Chip walked to the door and dismissed the guards. From their tone, Liza could tell that they weren't too happy about that, and she could hear their footsteps echo down the hall and fade away. Chip stood at the door, playing look-out.

"What do you want?" she asked, finally.

"First of all, your friend is fine. He's locked in a cell on another floor. Alis won't kill him yet. She hopes to use him as leverage against you," Lynwood said. Liza scowled. "Second of all, your stay here will be short but unpleasant."

"What do you mean?" Lynwood merely smiled.

"Alis plans to use you for experiments, but when the timing is right, you'll have your chance to escape," Lynwood said.

Liza pushed herself off the cot and stood up, facing Lynwood. "Why are you telling me this?"

"Don't ask questions. You'll live longer," he said, half turning towards the door. Liza stared at him, all of the questions scrambling at the tip of her tongue. "Just trust me."

"I don't even know you," Liza countered. Lynwood shrugged.

"That's up to you, then," he said and walked towards the door. Chip nodded and stepped outside, Lynwood following. The door closed before Liza could reach it, and a click of the lock echoed inside the cell. She slumped forward, her palms flat against the door. She was confused, even more, confused than she was when she first woke up. She turned from the door and slunk back to the cot, where she sat down and sank into the springs that held the canvas to the frame.

Her thoughts whirled. Why would the assistant director of the SSA be willing to help her out? What was in it for him? And clearly, his assistant was in on whatever plans he had. But she had to deal with these so-called experiments that the director wanted to perform on her. Liza had a flash of memory, not her own memory, but Jeffry Morre's memory. Of the Synth-gen chip installed in his spine, sending his ability into complete overload. Liza shuddered at the thought.

She was just about asleep again when the door to her

cell opened once more. This time, several men and women in brown uniforms with gray stripes entered the room. Fake Kathos. Before attempting to fight them, a powerful force surrounded her, pinning her arms to her sides. She felt her willpower bend, and she fought like hell to push it back, to keep them from Snapping her. But without her full strength, she couldn't win against several Kathos, even Fake ones. Her willpower bent enough that her legs lifted her up off the cot and forced her to follow the Fakes from the cell and down the hallway. To where Liza had no idea.

64

Pioneer slipped from the Sun Station docking bay and out into open space. Gael sat at the controls with Vely in the passenger seat. She looked out at space, how busy it was, with ships darting here and there. Gael navigated expertly through the mess until the tiny ship was away and heading towards the SSA headquarters.

Vely was terrified. She was sure that someone at the SSA would remember her face or her name and capture her, or worse, kill her. But Gael promised he wouldn't let anything happen to her, as long as she didn't let anything happen to him. He again mentioned the TK blasts, but Vely was having difficulty figuring out how she was supposed to protect him from such an attack. She felt that Liza would be better for the job because she could just bend their willpower until they couldn't attack. Vely hadn't yet mastered her ability, and she was still trying to learn how to send it in specific directions rather than all over the place. All she could hope to do was to try and form a wall of Tranquility around Gael and hope that it was enough. She also had to be careful not to touch him, or he'd go slack.

Vely chewed on her fingernail until Gael gave her a sharp look. She dropped her hand into her lap and blushed, staring off into space.

"No need to be nervous," Gael said. "I've been dealing with Alis for years. I'm not afraid of her. And I think you'll do just fine."

Vely wanted to deny him, to say that no, she wasn't going to do fine. That she wasn't ready. That she hadn't spent enough time practicing her ability. But that wasn't the right thing to do. She had to pretend to be strong. She was a Cosmic Resistance spy, after all. She imagined that the other spies around the Solar System didn't tell the people they were spying on that they had no confidence in themselves. Instead of biting her nail, Vely twisted her fingers around in her lap.

The SSA headquarters came into view. It was a huge structure floating in space. It was surrounded by ships, more than Vely saw at the Sun Stations. These ships, however, were much larger and intimidating. Weapons seemed to jut off in all directions. Vely pictured Liza at the Master Gunner station, having a field day with all the extra weapons. That made her smile, and she felt a little better.

Gael piloted *Pioneer* into the docking bay of the headquarters. The small ship settled quickly into a docking port, and he shut off the engines. The hatch opened, and together, Gael and Vely climbed out. For the first time, and hopefully the last, Vely stepped her foot into the SSA Headquarters.

When her foot connected to the catwalk, a strange feeling came over her. Something familiar. She looked around but saw no one she knew. And she had obviously never been to the headquarters before, so it wasn't as though she recognized anything. But the familiar feeling stayed with her, even as she walked with Gael down the catwalks and into the main lobby.

Vely wanted to focus on the feeling, to figure out what it meant, but two men approached wearing black uniforms. The taller had silver piping on his uniform. He smiled at Gael and extended a hand.

"Good to see you again, Gael," he said, shaking Gael's hand.

"And you, Lynwood."

"Who is this?" the man called Lynwood asked, nodding his head towards Vely. She mustered up a smile.

"This is Karina Malik, my new assistant," Gael said. Lynwood blinked once, then narrowed his eyes at her. He extended his hand out to her, and Vely shook it, trying her best not to leak Tranquility everywhere. She stared up at Lynwood's eyes, and she thought she saw something there. Recognition. But she'd never seen this man before in her life.

He released her hand and waved it towards the man beside him. "And you remember Chip Wilson," Lynwood said. Gael nodded and shook the man's hand, and Vely followed suit. After the introductions were complete, Lynwood nodded, turned, and began to walk down a corridor towards a lift. Vely hurried to keep up.

As they walked through the corridors of the headquarters, the familiar feeling persisted in the pit of Vely's stomach. When they stopped at a set of large, double doors, Liza came into Vely's mind. The doors opened, revealing a tall, slim woman with a cloud of black hair.

The feeling of familiarity clicked in Vely's brain. Like the last puzzle piece, slipping into place.

Liza was here.

She was somewhere in the headquarters, probably a prisoner. How did the SSA get their hands on her? Panic gripped Vely, and she had to work hard to control her features as introductions to Director Alis Foste were made. The woman made no move to shake Vely's hand, which was OK with her. The woman was terrifying. Vely looked into her eyes and saw nothing there. No happiness. No joy. Nothing. Only a blank stare that could morph into a glare at a moment's notice. Director Foste's gaze bore into Vely's skull, and a strange, sick smile formed on the woman's lips.

A cool sensation wrapped around Vely's body, but it was unfamiliar. She pushed it away, and when she was escorted into the room, she saw several people standing along the edges of the room. They wore black uniforms with colored stripes on their sleeves, but Vely didn't know what the colors meant. They stared at her as she walked by, and she tried her hardest not to shrink under their gaze.

Gael nudged Vely in the arm and jerked his chin

towards the people on the edges of the room. "They're her supersensors," he said. Vely nodded. She could feel a chill tickling her from all angles, but she brushed it away again. She felt a push on her willpower, but she fought back, trying not to squeeze her eyes shut in the process. The effort made her feel weak, but she had work to do.

With no idea what to do, Vely took a chance. She imagined a blanket of Tranquility wrapped around Gael, protecting him from the supersenors around them. She casually lifted her hands until the blue mist formed into the air, swirling around Gael. But she kept enough space between the mist and Gael that he wouldn't be affected by her ability. She made the blanket thicker until he was completely covered in a wall of blue. She neglected to protect herself, however. She had to fight off the other supersensors who were trying to attack her mind. She brushed them away, again and again, forcing herself back against their attempts to bend her willpower. At the same time, she tried to listen to Gael and Alis' conversation, but her ears buzzed with the effort of maintaining his shield and blocking the others from entering her mind.

"Where are my ships?"

"We're working on them, but progress is slow."

"Why? I'm paying you enough money."

"It's not money; it's talent. We don't have the number of people needed to fill such a large order in a short amount of time."

"Well, then get more talent!"

"That comes at an additional expense. People have to be trained to do this work, Alis."

"You're the largest manufacturer of ships, and you don't have the talent?"

Silence. "I don't know what to tell you, Alis."

"Do what you have to do. I'll push more money your way if you just get those ships built!"

"Alright, I'll do my best."

The conversation devolved into buzzing in Vely's ears. Alis Foste looked angry, while her assistant director had a bemused expression on his face. Vely's eyes would flick towards him every once in a while, only to find that he was staring at her.

Vely was nearing collapse. Finally, Gael turned and headed towards the door. Vely let her wall around him dissipate. A heaviness settled over her limbs, and she had to force herself to follow Gael without falling on the ground. Lynwood and Chip directed them back to the docking station, where they climbed back into *Pioneer*. Once seated and her restraining harness secured, Vely let herself drift off to sleep.

65

Liza was dragged through the SSA headquarters, attempting to walk but finding it difficult to use her legs and feet. The Fakes who came to fetch her held her up by the arms, pulling her beside them. Liza didn't want to know what awaited her at their final destination. Every once in a while, she could feel one of them prod at her willpower, pushing it. She didn't have the energy to fight back, but she tried anyway. She didn't even have the energy to draw off their willpower to strengthen her own. She would have to find out what was going to happen to her the hard way.

The group entered a lift, and it shot up several floors of the headquarters until it slid smoothly to a stop. The doors opened to reveal a long, white hallway. The lights recessed in the ceiling were blindingly white. Liza closed her eyes against the glare. The Fakes dragged her along. They stopped in front of a door, and one of them swiped his badge on the card reader, and the door slid open. They pulled Liza inside.

The room reminded her of the Research room back at the Supersensory training facility. There were computer consoles everywhere, tubes like the one Liza had blasted apart on accident, and a medical bed in the center of the room. Several people in lab coats hurried around the room. Liza flashed back to the time she nearly killed everyone in a blast of Kathokinetic power. She wondered if whatever they were going to do to her would end up the same way.

Liza was dragged towards the medical bed. The Fakes lifted her off the ground and put her in the bed. She flopped down without much control over her limbs. Once she was in bed, metal restraints emerged and snapped around her wrists and ankles while one reached up around her neck. She tried to dodge it, but it was too quick for her. She couldn't move, even if she wanted to. Her willpower flexed back into place, meaning the Fakes weren't bending it any longer. Her escorts moved away from the table and stood nearby, perhaps to keep watch should Liza free herself from her bonds.

One of the people in a white lab coat approached Liza with a tablet in hand. The woman tapped her finger on the tablet a few times, then looked at Liza.

"According to a recent report, you seemed to have drawn on additional energy, aside from willpower," the woman said. Liza attempted to shrug her shoulders. "We have a theory about that." Liza was curious but said nothing. She wouldn't give them the pleasure. The woman seemed to be waiting for Liza to ask, but the woman went on anyway when she didn't. "We believe you drew on dark energy."

Liza frowned. She remembered hearing the term in school on the Moon, but she couldn't remember what it meant. It had something to do with outer space.

"Dark energy, as we know it, causes the Universe to expand," the woman said. "It permeates all things and is ever-present in our lives. We believe you somehow tapped into that power."

"That's crazy," Liza mumbled. Even when she was at the training facility for Supersensors, no one had ever mentioned dark energy as a possibility for power. Besides, she wasn't *supposed* to be drawing on any power. And if Morre was right, then Liza was an ordinary Katho with no special abilities. Not that she believed everything he had said, but he at least seemed to be an expert in the subject.

"It does sound crazy, yes," the woman said a slight smile on her face. Liza flinched at the small act of kindness. "But if it's true, then you might be the most powerful Katho we've ever seen. Or the most reckless."

Liza shook her head. "Morre said I was nothing."

The woman rolled her eyes. "Morre told that to everyone, especially the ones he liked, rest his soul." Liza jerked her head to look at the woman, blinking. Morre had hated her, didn't he? The woman must have read the confusion in Liza's eyes. She tilted her chin up and smiled down at Liza. "We believe Morre had an *unnatural* attachment to you."

"You're insane."

The woman shrugged. "Not for me to judge," she said. "Either way, we want to test and see if you can draw on dark energy again."

"I can't."

"Yes, you can."

"I'm not going to let you people do experiments on me again," Liza said. "I almost killed people the last time. I don't need another death on my conscience." The woman stared at her without expression. She turned and nodded to someone, who pressed a button. A screen lit up, showing the inside of a cell. Liza watched as Dom appeared, pacing the cell. He didn't seem to be aware that he was being watched. Liza tried to reach for him, with her limbs and mind, but she couldn't reach him.

"We won't do anything now, but don't think we won't if you continue to resist," the woman said, a cruel note in her voice. It reminded her of Alis Foste. Liza closed her eyes and sighed. She couldn't let anything happen to Dom. Lynwood Gammon's words rang in her mind. But still, she didn't know or trust the man. He could have been lying.

"Fine," Liza mumbled. The woman's face changed into a smile. She nodded to those standing around her, and they took several steps back.

"All we need you to do is to try and draw on the dark energy again." Liza closed her eyes to concentrate. "And don't go drawing too much willpower from us. We'll know."

Liza wanted to scoff. Morre had always been right about her. She couldn't control her powers, let alone *not* draw on the willpower of others; it was too natural and easy. But at the very least, she could try, if only to save Dom from being harmed.

Liza squeezed her eyes shut tighter and drew from the energy around her. A myriad of smells jumbled in her nose. She drew on willpower from the others in the room. She tried to imagine pulling from space and not from the others, but nothing happened.

She didn't know how she became so powerful before. She was just drawing on energy around her, and it happened to be there. Now, she could feel nothing except the willpower of the people around her. She opened her eyes, glanced at the scientist, and shrugged her shoulders.

"I can't do it," she said. The woman gave her a flat stare, and Liza looked away.

"Try again," she commanded. Liza heaved a breath, closed her eyes, and tried to draw on the energy beyond those in the room. For a brief moment, a smell filled her nose. It was strange yet familiar. Because she'd smelled it before. It was the metallic smell that cut away at her nose when she'd fought against Morre. But just as she tried to grasp for the energy, it was gone, leaving her with nothing but a lingering taste of metal in her mouth.

"I almost had it, but I can't do it," Liza said, opening her eyes once more. The woman stared at Liza, then looked around the room at the others, who shrugged. Clearly, they weren't any more knowledgeable about how to do it than Liza. The room remained silent for several minutes before the scientist moved away from Liza, picked up a clear box, and brought it near. Liza glanced at it, wondering what was inside but fearing the worst. The woman opened the box and picked something out, and held it between her fingers. Liza recognized it instantly.

It was astarte.

It glowed blue in the woman's hand, taunting Liza with its secret power. Liza shook her head.

"Please, don't," she said, hating the sound of desperation in her voice. The scientist smiled, knowing what the astarte would do to Liza, and evidently did not care. She touched the astarte to Liza's bare skin.

Her willpower swelled, larger and larger every second the astarte was against her skin. Liza closed her eyes tight against the whirling power, and in an act of desperation and stubbornness, she let go.

The room erupted.

66

Vely wasn't sure how she made it home. She was surprised when she opened her eyes and found herself lying on her bed in the rented apartment. She sat up, shaking the sleep from her mind. Her body felt heavy and exhausted from her efforts of protecting Gael at the meeting with that awful Alis Foste woman.

And Liza! Vely was sure that Liza was back at the SSA headquarters, probably locked away somewhere. How did they get their hands on her? Liza was too careful to be captured, wasn't she? *Or not*, Vely thought. Liza was too *reckless* and was more likely to be caught. Vely folded her hands together and twisted her fingers around, wondering. Should she try to save Liza from the clutches of the SSA or stick with the Cosmic Resistance's plan?

Vely rose from the bed. The movement took much effort and left her chest heaving. She shuffled her feet towards the door, which slid open at her approach. She stepped into the main living area and saw Sehen working on his computer console. Vely realized she didn't even know what day it was or even what time.

Sehen looked up when she walked into the room and smiled. Vely waved to him, and he turned in his chair and rose.

"When did I get home?" Vely asked, rubbing her head. Sehen chuckled.

"Yesterday afternoon," he said. "You were dropped off. You stumbled into bed and passed out. This is the first time you've woken up since then."

Vely blinked. She'd been asleep for over twenty-four

hours. "I still feel drained," she commented, pressing her hands to either side of her head. A look of concern crossed Sehen's face.

"What did you have to do?" he asked.

"I had to protect Gael from a TK blast by Alis Foste's Supersensors," Vely said. Sehen lifted an eyebrow.

"What's that?"

Vely shrugged her shoulders and made an attempt to explain. "It's sort of like when both a Katho and a Tranq exert their power on one person at the same time," she said. Sehen wrinkled his nose.

"That sounds unpleasant," he said.

"Apparently, it has happened to Gael before, and he wants to avoid that, for obvious reasons," Vely said. "It makes him too persuasive, and he needs to stay strong in the face of the SSA."

"I thought the SSA and Gael were partners," Sehen said, speaking slowly, one eyebrow raised. Vely bit her lip, wondering if she was giving too much away. She responded slowly, watching every word she said.

"He has an interesting relationship with the director," Vely said. "It's as if they are constantly playing one against the other, trying to get what they want without having to sacrifice anything of their own. I think Gael is not as evil as most people make him out to be." Sehen looked skeptical, but he said nothing. "I think-- I think he could be persuaded to our side."

"You sound a little crazy, Vely," Sehen said. Vely bristled, crossing her arms over her chest.

"Why does that sound crazy?"

"This man did nothing about a bunch of bodies that were found on a returning mining ship," Sehen said. "No compensation for the families, no regrets, nothing." Vely rolled her eyes.

"I know about the bodies. I'm the one who found them," she said. Sehen's mouth dropped open.

"I didn't know that," Sehen said. "So you must have been

with that pirate crew..." Vely nodded.

"I don't know what Gael did or didn't do about that," Vely said. "But I think there's more to it than we know. I... I trust him."

Sehen opened his mouth to speak but seemed to think better of it. He closed his mouth, nodded firmly, and reached out to Vely. He clapped a hand on her shoulder.

"I'm on your side," he said. "No matter what, we'll figure this out together. You're the one who is getting to know him, so I'll trust your judgment. As long as we can gain access to the Temple of the Black Moon, then you're doing your job."

Relief washed over Vely, and she released a long breath. She turned to a small dinette set and dropped into one of the chairs. Her limbs felt weak and heavy. She tried to muster up her energy to keep moving, but all she wanted to do was go back to bed.

"There's something else..." Vely said after a long silence. Sehen raised an eyebrow, listening. "I think the SSA has my sister."

"Really? Why do you think that?"

"I don't really know..." Vely said. "I could just tell that she was there, at the SSA Headquarters. We are a dyad, after all."

"What? You're a dyad, and you're apart?" Sehen asked, genuine surprise on his face. Vely shrugged her shoulders.

"We wanted different things," she said. "I left to find my own path." Sehen smiled and approached her. He knelt down in front of her and slipped his hands over hers.

"I'd say you found the right path," he said, his eyes shining.

"Have I?" she breathed.

"You're helping the Cosmic Revolution shape the future of our Solar System. You may not think your role is important, but you're probably the most important person in the Cosmic Resistance right now."

"No pressure," Vely muttered. Sehen chuckled.

"You can do it. Ren, Maggie, and I all have faith in you. You're going to save the Solar System."

At that, Sehen tilted his face up and pressed his lips against hers. His grip on her hands tightened, and she squeezed back in return. A rush of emotions whisked through her body, igniting her senses. Her suspicions had been right, after all. Sehen did care for her as more than just another Cosmic Resistance spy.

But what about Cedrick?

Vely pulled away, squeezing her eyes closed. She felt Sehen press a hand against her cheek. Vely's eyes popped open and met Sehen's gaze.

"I want this," she whispered. "I really do." A confused expression crossed Sehen's face.

"Then what's wrong?" he asked.

"It's just that… well, I feel guilty," she said, averting her eyes from his.

"About what?"

"I left someone behind on Mars," she said. Sehen removed his hands from hers. "I think we, well, I don't know what we were, but I don't think we're that anymore. I left him in a Tranq den." Sehen winced.

"Was he your first?"

"Yes, I mean, what?" Sehen gave her a significant look. "No!" Sehen chuckled and placed his hands back on Vely's. "You know that dating wasn't really an option on the Moon."

"You're right," he said. "But we're not on the Moon anymore."

"I know…"

"You don't have to feel guilty. It's part of life," he said. "We are lucky to have a choice, now that we're free from the confines of the Moon."

Vely thought about this for a moment. Could she move on from Cedrick and try something with Sehen? Just because he was her first kiss didn't mean she owed him her life. She smiled at Sehen and leaned forward, pressing her lips to his.

He wrapped his arms around her shoulders and pulled her towards him, off the chair, and into his chest. Vely allowed the kiss to deepen as she closed her eyes.

67

She was coming apart like her skin was made of thread, and each stitch was coming undone. Her willpower flowed freely from her body, from every pore, touching everything in the room. Liza couldn't control it. Scents of the other people in the room flooded inside her brain. Not only was she releasing her willpower, but she was drawing on the willpower of others. She tightened her body in response, trying to reign in the unyielding power. She was vaguely aware of her own screams.

"Stop!"

The heat from Liza's skin disappeared, and her willpower began to calm. Air rushed through her lungs as she tried to keep up with the amount of breath her blood needed to course through her body. Every fiber of her being was in pain, like an electric shock that touched every inch of her. Her power crackled between her fingers, curling around her palm and twisting itself around her wrist. She willed it away, but she was too weak. Her full power had been unleashed, and there was nothing she could do about it.

Liza opened her eyes. She stared at the ceiling, not wanting to know what damage she did to the room or the people in it. With a heavy breath, she turned her head to one side. The room was destroyed. Scientists and other SSA agents in their uniforms picked themselves up off the ground and dusted themselves off. The doors to the room opened, and Alis Foste stormed in like a demon out of hell, her face contorted with fury. Her wild, black hair flew around her head like a storm cloud. `

"What the hell happened here?" she shouted into the

room, storming across the floor. She stopped by the table where Liza was strapped down and glared at her. Liza could see her power crawling up and down her skin, but she knew Alis couldn't see it. Otherwise, she'd be more afraid. The woman who pressed the astarte to Liza's skin rushed forward, her hair a disheveled mess.

"Ma'am, the astarte!"

"What happened?"

"You unleashed a monster," Liza said from her position on the table. Alis' gaze shot to her, eyes boring into Liza's skull.

"What?"

"You used that damn stone on me," Liza said, her voice low and growling. "I can't control my ability anymore." Alis continued to stare at her, seemingly waiting for an explanation. Liza unfurled her hand briefly, and a burst of power erupted from her palm. It hit the ceiling, denting the metal. Alis flinched as a metal note rang through the air. The scientist shrunk backward away from Liza.

"You wanted to see what would happen," the scientist said, speaking softly to Alis. "This is what happens." Alis whirled on the woman, her eyes blazing. Liza turned her attention back to herself. She focused on the bindings that held her to the table. She sent her willpower after them, searching for their weakest point. She found it and pulled back on her willpower, bending the binding until they broke free. Liza pushed herself up on the table and tried to make a run for it, but her body hit against an invisible wall of willpower. She stopped dead in her tracks and fell backward, barely catching herself before she landed on her tailbone again.

The Fakes rushed forward and gripped her around the arms, but Liza's unleashed power pushed them backward. They stumbled over each other, regained their footing, and rushed her again, this time, their arms outstretched, sending a wave of willpower over her. A sensation like a heavy blanket rested over her head and shoulders, and she dropped down to one knee, trying to force herself back up. But their combined power was too strong. If only she hadn't unleashed so much power, she'd be stronger and more rested. But her muscles betrayed her, and the willpower forced her to the ground. A Fake hurried towards her and clamped a pair of handcuffs around her wrists, though Liza thought they'd do little to restrain her.

"Throw her back in the cell," Alis commanded. The Fakes jumped to obey, and they lifted Liza up, all of them fighting against the willpower that rushed over Liza's skin. For good measure, she saw swing a fist, colliding with the side of her head. The pain was enough to send her world into darkness.

When Liza awoke, she was once again in the cell, lying prone on the cot. Her head throbbed fiercely. With a groan, Liza pushed herself into a sitting position. Her power appeared again on her skin, crawling and twisting around. There was no way they could keep her in the cell, not with her power like this. If they allowed her to regain her strength, then she could destroy everyone. Maybe the entire SSA Headquarters. But that was the hitch. They would never allow that. It was crazy to think they didn't know that about Psychogens, with all their research.

Liza rolled herself to the floor and stood up painfully. Her body ached so much, she wished for the cooling sensation of Tranquility, even if she could just sleep for a while. If only Vely were here...

If and when she got out of this mess, she would rest up and avoid action for a long time.

Liza's ears perked up when she heard footsteps outside in the hall. She turned to face the door and waited. The footsteps grew closer until they were just outside of her cell. She heard the guards dismissed and their grumbles as they disappeared from the cell door. It opened, revealing the two men who had come and talked to her before-- Lynwood and Chip. Once again, Chip stayed in the doorway, watching the hallway, as Lynwood made his way inside the cell. He stood at attention before her, his hands folded behind his back.

"Don't get too close," Liza warned. A smile formed on Lynwood's face.

"I heard about what happened. Alis is furious that you destroyed her lab," he said. Liza scoffed.

"She shouldn't have put that stupid stone on me," Liza said, looking down at her hands, at the bands of energy that Lynwood could not see.

"I understand," Lynwood said. "I hope we can rectify this." Liza glanced at him and raised an eyebrow.

"What do you mean? Why would you care?" Lynwood inhaled through his nose and took a step closer to her. Liza instinctively stepped back.

"I can't tell you everything," he said. "It's too dangerous. But I'm giving you a chance to get out of here alive."

"What about Dom?"

"The other pirate?" Liza nodded. "He goes free as well."

"But why?" Lynwood shook his head. Liza crossed her arms over her chest. "Fine. Keep your secrets. But how am I to escape? They've got Fakes and Psychos everywhere."

"There will be a convenient distraction," Lynwood said. His eyes flashed deviously. Liza narrowed her own eyes but didn't ask him to elaborate. She knew he wouldn't. "I imagine that once the guards are gone, you'll have no trouble blasting your way out of here."

"Hopefully. I'm pretty beat," Liza said, gesturing towards her body. "Literally." For a moment, Liza thought Lynwood actually looked apologetic.

"Your friend is on the floor up from here. Cell number 700."

"Thanks." Lynwood turned towards the door and nodded to her.

"Good luck, Liza Strange."

He disappeared from the room, and the door clanged shut.

68

The following morning, a black car appeared outside of Vely and Sehen's rented apartment. The Walnad logo was emblazoned on the front doors. Vely stepped outside to the street and walked around to the driver's side door. A young man rolled down the window.

"Vely Strange?" he asked, almost as if he were holding back a laugh. Vely scowled.

"That's me."

"Gael sent me to pick you up," he said. Vely nodded and circled around to the backseat, and climbed inside. She pulled the door closed, and the car drove off, heading towards the Walnad headquarters. Vely wondered if Gael would be mad that she didn't show up the previous day, but she'd slept half the day away. Maybe he'd be understanding, but she didn't think it looked very good for her first week.

The ride was short and silent. The driver made no attempts at conversation, so Vely remained quiet. Her mind was occupied, anyway, with thoughts of the previous night.

The car pulled up in front of the main entrance of the building, and Vely climbed out of the car. She crossed the sidewalk and walked through the sliding glass doors. When the lobby receptionist saw Vely, she rose and waved to her. Vely approached.

"Mr. Daniels left a message to send you right up to his office," she said. She handed over a key card with a clip on it. It had Vely's fake name printed on it. "Use this in the lift to reach his floor."

"Thank you," Vely said and took the key card. She turned

away and headed towards the bank of lifts. She saw a place to swipe her badge, and she pressed the button for the fourth floor. The lift chimed and began its short ascent. The doors slid open, and she stepped out into the silent hallway. She remembered that Gael's office was at the end of the hall, so she made her way down towards the closed door. When she reached it, she knocked.

The door immediately slid open. Vely stepped through into Gael's office. She saw him sitting behind his desk, working on his computer terminal. When she entered, he glanced up and smiled.

"There you are. I hope you're rested."

"I'm sorry I didn't show up yesterday. I-"

Gael cut her off. "It's alright. I know you were working hard to keep me protected." Vely released a sigh of relief. She dropped into a chair opposite Gael. He folded his hands and leaned forward. "I have called a gathering of the temple."

"You did?"

Gael nodded. "To discuss the current affairs of the Solar System. There's just something you'll have to do." A knot formed in Vely's stomach.

"What?"

"You'll have to be initiated." Vely's eyebrows rose.

"What exactly does that mean?"

"You're going in deep, Vely Strange. You're going to become a member of the Temple of the Black Moon."

"Is that necessary?"

"I believe it is, considering what you are trying to accomplish. You'll have to become a member and convince them to fall to your line of thinking." The knot in Vely's stomach tightened. "I've already submitted the request for you to be initiated."

"I don't know if I can do this," Vely said. "What is the initiation like?"

"I am a Legacy member," Gael said. "I didn't have to go through initiation because I'm a third-gen member." Vely twisted her hands together in her lap. This was the plan, wasn't it? And Gael was paving the way for her to succeed. She had to be strong. She was trying to save the entire solar system, after all.

A chime sounded from his computer terminal. Gael glanced at the screen and grinned.

"Well, although you have no record of a past, they agree to allow you to be initiated. The date is set for tomorrow." He grinned. "My word carries a lot of weight within that organization." A thrill of excitement and nervousness ran through Vely's bloodstream. What would the initiation entail? "Why don't you head home for the day and prepare mentally for whatever they're going to throw at you," Gael said. "I want you rested and prepared."

"But if I don't know what's going to happen, how can I prepare?" she asked.

"Fortify yourself. Practice your Tranquility, just in case." Vely bit her lip and nodded. Gael opened a drawer on his desk and pulled out a small communication device. He handed it over to Vely. It had a screen for text-based messages and a small microphone and speaker for audio messages. She turned it on, and the screen lit up. "Keep that with you, just in case. Especially if you get into trouble."

"Okay," she said and stowed the device in her pocket. She rose from the chair and stood before him.

"I'll pick you up in the morning, and we'll go to the Temple together. But after we enter the building, I won't see you again until the end." Vely nodded. "Now go and rest."

She tried to smile and turned towards the door. Her whole body shook. Vely headed back into the hallway and down the lift to the main floor. Her legs felt like jelly as she walked, and her heart thumped wildly in her chest. She had to be prepared for anything.

Vely made her way back to the apartment and, when she walked inside, saw Sehen sitting at his computer terminal, working away. The door closed behind her and caught his attention.

"You're home early," he said, pushing his chair away from the desk and standing up. "Is everything alright?"

"More than alright," Vely said, a nervous smile on her face. "Tomorrow, I'm being initiated into the Temple of the Black Moon."

Surprise bloomed on Sehen's face.

"How did you manage that?" he asked, stepping towards her and grasping her upper arms. Vely felt a blush explode across her face.

"Gael got me a pass into the initiation, so I'll become a full-fledged member of the Temple. And then I can try to convince them to join our cause."

In one swift motion, Sehen leaned forward and kissed Vely on the lips.

"This is great! You're amazing!"

The blush on her cheeks deepened, but she smiled.

"Come on. Let's call Maggie and Ren and tell them the good news." Sehen rushed to the computer terminal and began to type. Vely approached his side, smiling, her nervousness dissipating, replaced with excitement.

69

Liza paced the cell, her arms behind her back, thinking and waiting. She didn't know *when* this supposed distraction would take place, so she was afraid to sleep. What if she missed it? Her eyelids grew heavy as she paced, threatening to close. So, she continued to pace.

She heard the guards mumbling to each other outside the door, but she couldn't catch what they were saying. She moved closer to the door, listening, only to have it wrench open. Liza nearly lost her balance, and she backed up into the center of the room.

Standing in the doorway was Alis Foste. An angry scowl was painted on her face. She stepped into the room, clutching a box in her hand. Liza did not want to know what was inside the box, but she had an inkling.

"How many times are you going to make me destroy your headquarters?" Liza asked while Alis opened the box in her hands. Alis smirked.

"Morre was right about you," she said, her voice low. "You are a terrible Kathokinetic. You can't control your powers."

Liza knew Alis was just trying to get into her head, just like Morre did before. But she wasn't going to let that happen again. She glanced down at her hand, at the power crawling around her clenched fist. From the box she held, Alis pulled out a piece of astarte. She turned and pulled the door closed behind her, leaving the guards on the outside. Approaching Liza, she held out the stone. Liza backed up, holding her hands up in front of her. She didn't want to kill Alis, not yet anyway, not before she was able to escape and find Dom. She didn't trust the word of Lynwood. So far, there had been no distraction.

"You will hold onto this stone and control your power," Alis said, reaching towards Liza, who shook her head and backed up until she was pressed against the wall. She could feel the cool metal of the walls under her clothing.

"Don't make me kill you," Liza said through clenched teeth. Alis laughed and edged closer.

"You can't kill me," she said. And with that, she thrust her hand out and pressed her palm against Liza's cheek, the astarte digging into the skin. Liza's power exploded.

"Control it!" Alis shouted at her. Her hair blew back as Liza's power forced its way out of her body and into the room, creating a vortex in the center. Liza gritted her teeth and closed her eyes, the blue stone burning against her skin, sending her power into overdrive. She pulled back on her power, inching ever so slightly, back under her control. Alis pushed harder against Liza's face. Liza could smell Alis in her nose, and she smelled like death.

"You're weak! Control your power!" Alis shouted at Liza, but Liza closed her eyes and shook her head. Alis pressed harder until Liza's other cheek almost touched the wall behind her. She pulled and pulled, trying to stop the unleashed power from spiraling in the room. She could feel her own willpower bending and bending, so close to Snapping until--

A sudden calm washed over her. Almost like Tranquility, but it came from within herself. Her power halted, the vortex stalled. Liza opened her eyes. Alis was looking around the cell, her eyes wide, a sick smile on her face.

"It can be done," she said and turned her attention back to Liza, who was panting.

She gained control over her power.

"I knew it!" Alis cried, removing the astarte from Liza's cheek. "It is possible."

Liza felt her power dim, now that the stone was no longer touching her. But only slightly, to where it didn't take as much effort to keep it under control.

"I will have the most powerful Kathos in the entire galaxy," she said, pressing the stone to her chest.

"You'll kill them," Liza growled.

"I didn't kill you, did I?"

"You tried."

Alis shrugged her shoulders and turned away, leaving her back exposed to Liza. *Attack her*, Liza thought. But she shook the thought away. If she did that, she might ruin the chance to escape. She'd alert the guards, and now that Alis knew a Katho could control their power with the stone, then there was no use for Liza any longer. Her lips pressed into a line, she allowed Alis to walk out of the cell unscathed. The door closed behind her, ending her chance to kill the woman.

Liza turned her thoughts and awareness inward, searching for her power. She could feel it swelling against her hold. But something like calm radiated from her core, keeping the power from lashing out. It was a strange feeling, something Liza had never felt before, aside from her few brushes with Tranquility. It was almost a glow, the feeling inside of her. And for some reason, she felt *happy* and *hope*.

That in itself was unusual.

Especially considering the circumstances.

Perhaps she was Snapped. That might explain the feelings, but it seemed unlikely. She didn't feel compelled to kill herself like they said happened to Snapped people. In fact, she felt the complete opposite.

Time passed, and the glow faded slightly. But Liza still felt hope, hope that Lynwood would come through for her and that she and Dom would be able to escape.

More time passed, and Liza began to wonder if Lynwood had been leading her on. Perhaps some trick that Alis set him to. It would seem likely. Although he didn't exactly give her a timeline. It could be days.

Liza was about to give up and go to sleep when she heard an alarm blare. It was loud and piercing, and from the outside of the cell, she could hear the guards shouting at each other.

A computerized voice spoke over the loudspeaker. *"All units to the fourth floor."* And the alarm continued to blare.

Was this the distraction?

Liza stood at the door and pulled herself up on her tiptoes to look through the small window. The guards were no longer standing by her door, and other guards were running down the hall. Liza shook the door, but it was locked tight. How was she supposed to get out? Blast it? A face appeared on the other side of the cell door. It was that other man, Chip Mann. The door unlocked and swung open. Chip nodded to her.

"Come on. We have to release your friend," Chip Mann said. Liza nodded and followed him from the cell. They ran down the hallway, passing other cell doors. She could hear the prisoners calling out to them, begging for release. But Chip ignored them, so Liza did as well. They reached the lift at the end of the hall, and Chip pressed the button for the next floor. The door closed and slid upwards. The doors opened again, and Chip ran out into the hallway. Liza followed, concentrating on her power. Little arcs of power crisscrossed her arms and hands, ready for an attack.

Chip stopped at cell 700 and held his hand against the biometric scanner. The device beeped, and the door swung open. "Come on, young man," Chip said into the cell. Liza stepped around Chip to peer inside. Dom sat on the cot, staring at Chip with a confused expression on his face. He looked beat up. There was a shadow of a bruise under his eye. Liza's hands clenched. She would kill whoever did that to him.

Dom spotted Liza. He rose up. "Liza!" He jogged to the doorway, and Chip stepped aside, allowing him out of the cell. "What's going on?" he asked, pulling Liza against his chest. Liza squeezed him back but pulled away quickly.

"We're getting out of here. We have to go now."

"Okay...?" Liza shook her head. She could explain later. Chip turned to them and pulled a gamma pistol from his hip, and handed it over to Dom.

"I assume you can protect yourself," he said to Liza. She nodded. "Take the lift to the Zero floor. Follow the hallway to the end and take a right. Steal a speeder and get the hell out of here. We don't have much more time."

"Okay. Thank you," Liza said. Chip nodded. Liza grabbed Dom's hand and pulled him along the hallway, back towards the lift.

70

"Lynwood! Where are you?" Alis cried over the communicator. His voice came through, but it was distorted and hard to understand.

"Sec- Fl-. -Ab. -he's -tta-ing." Alis frowned at the device but thought she could make it out. He was on the second floor in the lab, and someone was attacking everyone. Alis shoved her communicator in her pocket and reached down to the lower drawer of her desk. She ripped it open and pulled out a gamma pistol and a laser blaster. Holding both, she ran from her office and headed towards the nearest lift. She took it down to the second floor, and when the doors opened, she burst out into the fray. Enforcers stood everywhere, their gamma pistols aimed at the door to the lab. From inside the room, she could hear crashing and shouting and the sounds of gamma pistol blasts hitting the walls. Alis clenched her teeth in annoyance. They were making her lab worse than it already was.

Alis pushed through the group of Enforcers and walked into the room. Lynwood stood near the side of the room, his back pressed against the wall. He gripped a gamma pistol in his hands. Standing in the center of the room was Gwen Adan. Her face was fury. Around her, anything not secured to the floor swirled in a vortex of her power. Alis could feel the pressure against her body, and she could feel her Willpower bending.

"Stop this!" Alis shouted, pointing her double gamma pistols at Gwen. The young woman lowered her hands, and the vortexes stopped, but Alis could still feel the pressure against her body. She tensed, trying to keep control of her own Willpower. But Alis lacked the power to control it.

"Who are you?!" Gwen shouted, pointing to Alis, who frowned.

"What are you talking about?" Alis asked. "You know very well who I am."

"No, I don't. But you've trapped me here, didn't you? You controlled me."

For a brief moment, Alis' eyes went wide. Her programming. Gwen was no longer under Alis' control.

"Lynwood, what's going on?" she asked, turning towards him. He had lowered his gamma pistol and taken a few steps forward.

"Her programming. It's failed!"

"How is this possible?" she asked, but Lynwood shook his head. He didn't know. Alis turned her attention back to Gwen.

"Gwen Adan. Pandora, Galatea, Hydra, Carpo." Alis shouted. But nothing happened. Gwen glared at Alis from across the room. Gwen lifted one hand, and a blast of Kathokinetic energy hit Alis, full force in the chest. She flew backward and collided with an Enforcer. The man grabbed Alis to keep her from falling to the ground. Alis brushed him away once she regained her balance.

"Let me out of here, or I'll kill you all," Gwen said. Alis believed that the woman would do just that. And it appeared that she no longer had control over her.

Which meant that Alis needed to kill her first.

She aimed both of her weapons at Gwen and fired. Gwen raised both hands, and the blasts deflected to the ceiling causing two concave divots. Alis growled.

"Get the other Kathos in here and bring her down!" Alis shouted to Lynwood, who nodded and got on his communicator. Gwen stood in the center of the room, glaring at Alis, her hands clenched into fists. Alis stared back, willing the woman to return to her programming, but Alis knew it was futile. Something happened that broke Gwen's programming, and who knew how long it would take to bring her back under.

And was it even worth it?

Maybe it was.

The thudding of boots sounded behind her. She saw a large group of Kathos, both Supersensors and Synth-gens, flooding the hallway when she turned.

"Bring her under control!" Alis shouted at them. They filed into the room and circled Gwen, who seemed as calm as if nothing were happening. The Kathos and Synths fired their willpower at Gwen; Alis could feel the pressure of their power filling the room, but Gwen resisted, mightily. She never so much as bent her knee to the effects of the Kathos and Synths, and finally, she pushed their power away with her clenched fists.

And she broke into a run.

She ran through the room and shoved Alis to the side with a burst of power. Alis stumbled and fell, landing hard on the ground, in her most prone position. She screamed and pushed herself up, scrabbling to get her feet under herself. The others stood around as if they didn't know what to do.

"Follow her and *bring her down,*" Alis shouted. Her Enforcers, Kathos, and Synths followed after Gwen, who was gaining ground against them down the hall. She reached a lift and stepped into one, disappearing behind the door.

Lynwood appeared at her side.

"How could you let this happen?" Alis shouted at him, to which Lynwood merely stared at her.

"Why would I allow this to happen?" he asked her, his voice calm, irritatingly so. Alis ignored him and followed after her small army. They got held up at the lifts, and Alis pushed her way to the front of the line, shoving her people to the side as she moved through them. A few grumbled, but when she shot them a glare, they clammed up immediately.

Alis rapidly pressed the button for the lift. "Which direction did she go?" Alis asked.

"We think she's heading for the docking bay," someone answered. Alis nodded, and finally, the lift arrived. She stepped in and was soon crowded with many others, squeezing her against the back wall. She stood with her arms flat against her sides, waiting for the lift to arrive on the docking bay floor. Alis burst through her people into the hallway when the doors slid open and ran, chasing after Gwen.

But she was nowhere in sight.

"Where is she?" Alis asked.

Another alarm blared through the halls of the headquarters. Alis ran for the docking bay.

But she was too late.

A small speeder undocked and sped out into the tiny airlock. Alis barely recognized Gwen inside the speeder but knew it was her. Her Space Enforcer division was already climbing into their own ships to chase after her.

All Alis could do was wait.

She couldn't waste more resources going after one girl. After all, what was the worst that could happen?

"Ma'am!"

Alis turned in the direction of an Enforcer, who was reaching out to her with a closed hand. She frowned.

"What is it?"

"We found these. She dropped them before she got into the speeder."

The Enforcer opened his hand, revealing two pieces of astarte.

71

For a man whose family accumulated so much wealth on the backs of others, Gael Daniels lived rather modestly. His penthouse sat atop an affluent hotel, surrounded by high-priced shopping centers and restaurants. Yet inside, Gael had minimal furniture, merely functional areas to eat, sit, and work. His bedroom was no different. A place to sleep and a place to store clothes. A washroom down the hall.

Gael stood barefoot in his bedroom, pulling out a set of Temple robes from the back of his closet. He needed to have them laundered before Vely's initiation ritual scheduled for the following day. Gael had to look the best, as he was the sponsor of the young lady, and it had not been easy to convince them to allow such a young woman with no background into the Temple. But when they heard about her actions on the Moon, they became much more interested. Anyone who could rile up the SSA was a good candidate in their book.

He held up the robes and dusted off the shoulders. The silver embroidery shone out against the black of the robes, denoting his place among the Temple; an upright rocket ship and the symbol of Jupiter stitched over the left breast. *If only I were the Eminence,* Gael thought to himself, turning and laying the robes out on his bed. *I could get some real work done.* He ran a hand over the soft material.

"Ah well," he said, speaking to the robes. "Now is not the time to dwell." He returned to his closet and chose an outfit to wear under the robes, something lightweight as the robes tended to be very warm. Just as he laid out the clothes next to his robes on the bed, he heard his video communicator chiming. Gael left his room, sat down at the desk in the main living area, and pushed the button to answer the call. It came from the SSA headquarters.

Gael was a little surprised to see Charles Mann's face appear. He would have expected Alis to disturb him at home. That was more her style.

"Charles, is something wrong?" Gael asked, noting the worried expression on his face.

"In a way," Charles said. "I found out rather devastating news that I thought I should share with you." Gael's stomach tensed.

"Go on..."

"I know what happened to your sister," Charles said.

Gael blinked. Once. Twice. Gwen? He stared at Charles through the screen. *His sister?*

"She's dead," Gael said, the lie coming easily to him, as he'd spoken it for so many years. Yet, was it a lie? Or just a story he told himself to make things easier.

Charles shook his head.

"She's a Kathokinetic. She's been under the SSA's thumb for many years. She was programmed to be a sleeper agent. She escaped the SSA a few months ago with another Kathokinetic by the name of Liza Strange. Somehow, Lieutenant Jeffry Morre was able to activate her, and she helped the SSA bring down a fleet of pirates."

Gael opened his mouth but found that no words would come to him. *Liza Strange? Vely's sister, perhaps? And his* sister *was alive?*

"Where is she now?" Gael asked after several moments of silence.

"She broke through her programming and is on the run. She just escaped from the SSA headquarters, but Alis is sending Enforcers to bring her back. She and that Strange girl-- they're different."

"How so?"

"They can control their Kathokinetic powers even when

holding onto astarte. We think that's how Gwen broke her programming."

Words swirled in Gael's head. He knew that Alis was experimenting with astarte and Supersensors, but he didn't know the extent of her "research." And if she had been performing research on his sister this whole time...

His hands clenched into fists. Emotions roiled over him, and he struggled to maintain his composure in the face of Charles. He had to find a way to get his sister back and protect her from that evil, vile woman.

"I want you to track her the best you can," Gael said. "Find out where she's going or where she ends up. Keep me updated regularly."

"I'll do my best, sir," Charles said, nodding to him.

"What else do you know?" Gael asked, but Charles shook his head.

"I'll keep digging and try to come up with more information. And I'll have someone track her for you. We'll find her and bring her back."

"Yes, please."

Charles signed off with a wave goodbye, and the video communicator went dark. Gael sat back in his chair. His body was tense, and an unpleasant fluttering made his stomach feel weak. Gwen was *alive?* She'd disappeared at such a young age. He knew she was special and had Supersensory abilities, but their parents were so against her developing them. Did she run away? Or was she kidnapped by Alis?

Charles would get to the bottom of this. Gael hoped, anyway. Otherwise, he'd take matters into his own hands.

This new development certainly threw a wrench in Gael's plans. He'd only had to look out for himself for so many years, and now that he knew his sister was alive, things were different. And Vely. And the Temple. He had to stay focused. Nothing could go wrong with Vely's initiation, or his entire plan would be ruined. But in an instant, with only a few words, Charles Mann had completely changed Gael's life.

Gael dialed up the call number that Vely had given him. He waited while the connection was established, and finally, Vely's face appeared on the screen.

"Mr. Daniels," she said, seemingly unsurprised that he was calling on her.

"Vely. I wanted to check up on you. Are you ready for tomorrow?"

"As much as I can be, I think," she said, a nervous tremor in her voice. "I've been practicing my Tranquility, and I got those robes you sent over. Is there anything else?"

Gael almost told her about Gwen. It was on the tip of his tongue. But he held back. No need to distract her with other information that wasn't necessary for the next few days. Besides, it was crazy to think that Vely would even know who Gwen was in the entire solar system, considering his sister had been trapped by the SSA. But maybe she did… if Gwen ran around with Vely's sister.

"I just wanted to make sure you were ready," Gael said, nodding to her through the screen. "You'll do great. I know it."

"Thank you, Mr. Daniels."

He nodded to her and signed off. Gael stood up from his chair and began to pace, his hands linked behind him, deep in thought.

72

Alarms blared through the SSA headquarters, and Enforcers rushed in all directions. This "distraction" was making it more difficult for Liza and Dom to escape. They managed to find an empty room to hide in, and with the door opened just enough to peer through, they waited for their chance to move.

"What do you think is going on?" Liza whispered.

"No idea," Dom said. "Some disaster, apparently."

Liza rolled her eyes and peered out into the corridor. For the moment, the coast was clear. She grabbed Dom's hand, pushed open the door, and they stepped out. Inching along the hallway, they came to an intersection. A plaque on the wall pointed in the direction of the docking bay, among other locations with the SSA. Liza was tempted to pay a visit to Alis Foste, give her a little payback for the trouble she caused, but the rational part of Liza's mind, one that sounded an awful lot like Vely, reminded her that her temper was the reason they were stuck in this mess, to begin with.

"Come on."

Together, they inched around the corner and headed down the hallway. A lone Enforcer appeared at the other end, running down the hall towards them. Liza felt Dom tense up beside her, and she called upon her power, just in case. But the Enforcer barely paid them any attention. He ran on down the hall and disappeared around a corner. Both Liza and Dom released a sigh.

"Keep moving," Dom said, prodding Liza in the back. She nodded and moved forward down the hall. Just as they reached the next intersection, following the signs on the wall, another alarm blared, intermixing with the other two that were already going off.

"*Escaped Prisoners. Escaped Prisoners. Escaped Prisoners.*"

"Shit."

Liza and Dom hurried down the hall towards the docking bay. They almost reached the next intersection of hallways when a group of Enforcers appeared.

"Is that them?" someone asked.

"Yes!"

Gamma pistols rose up, their barrels pointed at Liza and Dom, who skidded to a halt, changed directions, and headed back the other way. When Liza heard the sound of the gamma pistol going off, she threw up a shield of willpower behind her, deflecting the blast up into the ceiling. A harsh metal note rang through the air, making her want to cover her ears from the cacophony of noise. Liza was surprised at how effortless the deflection was. The last time she'd escaped from the SSA, deflecting gamma blasts had taken an extreme amount of effort.

More gamma pistols fired in their direction. The blasts continued down the hall and hit the far wall, denting the metal. Liza missed one blast, but Dom pulled her to the ground to avoid it. The Enforcers moved again, chasing after them. Dom and Liza pushed off the ground, their boots slipping on the smooth metal floor. They ran as fast as they could down the hall, knowing full well they were going in the wrong direction.

"We need to go back that way," Liza shouted to Dom. He nodded, turned, and fired his own blaster towards the Enforcers. They ducked and scattered, but one Enforcer did not make it out of the way. His body flew backward, blood spraying in all directions. Liza's stomach lurched at the sight as memories of her father conjured up in her mind.

"No, not now," she mumbled to herself. She lifted her hands and sent a blast of willpower down the hall at the

Enforcers, who were now trying to stand back up. They took a full blast to the face and flew backward, landing in a heap in the middle of the hallway.

"Let's go," Dom shouted, grabbed Liza by the hand, and pulled her back in the direction of the Enforcers, who were attempting to untangle themselves from each other. Liza sent willpower blasts at the Enforcers as they ran by, keeping them from gaining any footing. Liza and Dom managed to clear the group of Enforcers and turned down the next hallway.

They continued to run until they encountered the biggest problem yet.

Alis Foste and a group of Enforcers stood in their way, blocking the main doors to the docking bay. She was already holding a gamma pistol in her hands and was shouting at the Enforcers around her.

"What is going on? What prisoners escaped?" she was asking them.

"That'd be me," Liza called out. Alis spun, and her dark eyes latched onto Liza's. She bared her teeth most unpleasantly and aimed her gamma pistol at Liza's head.

"Get them," Alis shouted to her Enforcers, who jumped into action.

They ran down the hall, their pistols raised, firing off shots. Liza managed to deflect most of the shots, but they were forced to their knees to avoid the rest. Liza jumped back to her feet as best she could; the aching in her body was getting worse despite the adrenaline running through her veins. She pushed a wall of willpower against the Enforcers, pushing them backward, bending their will. Her nose filled with their smells, a confusing array of alcohols, and something sweet. She bent them further, unable to decide if she should Snap them or not. It would be irresponsible for her to Snap a whole crowd of Enforcers, but they were in her way.

Instead, she gave a heavy push, and the Enforcers flew backward, losing their footing. One of the Enforcers collided with Alis Foste, sending her to the ground. Liza and Dom took their chance and ran for the doors to the docking bay. From the ground, they could hear Alis swearing and struggling to stand back up, but the bodies of several Enforcers kept her on the ground. Liza and Dom leaped over the pile of bodies and passed through the doors to the docking bay.

"Right there," Dom said, pointing. A small speeder sat, almost as if it had been waiting for them. They ran to the ship, Liza blasting Enforcers out of the way as they went. Dom jumped in first, and Liza followed, pulling the hatch down behind her. The hatch sealed, and Dom kicked on the engines. Liza glanced back at the doors to the docking bay. It appeared that Alis and her goons had managed to get themselves upright and were spilling into the docking bay, ready to take off after them.

"We need to go *now*," Liza urged.

"I'm working on it," Dom said.

The ship pulled away from the docking arms, and Dom navigated towards the speeder ship airlock. They reached it, and Dom sent a signal to the airlock to close behind them and open up in front of them. The speeder shot out into the space.

73

For the second time that day, Alis watched one of her speeders disappear into space. She stood with her hands clenched at her sides, her jaw tight, teeth grating against each other. She spun and faced the gathered Enforcers who failed to capture Gwen and Liza.

"You are all useless!" she shouted, brushing past them, not making eye contact with anyone. The crowd parted as she made her way back into the headquarters. A few mumbled apologies, but that was not good enough. She needed those two women *caught* and brought back to her. Now that they knew they could control the astarte, there would be no limit to the havoc they could cause for the SSA.

This also meant that her experiments with her current Kathos would need to ramp up. No more dawdling. Her Supersensors would learn to control the astarte and become more powerful than Liza and Gwen.

But what about the incident with Morre? Liza had pulled on something else besides astarte that made her even more powerful and dangerous. But Morre died before anyone could determine what she did. And now Liza Strange was gone, and Alis would have to spend precious resources to get her back.

Alis stormed her way up to her office and allowed the doors to close and lock behind her. She sat down at her desk and brought up her video communicator. She dialed a number for a nearby ship.

Warwick's face appeared.

"Ah, hello, Alis," he said, smiling that disgusting grin of his. Alis had no time for pleasantries.

"Where are you?" she asked.

"Nearby the headquarters, waiting on *you*," he said. "What's the hold-up? I thought I'd get my hands on that little worm."

Alis shook her head.

"Liza escaped, and so did my sleeper agent, Gwen Adan. Get. Them. Back."

Warwick raised an eyebrow and stared at her through the communicator screen.

"You lost her?"

"She *escaped*. I don't know how, yet, but I'm going to find out and kill whoever was involved." Warwick snorted but said nothing else. "Now go after her. Do not kill her. I am not done with her yet."

"It's going to cost you," Warwick said. Alis growled.

"Fine. Whatever you want. Just get that girl back here immediately."

"Aye, aye," Warwick said with a mock salute. He signed off, and the screen went dark. Alis leaned back in her chair. The Corsairs would bring them back. They had to. In the meantime...

She needed a new Lieutenant for the Kathos in her Supersensory Division, now that Morre was dead. And she had an idea.

Alis dialed down to her Enforcer training division and requested a certain man's presence. It wasn't long before there came a knock at her door. She pressed a button on her desk, and the doors slid open, revealing a hulking man. He stepped through the door, ducking as he did so, and walked into the room. His hair was cut short against his scalp, and his light-colored eyes shone at her with interest. Alis could feel his power press against her, gently touching her willpower. She frowned at him.

"Keep your willpower to yourself," she ordered, and the touch faded.

"What can I do for you, ma'am?" the man asked.

"Hayeson Zachiel," she said, rising from her chair. "I have a proposal for you."

"I'm listening."

"I'm giving you a promotion. You will now be in charge of the Kathokinetics in the Supersensory Division." Alis said. Hayeson's eyebrows rose.

"Interesting proposal. What happened to Lieutenant Morre?"

"Dead. By the hand of a slithering little snake that deserves proper punishment for the trouble she has caused me," Alis said. "I need you to take his place."

Hayeson Zachiel grinned.

"When do I start?" he asked.

"Immediately." A slow smile spread across Hunter's face. "You are now promoted to Lieutenant of the Supersensory Division. Report there tomorrow to convene with Howards and Carte. They'll show you around. Your first mission is to increase experiments with astarte and Kathos. I need all of my Kathos to control their powers when subjected to the astarte."

"That's impossible," Hayeson commented.

"I've seen it twice today," Alis grunted. "It's possible." Hayeson's eyes went wide. "Train these Supersensors to be smarter and tougher than the Enforcers. They are my elite soldiers, and I need them ready and prepared for what's to come."

"And, if I may ask, what is coming?" Hayeson asked.

Alis smiled. "Something big."

74

Vely rose early before the artificial lights of the Sun Station came on. She picked through her clothes, selecting the least worn pair of pants and tunic shirt that she owned. Her ass-kicking boots were the only boots she had with her, so she drew them on over her pants. Sitting on the edge of the bed, she looked back at Sehen, who was still asleep, bundled under the blankets. Her lips turned up in a smile, and she gently stood up from the bed and moved into the living area.

In the small kitchenette, Vely hunted for food. She knew Sehen had bought food, but nothing appealed to her. Her stomach was in knots of nerves. She turned away and stood in the center of the room, feeling the fabric of the robes hang over her hands and brush against her neck. She grabbed at the collar and tugged it away, not liking the feeling of being so closed in. With nothing else to do until Gael picked her up, she paced the room, back and forth, thinking and worrying about what lay ahead.

While she paced, Sehen appeared in the doorway, tousled from sleep. He inched his way out into the living area, wiping his eyes.

"Why are you up so early?" he asked. Vely stopped pacing.

"Couldn't sleep," she said. "Too nervous."

Sehen crossed the room. He placed his hands on her shoulders and gave her a little shake.

"You'll do great today, I promise," he said. "You're going to bring us even closer to accomplishing our goal." Vely blushed, but there was no way he could see in the low light of the morning.

Outside the apartment, a black car rolled to a stop. Vely glanced over her shoulder and looked out the window. "That's my ride," she said. Sehen nodded and released her. Before she could turn the whole way, Sehen pecked a kiss on her lips, then spun her around and prodded her towards the door.

"Good luck!" he said. Vely shook her head with a smile. She walked to the door and stepped outside in the cool air of the regulated morning. The car's back door opened, and inside, Vely could see Gael, dressed in his own black robes. She climbed into the car and shut the door. The car pulled away from the curb and onto the street, heading in the direction of the Temple of the Black Moon.

ABOUT THE AUTHOR

N.C. Madigan is the author of the *Galactic Syndicate Cycle*, including book 1, titled *Psychogen*. She is super excited to share the second book with the world and hopes that readers will enjoy Liza and Vely's journey as much as she has enjoyed writing it. N.C. Madigan lives in Metro Detroit with her boyfriend, dog, and snake.